THE SECRET HOUR

scott westerfeld

MIDNIGHTERS

vol. 1   THE SECRET HOUR

An Imprint of HarperCollins*Publishers*

Eos is an imprint of HarperCollins Publishers

The Secret Hour
Copyright © 2004 by 17th Street Productions, an Alloy company, and
Scott David Westerfeld

Produced by 17th Street Productions,
an Alloy company
151 West 26th Street, New York, NY 10001

Library of Congress Cataloging-in-Publication Data

Westerfeld, Scott
  The secret hour / Scott Westerfeld.— 1st ed.
    p. cm. — (Midnighters ; v. 1)
    Summary: Upon moving to Bixby, Oklahoma, fifteen-year-old
Jessica Day learns that she is one of a group of people who have special
abilities that help them fight ancient creatures living in an hour hidden at
midnight; creatures that seem determined to destroy Jess.
      ISBN 0-06-051951-7 — ISBN 0-06-051952-5 (lib. bdg.)
[1. Science fiction.] I. Title.   2003006986
PZ7.W5197Se 2004
[Fic]—dc21

1 2 3 4 5 6 7 8 9 10

First Edition

1

REX

The halls of Bixby High School were always hideously bright on the first day of school. Fluorescent lights buzzed overhead, their white honeycombed plastic shields newly cleaned of dead insect shapes. The freshly shined floors dazzled, glinting in the hard September sunlight that streamed in through the school's open front doors.

Rex Greene walked slowly, wondering how the students jostling past him could *run* into this place. His every step was a struggle, a fight against the grating radiance of Bixby High, against being trapped here for another year. For Rex summer vacation was a place to hide, and every year this day gave him the sinking feeling of having just been discovered, caught, pinned like an escaping prisoner in a searchlight.

Rex squinted in the brightness and pushed up his glasses with one finger, wishing he could wear dark shades over their thick frames. One more layer between him and Bixby High School.

The same faces were all here. Timmy Hudson, who had

beaten him up just about every day in fifth grade, passed by, not giving Rex a second glance. The surging crowd was full of old tormentors and classmates and childhood friends, but no one seemed to recognize him anymore. Rex pulled his long black coat around himself and clung to the row of lockers along the wall, waiting for the crowd to clear, wondering exactly when he had become invisible. And why. Maybe it was because the daylight world meant so little to him now.

He put his head down and edged toward class.

Then he saw the new girl.

She was his age, maybe a year younger. Her hair was deep red, and she was carrying a green book bag over one shoulder. Rex had never seen her before, and in a school as small as Bixby High, that was unusual enough. But novelty wasn't the strangest thing about her.

She was out of focus.

A faint blur clung to her face and hands, as if she were standing behind thick glass. The other faces in the crowded hall were clear in the bright sunlight, but hers wouldn't resolve no matter how hard he stared. She seemed to exist just out of the reach of focus, like music played from a copy of a copy of an old cassette tape.

Rex blinked, trying to clear his eyes, but the blurriness stayed with the girl, tracking her as she slipped further into the crowd. He abandoned his place by the wall and pushed his way after her.

That was a mistake. Now sixteen, he was a lot bigger,

his dyed-black hair more obvious than ever, and his invisibility left him as he pushed purposefully through the crowd.

A shove came from behind, and Rex's balance twisted under him. More hands kept him reeling, four or five boys working together until he came to a crashing stop, his shoulder slamming into the row of lockers lining the wall.

"Out of the way, dork!" Rex felt a slap against the side of his face. He blinked as the world went blurry, the hall dissolving into a swirl of colors and moving blobs. The sickening sound of his glasses skittering along the floor reached his ears.

"Rex lost his spex!" came a voice. So Timmy Hudson did remember his name. Laughter trailed away down the hall.

Rex realized that his hands were out in front of him, feeling the air like a blind man's. He might as well be blind. Without his glasses, the world was a blender full of meaningless color.

The bell rang.

Rex slumped against the lockers, waiting for the hall to clear. He'd never catch up with the new girl now. Maybe he'd imagined her.

"Here," came a voice.

As he raised his eyes, Rex's mouth dropped open.

Without glasses Rex's weak eyes could see her perfectly. Behind her the hall was still a mess of blurred shapes, but her face stood out, clear and detailed. He noticed her green eyes now, flecked with gold in the sunlight.

"Your glasses," she said, holding them out. Even this close, the thick frames were still fuzzy, but he could see the girl's outstretched hand with crystal clarity. The Focus clung to her.

Finally willing himself to move, Rex closed his mouth and took the glasses. When he put them on, the rest of the world jumped into focus, and the girl blurred again. Just like the others always did.

"Thanks," he managed.

"That's okay." She smiled, shrugged, and looked around at the almost empty hall. "I guess we're late now. I don't even know where I'm going."

Her accent sounded midwestern, crisper than Rex's Oklahoma drawl.

"No, that was the eight-fifteen bell," he explained. "The late bell's at eight-twenty. Where're you headed?"

"Room T-29." She held a schedule card tightly in one hand.

He pointed back at the doorway. "That's in the temps. Outside on the right. Those trailers you saw on the way in."

She looked outside with a frown. "Okay," she said hesitantly, like she'd never had class in a trailer before. "Well, I better get going."

He nodded. As she walked away, Rex pulled off his glasses again, and again she jumped into clarity as the rest of the world became a blur.

Rex finally allowed himself to believe it and smiled. Another one, and from somewhere beyond Bixby, Oklahoma.

Maybe this year *was* going to be different.

Rex saw the new girl a few more times before lunch.

She was already making friends. In a small school like Bixby, there was something exciting about a new student— people wanted to find out about her. Already the popular kids were staking a claim to her, gossiping about what they'd learned about her, trading on her friendship.

Rex knew that the rules of popularity wouldn't allow him near her again, but he hovered nearby, listening, using his invisibility. Not really invisible, of course, but just as good. In his black shirt and jeans, with his dyed-black hair, he could disappear into shadows and corners. There weren't that many students like Timmy Hudson at Bixby High. Most people were happy to ignore Rex and his friends.

It didn't take Rex long to find out a few things about Jessica Day.

In the lunchroom he found Melissa and Dess in the usual place.

He sat across from Melissa, giving her space. As always, her sleeves were pulled down, almost covering her hands against any accidental touch, and she wore headphones, the hiss of metal power chords audible from them like an insistent whisper. Melissa didn't like crowds; any sizable number of regular people drove her crazy. Even a full classroom tested her limits. Without headphones she found the bickering, striving chaos of the lunchroom unbearable.

Dess ate nothing, didn't even push her food around, just folded her hands and peered at the ceiling through dark sunglasses.

"Here again for another year," Dess said. "How much does this suck?"

Rex reflexively started to agree but paused. All summer he had dreaded another year of awful lunches, hiding from the blazing skylights here in the dimmest corner. But for once he was actually excited to be in the Bixby High lunchroom.

The new girl was only a few tables away, surrounded by new friends.

"Maybe, maybe not," he said. "See that girl?"

"Mmm," Dess answered, her face still raised to the ceiling, probably counting the tiles up there.

"She's new. Her name is Jessica Day," Rex said. "She's from Chicago."

"And I'm interested in this why?" Dess asked.

"She just moved here a few days ago. Sophomore."

"Still bored."

"She's not boring."

Dess sighed and lowered her head to peer through her sunglasses at the new girl. She snorted. "First day at Bixby and she's already right in the middle of the daylight crowd. Nothing interesting about that. She's exactly the same as the other hundred and eighty-seven people in here."

Rex shook his head, starting to disagree, but stopped. If

he was going to say it out loud, he had to be right. As he
had a dozen times that day, he lifted his thick glasses an
inch, looking at Jessica Day with just his eyes. The cafeteria
dissolved into a bright, churning blur, but even from this
distance she stood out sharp and clear.

It was after noon, and her Focus hadn't faded. It was
permanent. There was only one explanation.

He took a deep breath. "She's one of us."

Dess looked at him, finally allowing an expression of interest to cross her face. Melissa felt the change between her
friends and looked up blankly. Listening, but not with her ears.

"*Her?* One of us?" Dess said. "No way. She could run
for mayor of Normal, Oklahoma."

"Listen to me, Dess," Rex insisted. "She's got the Focus."

Dess squinted, as if trying to see what only Rex could.
"Maybe she got touched last night or something like that."

"No. It's too strong. She's one of us."

Dess looked back up at the ceiling, her expression sliding again into totally bored with the ease of long practice.
But Rex knew he'd gotten her attention.

"All right," she relented. "If she's a sophomore, maybe
she's in one of my classes. I'll check her out."

Melissa nodded too, bobbing her head to the whispered
music.

2

DESS

When Jessica finally collapsed behind a desk for her last class of the day, she was completely exhausted. She crammed the wrinkled schedule into her pocket, hardly caring if she was in the right room anymore, and gratefully dropped her book bag onto the floor. All day it had been gaining weight like a new employee at Baskin-Robbins.

No first day of school was ever easy. But at least back in Chicago, Jessica had had the same old faces and familiar halls of Public School 141 to look forward to. Here in Bixby everything was a challenge. This school might be smaller than PS 141, but it was all spread out on ground level, a maze of add-ons and trailers. Every five-minute change of classes had been traumatic.

Jessica hated being late. She always wore a watch, which she set at least ten minutes fast. Today, when she already stood out as the new girl, she'd dreaded having to creep into a class late, everyone's eyes on her, looking sheepish and too dumb to find her way around. But she'd made it again. The bell hadn't rung yet. Jessica had managed to be on time the whole day.

The class filled slowly, everyone looking end-of-the-first-day frazzled. But even in their weariness a few noticed Jessica. They all knew about the new girl from the big city, it seemed. At her old school Jess had been just one student out of two thousand. But here she was practically a celebrity. Everyone was friendly about it, at least. The whole day she'd been shepherded around, smiled at, asked to stand up and introduce herself. She had the speech down pat now.

"I'm Jessica Day, and I just moved here from Chicago. We came because my mom got a job at Aerospace Oklahoma, where she designs planes. Not the whole plane, just the shape of the wing. But that's the part that makes it a plane, Mom always says. Everyone in Oklahoma seems very nice, and it's a lot warmer than Chicago. My thirteen-year-old sister cried for about two weeks before we moved, and my dad's going nuts because he hasn't found a job in Bixby yet, and the water tastes funny here. Thank you."

Of course, she'd never said that last part out loud. Maybe for this class she would, just to wake herself up.

The late bell rang.

The teacher introduced himself as Mr. Sanchez and called the roll. He paused a little when he got to Jessica's name, glancing at her for a second. But he must have seen her weary expression. He didn't ask for the speech.

Then it was time to pass out books. Jessica sighed. The

textbooks Mr. Sanchez was piling onto his desk looked dauntingly thick. Beginning trigonometry. More weight for the book bag. Mom had talked the guidance counselor into starting Jessica in all advanced classes here, dropping back to a normal level later if she needed to. The suggestion had been flattering, but after seeing the giant physics textbook, the stack of paperback classics for English, and now this doorstop, Jessica realized she'd been suckered. Mom had always been trying to get her into advanced classes back in Chicago, and now here Jessica was, trapped in trig.

As the books were being passed back, a tardy student entered the room. She looked younger than the others in the class. She was dressed all in black, wearing dark glasses and a lot of shiny metal necklaces. Mr. Sanchez looked up at her and smiled, genuinely pleased.

"Glad to see you, Desdemona."

"Hey, Sanchez." The girl sounded as tired as Jess felt, but with much more practice. She regarded the classroom with bored disgust. Mr. Sanchez was practically beaming at her, as if she were some famous mathematician he'd invited here to talk about how trigonometry could change your life.

He went back to passing out books, and the girl scanned the classroom for a place to sit. Then something strange happened. She pulled off the dark glasses, squinted at Jessica, and made her way purposefully to the empty desk next to her.

"Hey," she said.

"Hi, I'm Jessica."

"Yeah," the girl said, as if that were terribly obvious. Jessica wondered if she'd already met her in some other class. "I'm Dess."

"Hi." Okay, that was *hi* twice. But what was she supposed to say?

Dess was looking at her closely, trying to figure something out. She squinted, as if the room were too bright for her. Her pale fingers played with the translucent, yellowish beads on one of the necklaces, sliding them one way and then the other. They clicked softly as she arranged them into unreadable patterns.

A book arrived on Jessica's desk, breaking the spell that Dess's fingers had cast.

"When you get your book," Mr. Sanchez announced, "carefully fill out the form attached to the inside cover. That's *carefully*, people. Any damage you don't record is *your* responsibility."

Jessica had been through this drill all day. Apparently textbooks were an endangered species here in Bixby, Oklahoma. The teachers made everyone go through them page by page, noting every mark or tear. Supposedly there would be a terrible reckoning at the end of the year for anyone criminal enough to damage their books. Jessica had helped her dad do the same thing for their rental house, recording every nail hole in the walls, checking every electrical socket, and going into detail about how the automatic garage door didn't go up the last foot and a half.

Moving had been annoying in all kinds of unexpected ways.

She began going through the textbook, dutifully checking every page. Jess sighed. She'd gotten a bad one. *Underlined words, page 7. Scribbles on graph, page 19 . . .*

"So, how do you like Bixby so far, Jess?"

Jessica looked up. Dess was leafing through her book distractedly, apparently finding nothing. Half her attention was still on Jess.

The speech was all ready. *Everyone in Oklahoma seems very nice, and it's much warmer than Chicago.* But somehow she knew that Dess didn't want the speech.

Jess shrugged. "The water tastes funny here."

Dess almost managed to smile. "No kidding."

"Yeah, to me anyway. I guess I'll get used to it."

"Nope. I was born here, and it still tastes funny."

"Great."

"And that's not all that's funny."

Jess looked up, expecting more, but Dess was hard at work now. She'd skipped to the answers at the back of the trig book. Her pen leapt from one to another in no apparent order while her other hand fiddled madly with the amber beads. Occasionally she would make a change. She noted each one on the form.

"Several moronic answers corrected by nonmoron, page 326," she muttered. "Who checks these things? I mean, if you're going to be all new-mathy and put the answers in the back, they might as well be the right ones."

Jessica swallowed. Dess was checking the answers for chapter eleven, and they hadn't even started the book yet. "Uh, yeah, I guess. We found a mistake in my algebra textbook last year."

"*A* mistake?" Dess looked up at her with a frown.

"A couple, I guess."

Dess looked down at the book and shook her head. Somehow Jessica felt like she'd said something wrong. She wondered if this wasn't Dess's way of hassling the new girl. Or some weird way of showing off for her benefit.

Jessica went back to her own book. Whoever had owned it last year had dropped the class or had just lost interest. The pages were pristine now. Maybe the whole class had only gotten halfway through the book. Jessica hoped so— just leafing through the final pages of dense formulas and graphs was starting to scare her.

Dess was mumbling again. "A handsome rendering of the gorgeous Mr. Sanchez, page 214." She was doodling on one corner of a page, marking up the book and then recording the damage.

Jessica rolled her eyes.

"You know, Jess," Dess said, "Bixby water isn't just tasty. It gives you funny dreams."

"What?"

Dess repeated herself slowly and clearly, as if talking to some textbook-answer-checking moron. "The water in Bixby—it gives you funny dreams. Haven't you noticed?"

She looked at Jessica intensely, as if awaiting the answer to the most important question in the world.

Jessica blinked, trying to think of something witty to say. She was tired of Dess's games, though, and shook her head. "Not really. With moving and everything, I've been too tired to dream."

"Really?"

"Really."

Dess shrugged and didn't say another word to her the whole class.

Jessica was grateful for the silence. She struggled to follow Mr. Sanchez as he zoomed through the first chapter like it was old news and assigned the first night's homework from the second. Every year, by law, there was at least one class in her schedule designed to make sure that school didn't accidentally become fun. Jess was pretty sure that beginning trigonometry was this year's running nightmare.

And to make things worse, she could feel Dess's eyes on her the whole period. Jessica shivered when the last bell rang and headed into the crush of the loud and boisterous hallway with relief.

Maybe not everybody in Oklahoma was that nice.

3 | 12:00 A.M.

THE SILENT STORM

Jessica woke up because the sound of the rain just . . . stopped.

It changed all at once. The sound didn't fade away, trickling down into nothingness like rain was supposed to. One moment the whole world was chattering with the downpour, lulling her to sleep. The next, silence fell hard, as if someone had pushed mute on a TV remote control.

Jessica's eyes opened, the sudden quiet echoing around her like a door slam.

She sat up, looking around the bedroom in confusion. She didn't know what had woken her—it took a few seconds just to remember where she was. The dark room was a jumble of familiar and unfamiliar things. Her old writing desk was in the wrong corner, and someone had added a skylight to the ceiling. There were too many windows, and they were bigger than they should have been.

But then the shapes of boxes piled everywhere, clothing and books spilling out of their half-open maws, brought it all back. Jessica Day and her belongings were strangers here, barely settled, like pioneers on a bare plain. This was her new room, her family's new house. She lived in Bixby, Oklahoma, now.

"Oh, yeah," she said sadly.

Jessica took a deep breath. It smelled like rain. That was right—it had been raining hard all night . . . but now it was suddenly quiet.

Moonlight filled the room. Jessica lay awake, transfixed by how strange everything looked. It wasn't just the unfamiliar house; the Oklahoma night itself felt somehow wrong. The windows and skylight glowed, but the light seemed to come from everywhere, blue and cold. There were no shadows, and the room looked flat, like an old and faded photograph.

Jessica still wondered what had awakened her. Her heart beat quickly, as if something surprising had happened a moment ago. But she couldn't remember what.

She shook her head and lay back down, closing her eyes, but sleep wouldn't come. Her old bed seemed uncomfortable, somehow wrong, as if it didn't like being here in Bixby.

"Great," Jessica muttered. Just what she needed: a sleepless night to go with her exhausting days of unpacking, fighting with her little sister, Beth, and trying to find her way around the Bixby High maze. At least her first week at school was almost over. It would finally be Friday tomorrow.

She looked at the clock. It said 12:07, but it was set fast, to Jessica time. It was probably just about midnight. Friday at last.

A blue radiance filled the room, almost as bright as when

the light was on. When had the moon come out? High, dark clouds had rolled over Bixby all day, obscuring the sun. Even under the roof of clouds the sky was huge here in Oklahoma, the whole state as flat as a piece of paper. That afternoon her dad had said that the lightning flashes on the horizon were striking all the way down in Texas. (Being unemployed in Bixby had started him watching the Weather Channel.)

The cold, blue moonlight seemed brighter every minute.

Jessica slid out of bed. The rough timbers of the floor felt warm under her feet. She stepped carefully over the clutter, the moonlight picking out every half-unpacked box clearly. The window glowed like a neon sign.

When she looked outside, Jessica's fingers clenched and she uttered a soft cry.

The air outside sparkled, shimmering like a snow globe full of glitter.

Jessica blinked and rubbed her eyes, but the galaxy of hovering diamonds didn't go away.

There were thousands of them, each suspended in the air as if by its own little invisible string. They seemed to glow, filling the street and her room with the blue light. Some were just inches from the window, perfect spheres no bigger than the smallest pearl, translucent as beads of glass.

Jessica took a few steps backward and sat down on her bed.

"Weird dream," she said aloud, and then wished she hadn't. It didn't seem right saying that. Wondering if she were dreaming made her feel more . . . awake somehow.

And this was already too real: no unexplained panic, no watching herself from above, no feeling as if she were in a play and didn't know her lines—just Jessica Day sitting on her bed and being confused.

And the air outside full of diamonds.

Jessica slipped under her covers and tried to go back to sleep. *Unconscious* sleep. But behind closed eyelids she felt even more awake. The feel of the sheets, the sound of her breathing, the slowly building body warmth inside the covers were all exactly right. The realness of everything gnawed at her.

And the diamonds were beautiful. She wanted to see them up close.

Jessica got up again.

She pulled on a sweatshirt and rummaged around for shoes, taking a minute to find a matching pair among the moving boxes. She crept out of her room and down the hall. The still unfamiliar house looked uncanny in the blue light. The walls were bare and the living room empty, as if no one lived here.

The clock in the kitchen read exactly midnight.

Jessica paused at the front door, anxious for a moment. Then she pushed it open.

This had to be a dream: millions of diamonds filled the air, floating over the wet, shiny asphalt. Only a few inches apart, they stretched as far as Jessica could see, down the street and up into the sky. Little blue gems no bigger than tears.

No moon was visible. Thick clouds still hung over Bixby, but now they looked as hard and unmoving as stone. The light seemed to come from the diamonds, as if an invasion of blue fireflies had been frozen in midair.

Jessica's eyes widened. It was so beautiful, so still and wondrous, that her anxiety was instantly gone.

She raised a hand to touch one of the blue gems. The little diamond wobbled, then ran onto her finger, cold and wet. It disappeared, leaving nothing but a bit of water.

Then Jessica realized what the diamond had been. A raindrop! The floating diamonds were *the rain*, somehow hanging motionless in the air. Nothing moved on the street or in the sky. Time was frozen around her.

In a daze, she stepped out into the suspended rain. The drops kissed her face coolly, turning into water as she collided with them. They melted instantly, dotting her sweatshirt as she walked, wetting her hands with water no colder than September rain. She could smell the fresh scent of rain, feel the electricity of recent lightning, the trapped vitality of the storm all around her. Her hairs tingled, laughter bubbling up inside her.

But her feet were cold, she realized, her shoes soaking. Jessica knelt down to look at the walk. Motionless splashes of water dotted the concrete, where raindrops had been frozen just as they'd hit the ground. The whole street shimmered with the shapes of splashes, like a garden of ice flowers.

A raindrop hovered right in front of her nose. Jessica leaned nearer, closing one eye and peering into the little sphere of motionless water. The houses on the street, the arrested sky, the whole world was there inside, upside down and warped into a circle, like looking through a crystal ball. Then she must have gotten too close—the raindrop shivered and jumped into motion, falling onto her cheek and running down it like a cold tear.

"Oh," she murmured. Everything was frozen until she touched it, like breaking a spell.

Jessica smiled as she stood, looking around for more wonders.

All the houses on the street seemed to be glowing, their windows filled with blue light. She looked back at her own house. The roof was aglitter with splashes, and a motionless spout of water gushed from the meeting of two gutters at one corner. The windows glowed dully, but there hadn't been any lights on inside. Maybe it wasn't just the raindrops. The houses, the still clouds above, everything seemed to be incandescent with blue light.

Where did that cold light come from? she wondered. There was more to this dream than frozen time.

Then Jessica saw that she had left a trail, a tunnel through the rain where she had released the hovering rain. It was Jessica shaped, like a hole left by a cartoon character rocketing through a wall.

She laughed and broke into a run, reaching out to grab handfuls of raindrops from the air, all alone in a world of diamonds.

The next morning Jessica Day woke up smiling.

The dream had been so beautiful, as perfect as the

raindrops hovering in the air. Maybe it meant that Bixby wasn't such a creepy place after all.

The sun shone brightly into her room, accompanied by the sound of water dripping from the trees onto the roof. Even piled with boxes, it felt like *her* room, finally. Jessica lay in bed, luxuriating in a feeling of relief. After months of getting used to the idea of moving, the weeks of saying good-bye, the days of packing and unpacking, she finally felt as if the whirlwind were winding down.

Jessica's dreams weren't usually very profound. When she was nervous about a test, she had test-hell nightmares. When her little sister was driving Jessica crazy, the Beth of her dreams was a twenty-story monster who chased her. But Jessica knew that this dream had a deeper meaning. Time had stopped back in Chicago, her life frozen while she waited to leave all her friends and everything she knew, but now that was over. The world could start again, once she let it.

Maybe she and her family would be happy here after all.

And it was Friday.

The alarm rang. She pulled herself from under the covers and swung herself out of bed.

The moment her feet touched the floor, a chill ran up her spine. She was standing on her sweatshirt, which lay next to her bed in a crumpled pile.

It was soaking wet.

4

MELISSA

As Melissa got closer, the taste of school began to foul her mouth.

This far away it was acidic and cold, like coffee held under the tongue for a solid minute. She could taste first-week anxiety and inescapable boredom mixed together into a dull blur, along with the sour bile of wasted time that seeped out of the walls of the place. But Melissa knew the taste would change as school grew nearer. In another mile she would be able to distinguish the individual flavors of resentments, petty victories, rejections, and angry little skirmishes for dominance. A couple of miles after that and Bixby High would become almost unbearable, a buzz saw in her mind.

But for now she just grimaced and turned her music up.

Rex was standing in front of his father's house, tall and skinny, his black coat wrapped around him, the lawn under his feet dying. Even the tufts of weeds seemed to be battling some malign, invisible force. Every year since the old man's accident, the house had fallen further into disrepair.

Served the old guy right.

Melissa pulled her car up to the curb. Between the brown grass of the yard and Rex's long coat, she half expected cold winter air to rush into the car when he opened the door. But the hideous sun had already burned away the brief chill of last night's storm.

It was still early fall, still the beginning of the school year. Three months to go before winter, nine more months of junior year.

He jumped in and shut the door, careful not to get too close. When Rex scowled at the music's volume, Melissa sighed and turned it back down a notch. Human beings had no right to complain about music of any kind. The pandemonium that went on in their heads every waking hour was a hundred times noisier than any thrash-metal band, more chaotic than a bunch of sugar-rushing ten-year-olds with trumpets. If only they could hear themselves.

But Rex wasn't that bad. He was different, on a separate channel, free from the commotion of the daylight crowd. His had been the first individual thoughts she'd ever filtered from among the hideous mass, and she could still read him better than anyone.

Melissa could feel his excitement clearly, his hunger to know. She could taste his impatience, sharp and insistent over his usual calm.

She decided to keep him waiting. "Nice storm last night."

"Yeah. I went looking for lightning for a while."

"Me too, kind of. Just got soggy, though."

"Some night we'll get one, Cowgirl."

She snorted at the childhood nickname but muttered, "Sure. Some night."

Back when they were little kids, when it was just the two of them, they had always tried to find a streak of lightning. A bolt that had struck at exactly the right moment and gone to ground close enough to reach before time ran out. Once, years ago, they'd spent the whole hour biking toward a bright, jagged spur on the horizon. But they hadn't made it all the way, not even close. It'd been a lot farther away than it had looked. Riding back in the falling rain took much longer, of course, and by the time they'd made it home they were *soaking*.

Melissa had never been quite sure what they were supposed to do with a streak once they found one. Rex never said much about that. She could sense he wasn't totally sure about it himself. But he'd read something somewhere on one of his trips.

School grew nearer, the early morning collision of struggle and apprehension building from taste to clamor, the bitterness on her tongue expanding to a cacophony that assaulted her entire mind. Melissa knew she'd have to put her headphones on soon just to make it until classes started. She slowed the old Ford. It was always hard to drive this close, especially at the beginning of the year. She hoped her usual spot was free, behind a Dumpster in the vacant lot across the street from Bixby High. Parking anywhere else would take thinking. The school parking lot itself was too close to the maelstrom for her to drive safely.

"I hate that place," she managed.

Rex looked at her. His plain, focused thoughts made things better for a moment, and she was able to take a deep breath.

"There's a reason for all this," he said.

A reason for the way she was? For the agony she felt every day? "Yeah. To make my life suck."

"No. Something really important."

"Thanks." The Ford's suspension squealed beneath them as she took a turn too sharply. Rex's mind flinched, but not because of her driving. He hated hurting her, she knew.

"I didn't mean that your life wasn't—"

"Whatever," Melissa interrupted. "Don't worry about it, Rex. I just can't stand the beginning of the year. Too many melodramas all turned up to max."

"Yeah. I know what you mean."

"No, you don't."

The parking place was empty, and she pulled in, switching off the radio as she slowed. Melissa could tell that they were almost late—the crowd flowing into the building was harried, nervous. A bottle burst under one of her tires as the Ford ground to a halt. People snuck over here to drink beer at lunch sometimes.

Rex started to ask, so she beat him to it.

"I felt her last night. The new girl."

"I *knew* it," he said, hitting the dashboard in front of

him, his excitement cutting through the school noise with a clean, pure note.

Melissa smiled. "No, you didn't."

"Okay," Rex admitted. "But I was 99 percent sure."

Melissa nodded, getting out and pulling her bag after her. "You were totally scared that you might be wrong. That's how I knew how sure you were." Rex blinked, not understanding her logic. Melissa sighed. After years of listening to his thoughts she understood a few things about Rex that he didn't know himself. Things, it seemed, that he would never figure out.

"But yeah, she was out there last night," she continued. "Awake and . . ." Something else. She wasn't sure what else. This new girl was different.

As they walked toward Bixby High, the late bell rang. The sound always quieted the roar in Melissa's head, softening it to a low rumble as teachers established control and at least some students tried to concentrate. During classes she could almost think normally.

She remembered the night before, in the awesome silence of the blue time. Even in the dead of normal night she had to put up with the noise of dreams and night terrors, but the blue hour was absolutely still. That was the only time Melissa felt whole, completely free of daylight's chaos. For that one slice of each day she actually felt like she possessed a talent, a gift rather than a curse.

Melissa had known what Rex wanted her to do from the moment he'd come into the cafeteria on the first day of school. Every night this week she had crawled out of her window and up onto the roof. Searching.

It could take a few days to wake up for the first time. And she didn't know where the new girl lived. Dess had taken a long time to track down, out on the wild edge of the badlands.

Last night there hadn't been any lightning, not that she could see. Just one frozen flicker behind the motionless clouds. So Melissa had cleared her high perch of water splashes and sat down.

She had calmed her mind—so simple to do at midnight—and reached out across Bixby. The others were easy enough to feel. Melissa knew their signatures, the way they each met the secret hour, with relief, excitement, or calm. All of them were in their usual places, and the other things that lived in the blue time were in hiding, cowed by the energies of the storm.

A perfect night for casting.

Last night it hadn't taken long. The new girl lived close to her or was very strong. Melissa could feel her clearly, her new shape bright against the empty night. Melissa tasted a flicker of surprise at first, then long moments of wariness, then a slowly building torrent of joy that had lasted deep into the hour. Finally the girl had gone back to sleep, unworried by disbelief.

Some people had it so easy.

Melissa didn't know exactly what to think of the new girl. Below her shifting emotions was an unexpected flavor, a sharp metal taste, like a coin pressed against the tip of Melissa's tongue. The scent of unbridled energy was everywhere, but maybe that had just been the storm. And of course someone new was always full of unfamiliar flavors, unexpected faculties. Each of Melissa's friends felt different to her, after all.

But Jessica Day felt . . . more than different.

Melissa remembered to pull her headphones from her bag. She would need them to get through the halls to homeroom. As they crossed the street, Rex put a hand on her forearm, careful not to touch bare skin, steadying her as he always did this close to the distractions of school.

He pulled her to a stop as a car shot past.

"Careful."

"She's freaky, Rex."

"The new girl?"

"Yeah. Weird, even for one of us. Or maybe she's worse."

"Worse how?"

"Normal."

Melissa switched on her disc player as they continued, edging the volume up to push away the massive, approaching roar of school, pulling her sleeves down to cover her hands.

Rex turned to her as they reached the front door. He squeezed her shoulder and waited until she was looking at him. Rex alone knew that Melissa could read lips.

"Can you find her?"

She answered with deliberate softness—she hated people who yelled over the music in their headphones. "No problem."

"*Soon*," his lips formed. Was that a question or a command? she wondered. Something about his expression, and the worry in his mind, disturbed her.

"What's the big rush?"

"*I think there's danger. More than usual. There are signs.*"

Melissa frowned, then shrugged.

"Don't worry. I'll track her down."

She turned away from Rex, missing his reply, unable to concentrate as the school—with its noisy squall of anxiety, boredom, desire, misdirected energy, worry, competition, cheerleader pep, stifled anger, a little joy, and too much outright fear—swallowed her.

5

RURAL LEGENDS

"Okay, ten weird things about Bixby . . ."

Constanza Grayfoot folded back her notebook to a blank page and placed it primly on her knees. The other girls at the library table waited in silence as she wrote the numbers one to ten in a column down the left side.

"I've got one," Jen said. "Back two winters ago, when they found Sheriff Michaels's car out in the badlands." She turned to Jessica with eyebrows raised. "But no Sheriff Michaels."

"Number one: Disappearance of Sheriff Michaels," Constanza pronounced carefully as she wrote.

"I heard he was killed by drug dealers," Liz said. "They've got a secret airstrip in the badlands for when they fly stuff in from Mexico. He must have found out where it was."

"Or they were paying him off and they double-crossed him," Constanza said.

"No way," Jen said. "They found his uniform, badge, and gun, I heard."

"So what?"

"And also his teeth and hair. And his *fingernails*. Whatever's in the badlands is a lot worse than drug dealers."

"That's what the drug dealers want you to think."

"Oh, like you know."

Liz and Jen looked at Jessica, as if she was supposed to resolve the issue.

"Well," Jessica offered, "the badlands sound . . . bad."

"Totally."

"Girls," a voice called from the front desk of the library. "This is supposed to be a study period, not a chatting period."

"I'm just working on my article for the paper, Ms. Thomas," Constanza explained. "I'm editor this year."

"Does everyone in the library have to work on it with you?"

"Yes, they do. I'm writing about the ten things that make Bixby . . . special. Mr. Honorio said I need a wide variety of input. That's how I'm supposed to write it, so I'm working, not chatting."

Ms. Thomas raised one eyebrow. "Maybe the others have work of their own to do?"

"It's the first week of school, Ms. Thomas," Jen pointed out. "Nobody has any serious studying to do yet."

The librarian scanned her eyes across the five of them, then turned back to her computer screen. "Okay. Just don't get into any bad habits," she relented. "And try to keep it to a dull roar."

Jessica's eyes fell to her trig book. She actually *did* have some serious studying to do. Mr. Sanchez's class had moved through the first chapter with lightning speed, as if they'd started the book last year. Jessica was pretty sure she understood what Mr. Sanchez had covered in chapter two, but a few concepts kept popping up that were just incomprehensible. Mr. Sanchez seemed convinced that Jessica had been in advanced classes back in Chicago and that she only stayed quiet because she was way ahead of the rest of them. Not exactly.

Jessica knew she should be studying, but she felt too restless, too full of energy. Her dream the night before had done something to her. She wasn't sure what. She wasn't even positive it had been a dream. Had she actually gone sleepwalking? Jessica's sweatshirt had gotten wet somehow. But could you really walk around in driving rain without waking up? Maybe was she just going mildly nuts.

But whatever had happened last night, it felt wonderful. Her sister, Beth, had thrown her usual breakfast tantrum this morning, screaming that she could never start over in Bixby after spending the first thirteen years of her life in Chicago. Dad, with no work to go to, hadn't gotten up at all. And Mom had been in a huge rush to get to her new job, leaving Jessica the thankless task of getting her little sister out the door. But somehow this morning's dramas hadn't bothered her. The world seemed to be in focus today. Jess finally knew the way to all her classes, and her locker combination had spun from her fingers without a thought. Everything felt suddenly familiar, as if she had lived here in Bixby for years.

In any case, Jessica was way too restless to be reading a math book.

And listening to her new friends talk about the weird history of Bixby was much more interesting than trigonometry. Constanza Grayfoot was beautiful, with dark, straight hair and olive skin and just a trace of an accent. She and her friends were all juniors, a year older than her, but Jessica didn't feel younger around them. It was like being the new girl from the big city had mysteriously added a year to her age.

"I've got another one," Maria said. "How come there's a curfew here?"

"Number two: Annoying curfew," spelled out Constanza.

"Curfew?" Jessica asked.

"Yeah." Jen rolled her eyes. "Up in Tulsa, or even over in Broken Arrow County, you can stay out as late as you want. But in Bixby, if it's after eleven, you're busted. Until you're over eighteen. Don't you think that's weird?"

"That's not weird, that's just lame," said Liz.

"*Everything* about Bixby is weird."

"Everything about Bixby is *lame*."

"Don't you think Bixby's weird, Jessica?" Jen asked.

"Well, not really. I like it here."

"You're kidding," Liz said. "After living in Chicago?"

"Yeah, it's nice here." Jessica felt strange saying the words, but they were true. She'd been happy this morning, at least. But the other four girls were looking at her like they didn't believe her. "I guess there is some weird stuff about Bixby. Like the water. It tastes funny. But you guys know that already."

The others stared at her with blank expressions.

"But you know, I guess once I get used to it—" Jessica started.

"What about the snake pit?" interrupted Maria.

A momentary hush fell across the table. Jessica saw Ms. Thomas glance up, her interest piqued for a moment by the sudden silence, then turn back to her screen.

Constanza nodded. "Number three: Snake pit." Her voice was just above a whisper.

"Okay," Jessica said. "I'm going to guess that this snake pit is more on the weird side than the lame?"

"Yeah," Liz said. "If you believe in all that stuff."

"What stuff?" Jessica asked.

"Stupid legends," Liz said. "Like, supposedly a panther lives there."

"It escaped from a circus that came through a long time ago," Jen said. "There are articles about it in the library, from the *Bixby Register* in the 1930s or something."

"Articles *you've* actually read?" Liz asked.

Jen rolled her eyes. "Maybe *I* haven't, but everyone—"

"And this panther's, like, eighty years old?" Liz interrupted.

"Well, maybe not the 1930s . . ."

"Anyway, Jessica," Liz said. "The snake pit's just this lame place where you find old arrowheads. From the Indians. Big deal."

"We're called Native Americans," Constanza corrected.

"But this is from the *really* old days," Maria said, "before the Anglos moved all the other tribes here from the east. It was a village where the original natives of Oklahoma used to live—Stone Age cave people, not the Native Americans who live here now."

"You're right, that's not lame," Jessica said. "But it's hard to imagine a Stone Age Bixby."

"It's not only arrowheads," Jen explained seriously. "There's this big stone that sticks up out of the ground, right in the middle of the snake pit. People go there at midnight. And if you build this certain symbol out of rocks, it'll change right in front of your eyes exactly at the stroke of twelve."

"Change into what?"

"Well . . . the rocks don't change *into* anything," Jen said. "They're still rocks. But they move around."

"Lame," Liz declared.

"My older brother did it a year ago," Maria said. "It scared him to death. He won't even talk about it now."

Jen leaned forward, still talking in a quiet, ghost-story voice. "And even though archaeologists have been working there for a long time, you can still find arrowheads if you look. They're, like, a *thousand* years old."

"Ten thousand, you mean."

Jessica and the others turned to look across the library. It was Dess, the girl from Jessica's math class, sitting alone in a corner.

"Okay . . . ," Liz said slowly, her eyes rolling a little for the other girls at the table. Then she whispered, "Speaking of lame."

Jessica glanced back at Dess, who didn't seem to have heard. She had dropped her head back into her book, reading through dark glasses, as if no longer interested in their conversation. Jessica hadn't even noticed Dess, but she must have been there the whole period, camped in her corner of the library, books and paper splayed around her.

"Number four . . . ," Constanza began, her green pen poised above the paper. Jen giggled, and Maria made a silent hushing gesture.

Jessica looked down at her books, especially the heavy trig tome. Her energy was beginning its usual prelunch fade. She liked Constanza and her crew, but the way they'd teased Dess left a bad taste in her mouth. She remembered how things had been for her in Chicago, before she'd moved here and become Miss Popular.

Jessica looked over at Dess again. One of the books on the table was *Beginning Trigonometry*. If Dess was half as smart as she pretended to be, it might be worth asking her for help.

"I really should get some work done," Jessica said. "My mom went insane and put me in all these advanced classes. Trig is killing me already."

"Okay," Constanza said. "But if you think of anything else weird about Bixby, make sure you tell me. I want to get the new girl's perspective."

"I'll keep you posted."

Jessica gathered her books and moved over to the corner. She sat down in the other big chair across the low table from Dess. The girl's feet were propped on the table, shiny metal rings decorating her ankles over black stockings.

Jess thought she heard a whisper from back at the table but ignored it.

"Dess?"

The girl looked up at her without expression. Not impatient or annoyed, just strangely neutral behind the glasses.

Jessica's fingers started to tug her trig book from the stack.

"Do you think that . . ." Her question faltered. Dess's stare was so cool and unblinking. "I just wanted to ask you," Jess started again, "uh . . . do you always wear sunglasses when you read?"

"Not always. They make me take them off in class."

"Oh. But why—?"

"I'm photophobic. Sunlight hurts my eyes. A lot."

"Ow. They should let you wear dark glasses in class, then."

"They don't. There's no rule. But they don't."

"Maybe if you got a note from your doctor."

"What about you?" Dess asked.

"What about me, what?"

"Don't your eyes hurt from the light?"

"No," Jessica said.

"That's weird."

Jessica blinked. She was starting to wish she had stayed

at the other table. Dess had been interesting to talk to in trig class but not interesting in a fun way. The girls back at Constanza's table must be wondering what she was doing over here, talking to this girl. Jessica certainly was.

But she had to ask: "How is that weird?"

Dess pulled her glasses down half an inch and peered into Jessica's eyes, an intent expression on her face. "It's just that some people, *certain* people, who move to Bixby find that the sunlight here is hideously bright. They suddenly need to get sunglasses and wear them all the time. But not you?"

"Not me. Does that really happen to a lot of people?"

"A select few." Dess pushed her glasses back up. "It's one of the ten weird things about Bixby."

Jess leaned back in the chair and muttered, "Ten thousand, you mean."

Dess smiled back at her, nodding agreement. Seeing the pleased expression made Jessica feel better. In a way she felt sorry for Dess. The other girls had been rude, and Dess wasn't that bad.

"So, Jessica, do you want to know a *really* weird thing about Bixby?"

"Sure. Why not?"

"Check this out." Dess pulled a library book at random from the shelf behind her and handed it to Jessica.

"Hmm. *Vanity Fair,* except it's not a magazine, it's a five-hundred-page book. Scary."

"No, on the spine. The Bixby seal."

Jessica looked at the small white sticker that marked the book Property of Bixby High School Library. Under the bar code was a logo: a radiant sun.

"What, that little sun?"

"It's not a sun, it's a star."

"The sun is a star, I heard somewhere."

"In space, same thing. In symbology, they're different. See the little points coming out of it? Count them."

Jessica sighed and squinted at the sticker. "Thirteen?"

"That's right, Jess. It's a thirteen-pointed star. Look familiar?"

Jessica pursed her lips. It *did* look familiar. "Yeah, actually there's a plaque like it on our house. An antique. The real estate agent said that in the old days it showed you had insurance. The fire department wouldn't put out a fire at your house unless you had one."

"That's what everyone always says. But there's a plaque like it on every house in Bixby."

"So people didn't want their houses to burn down. What's weird about that?"

Dess smiled again, narrowing her eyes. "And there's a big star on the entrance to city hall. And one on the masthead of the *Bixby Register* and painted on the floor just inside every entrance to this school. All of those stars have thirteen points too." She leaned forward, speaking quickly and quietly. "The city council has thirteen members, almost every flight of stairs in town has thirteen steps, and *Bixby, Oklahoma* has thirteen letters."

Jessica shook her head. "Meaning?"

"Meaning that Bixby is the only city I've heard of where thirteen is considered a lucky number. And not just lucky, but *necessary*."

Jessica took a deep breath. She looked up at the bookshelves behind Dess's head. Now that Dess had pointed them out, she could see the little white stickers clearly, row upon row looming over the two of them. Hundreds of thirteen-pointed stars.

She shrugged. "I guess that is pretty weird, Dess."

"Are you having funny dreams yet?" the girl asked.

A chill traveled slowly up Jessica's spine. "What?"

"Remember in trig? I told you the water here would give you funny dreams. Have they started yet?"

"Oh, yeah." Jessica's mind started to race. For some reason, she didn't want to tell Dess about her dream. It had felt so perfect, so welcoming. And she was certain that Dess would say something to ruin the feeling that the dream had left her with. But the girl was staring at her so intently, her eyes demanding an answer.

"Maybe," Jess said slowly. "I kind of had one weird dream. But maybe it wasn't a dream at all. I'm not sure."

"You'll find out soon enough." Dess looked up at the library clock and smiled. "In 43,207 seconds, to be exact."

Seven seconds later the bell rang for lunch.

6

JONATHAN

Jessica headed to lunch, a fist of nerves clenched in her stomach.

Dess had given her the creeps again, just like that first day in trig. Jessica could see why Dess didn't have many friends. Every time Jess felt like they were starting to connect, the girl would make some weird, knowing observation, as if she wanted to convince Jessica that she had psychic powers. All Jessica had wanted was some help with trigonometry, not a course in the arcane ways of Bixby, Oklahoma.

Jessica sighed as she made her way toward the cafeteria. Now that she thought about it, Dess wasn't really all that mysterious. Just sad. She was pushing Jessica away on purpose. The befuddling twists and turns of her conversations were probably meant to shut people out. Messing with people's heads was easier than getting to know and trust them. Maybe she was afraid.

But Dess never seemed afraid, only calm and confident. However off the wall her lines were, she always delivered them in such a knowing way. Dess talked as if she lived in an alien world with completely different rules, all of which made perfect sense to her.

Which was another way of saying she was crazy.

On the other hand, something inside Jess felt as if Dess was actually trying to communicate with her. Was trying to help her understand her new town or maybe even warn her about something. Dess *had* been totally right about the weird dream. Of course, that didn't necessarily make Dess a mind reader and didn't mean the Bixby water supply had caused it. A lot of people had funny dreams when they went new places. Dess probably realized that Jessica was freaked out about moving and had decided it would be fun to freak her out a little bit more.

It had worked.

As Jess reached the lunchroom, the slightly rancid smell of frying swept out of the open double doors, along with the roar of hundreds of voices. Jessica's step slowed as she crossed the threshold. As the new girl, she still experienced a few seconds of minor panic while figuring out where to sit, not wanting to offend new friends or get stuck with people she wasn't sure about.

For a moment Jessica almost wished that Dad hadn't decided to start packing lunches for her. Waiting in line for official Bixby High School slop would have given her more time to scope out where to sit. Maybe that was why high school lunches had been invented. It certainly hadn't been for their nutritional value. Or their flavor.

As her eyes scanned the room, the butterflies in Jessica's stomach started fluttering again. There was Dess, looking straight at her. The girl must have used some quicker route to the lunchroom through the Bixby High maze. She sat at a table in a distant corner with two friends. Like her, they wore all black. Jess recognized the boy from the first day of school. She remembered that moment of anxiety entering Bixby High for the first time, terrified that she was late. The memory was strangely clear; the image of his glasses getting knocked off was cemented in her mind. Jessica wondered why she hadn't seen him around since then. With his long black coat the guy should have stood out at Bixby. There'd been a lot of kids like him and Dess back in PS 141, but there were only three or four here. It was too warm and sunny in Oklahoma to do the whole vampire thing.

Unless, of course, you were "photophobic," if Dess had even been telling the truth about *that*.

Now the boy was looking at Jessica too, as if he and Dess were both expecting her to join them. The other girl at the table was staring off into space, headphones over her ears.

Jessica looked around for somewhere else to sit. She wasn't up for any more head games today. She looked for Constanza or Liz, but she couldn't see them or any of the other girls from the library table. Her eyes searched for a familiar face, but Jess recognized no one. The horde of faces blurred together into a bewildering mass. The cafeteria slipped out of focus, the dizzying roar of voices assaulting her from all sides. Her moment of hesitation stretched out, suddenly transformed into total confusion.

But somehow her feet kept walking, bringing her closer to Dess's table. The girl and her friends were the only stable part of the room. Instinct carried Jessica toward them.

"Jessica?"

She turned, recognized a face out of the blur. A very attractive face.

"I'm Jonathan, from physics class. Remember?"

His smile cut through the fog enveloping her. His dark brown eyes were very much in focus.

"Sure. Jonathan. Physics." She *had* noticed him in class. Anyone would have.

Jessica stood there, unable to say anything more. But at least she had managed to stop walking toward Dess's table.

A look of concern crossed his face. "Want to sit down?"

"Yeah. That would be great."

He led Jessica to an empty table, in the corner opposite Dess's. Her dizziness began to subside. She gratefully dumped her book bag and lunch sack onto the table as she sat down.

"You okay?" Jonathan asked.

Jessica blinked. The cafeteria was back to its normal self: loud, chaotic, and a bit smelly, but no longer a roller coaster. Her disorientation had vanished as suddenly as it had arrived. "Much better."

"You looked like you were going to take a spill."

"No, I . . . Yeah, maybe. Tough week." Jessica wanted to

add that she didn't usually act like a zombie in front of cute guys but somehow couldn't find the right words. "I think I just need to eat."

"Me too."

Jonathan overturned his lunch bag, spilling its contents onto the table. An apple rolled perilously close to the edge of the table, but he ignored it. It stopped just before falling to the floor. Jessica raised an eyebrow as she looked at his pile of food. It included three sandwiches, a bag of chips, a banana, and a carton of yogurt in addition to the wayward apple.

Jonathan was thin as a rail. A hungry rail. He grabbed a sandwich from the pile, pulled off its plastic wrap, and tore into it.

Jessica looked at her own lunch. As always, Dad had gotten bored last night and created something complicated. Grated cheese, ground meat, chopped lettuce, and tomato all occupied their own corners of a multisection container. A couple of hard taco shells were visible through the plastic of another. The tacos were already broken. Jess sighed and popped open the containers, dumping all the ingredients together and starting to mix them up.

"Mmm, taco salad," Jonathan said. "Smells good."

Jessica nodded. The spicy aroma coming from the meat had taken the edge off the fried smell of high school cafeteria. "My dad's getting into southwestern cuisine in a big way."

"Beats sandwiches."

"That one looks good."

"They're peanut butter on banana bread."

"Peanut butter on banana bread? All three? That's a . . . time-saver, I guess."

"Saves slicing bananas. I can't ever wake up early enough to make anything fancy."

"But three of them?" she asked.

He shrugged. "That's nothing. Some birds eat their own body weight every hour."

"Sorry, I missed the feathers on you."

Jonathan grinned. He looked sleepy. His eyes never quite opened all the way, but they twinkled when he smiled. "Hey, if I don't get enough calories, I'm the one who's fainting." He opened the second sandwich and took a huge bite, as if talking this much had put him behind schedule.

"That reminds me," Jessica said, "thanks for saving me. That would have been a smooth move, falling on my face in front of the whole school my first week here."

"You could always blame the Bixby water."

Jessica's fork halted a few inches from her mouth. "You don't like it either?"

"I moved here more than two years ago, and I still can't drink it." Jonathan shuddered.

Jessica felt the fist of nerves in her stomach unclench a bit. She had started to think that everyone else in town had been born and bred here and that she was the first outsider they'd ever seen. But Jonathan was another stranger to this strange place.

"Where'd you move here from?" she asked.

"Philadelphia. Well, just outside, anyway."

"I'm from Chicago."

"So I heard."

"Oh, right. Everyone knows everything about the new girl."

He smiled, shrugged. "Not everything."

Jessica smiled back at Jonathan. They ate quietly for a while, ignoring the roar of the cafeteria around them. Her taco salad really was good, now that she paid attention to it. Maybe having a house dad wasn't so bad. And Jonathan's quiet feasting on his sandwiches was somehow reassuring. Jessica felt comfortable in a way she hadn't since coming to Bixby. She felt . . . normal.

"So, Jonathan," she said after a few minutes. "Can I ask you something?"

"Sure."

"When you first got here, did you think Bixby was kind of weird?"

Jonathan chewed thoughtfully.

"I *still* think Bixby's weird," he said. "And not kind of— very. It's not just the water. Or the snake pit or all the other funny rumors. It's . . ."

"What?"

"It's just that Bixby is really . . . psychosomatic."

"It's *what*?" she asked. "Doesn't that mean 'all in your head' or something?"

"Yeah. Like when you feel sick, but your body's really okay. Your mind has the power to *make* you sick. That's Bixby all over: psychosomatic. The kind of place that gives you strange dreams."

Jessica almost choked on a forkful of taco salad.

"Did I say something?" Jonathan asked.

"Mm-mm," she managed, clearing her throat. "People keep saying stuff that makes no . . ." Jess paused. "That makes too much sense."

Jonathan looked at her carefully, his brown eyes narrowing even further.

"Okay, I guess this might sound a little nuts," Jessica admitted. "But it sometimes seems like people here in Bixby know what's going on inside my head. Or I guess one person does, anyway. There's this girl—half the time she talks crazy, but the other half it's like she's reading my mind."

Jessica realized that Jonathan had stopped eating. He was looking at her intently.

"Do I sound insane?" she asked.

He shrugged. "I had this friend back in Philadelphia, Julio, who would go and see this psychic every time he had five bucks to blow. She was an old woman who lived in a storefront downtown, complete with a purple neon hand in the window."

Jessica laughed. "We had palm readers like that in Chicago."

"But she didn't read palms or look in a crystal ball," Jonathan said. "She just talked."

"Was she really psychic?"

Jonathan shook his head. "I doubt it."

"You don't believe in that stuff?"

"Well, not as far as she goes." Jonathan took a bite but

kept talking. "I went with Julio once to watch, and I think I figured out how it worked. The woman would say weird, random things, one after another, until something rang a bell with Julio and his eyes would light up. She'd keep pushing in that direction, and he'd start talking and telling her everything. His dreams, what he was worried about, whatever. He thought that she was reading his mind, but she was only getting him to tell her what was going on inside his head."

"Sounds like a good trick."

"I'm not sure it was just a trick," Jonathan said. "I mean, she really seemed to help Julio. When he was about to do something stupid, he wouldn't listen to anyone else, but she could always talk sense into him. Like when he'd decided to run away from home one time, she was the one who talked him out of it."

Jessica put down her fork. "So she wasn't just ripping him off."

"Well, the funny thing is, I'm not sure that she knew what she was doing. Maybe it was all instinct and she really thought she *was* psychic, you know? But she wasn't really psychic, just psychosomatic."

Jessica smiled, taking a thoughtful bite of her salad. The woman Jonathan had described sounded a lot like Dess. Her weird, probing questions and random statements, all delivered with total authority, had almost started Jessica believing that Dess had some kind of special power. Or at least they had fooled her enough to creep her out. Maybe it *was* all in her head. If Jessica *believed* that Dess had some special power, then in a way she did.

In any case, Dess certainly put the *psycho* back in *psychosomatic*.

"So it's possible," Jonathan continued, "that this girl you know isn't completely nuts. She might have a different way of communicating, but maybe she does have something important to say."

"Yeah, maybe," Jessica said. "But whatever it is, I kind of wish she'd just come out and say it."

"Maybe you're not ready to hear it."

Jessica looked at Jonathan with surprise. He blinked his sleepy brown eyes at her innocently.

"Well, maybe you're right," she said, shrugging. "But until then, I'm not going to worry about it."

"That makes sense."

Jessica smiled at those three words as Jonathan attacked his final sandwich. It was about time something made sense.

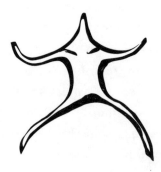

7

12:00 A.M.

DARK MOON

That night the blue dream came again.

Jessica had been lying awake and staring at the ceiling, relieved that it was finally the weekend. Tomorrow she was determined to finish unpacking. Searching through the fourteen boxes piled around her room was getting old. Maybe organizing her stuff would make her life feel a little bit more under control.

She must have been more tired than she'd realized. Sleep stole up on her so quietly that dreaming seemed to collide with consciousness. It was as if she blinked, and everything changed. Suddenly the world was blue, the low hum of the Oklahoma wind swallowed by silence.

She sat up, suddenly alert. The room was filled with the familiar blue light.

"Great," she said softly. "*This* again."

Tonight Jessica didn't waste time trying to go back to sleep. If this was a dream, she was already asleep. And it *was* a dream. Probably.

Except for the matter of that soggy sweatshirt, of course.

She slipped out from under the covers and got dressed in jeans and a T-shirt. The motionless rain had been wonderful, so she might as well see what wonders her subconscious had cooked up this time.

Jessica looked around carefully. Everything was sharp and clear. She felt very calm, without any dreamy muzzy-headedness. She remembered from a psych class she'd taken last year that this was called "lucid dreaming."

The light was exactly the same as in her dream the night before, a deep indigo that shone from every surface. There were no shadows, no dark corners. She peered into one of her moving boxes and could see everything inside it with equal and perfect clarity. Every object seemed to glow softly from within.

She looked out the window. There were no floating diamonds this time, just a quiet street, as still and flat as a painting.

"That's boring," she muttered.

Jessica crept to her door and opened it carefully. Something in this dream made her want to respect the deep silence; in the blue light the world seemed secretive and mysterious. A place to sneak through.

Halfway down the hall Beth's door was ajar. Jess pushed it open tentatively. Her sister's room was lit in the same deep blue as her own. It was wrapped in the same silence and flatness, though it was definitely Beth's clothing strewn chaotically around the floor. Her sister had accomplished even less on the unpacking front than Jessica.

A shape filled the bed. The small form was tangled uncomfortably in the covers. Since the move Beth hadn't been sleeping well, which kept her in a state of constant crankiness.

Jessica crossed to the bed and sat down gently, thinking about how little time she'd spent with Beth since they'd arrived in Bixby. Even in the months before the move her little sister's tantrums had made her impossible to hang out with. Beth had fought the idea of leaving Chicago every step of the way, and everyone in the family had gotten into the habit of avoiding her when she was in a bad mood.

Maybe that was why this dream had led her here. Having to get used to Bixby herself, Jessica hadn't thought much about her sister's problems.

She reached out and rested one hand softly on Beth's sleeping form.

Jessica jerked back, a chill running through her. The body under the covers felt wrong. It was hard, as unyielding as a plastic mannequin in a store window.

Suddenly the blue light seemed cold around her.

"Beth?" Her sister didn't move. Jessica couldn't see any sign of breathing.

"Beth, wake up." Her voice broke from a whisper into a cry. "Quit fooling around. Please?"

She shook her sister with both hands.

The shape under the covers didn't move. It felt heavy and stiff.

Jessica reached for the covers again, not sure that she

wanted to reveal what was underneath but unable to stop herself. She stood up, taking a nervous step away from the bedside even as she reached out and pulled the bedclothes away with a frantic jerk.

"Beth?"

Her sister's face was chalk white, as motionless as a statue. The half-opened eyes glimmered like green glass marbles. One white and frozen hand clutched the tangled sheets like a pale claw.

"Beth!" Jessica sobbed.

Her sister didn't move.

She reached out and touched Beth's cheek. It was as cold and hard as stone.

Jessica turned and ran across the room, almost tripping on the piles of clothing. She threw open the door and ran down the hallway toward her parents' room.

"Mom! Dad!" she screamed. But as Jessica stumbled to a halt in front of her parents' room, the cry died in her throat. The closed door stood cold and blank before her.

There was no sound from inside. They must have heard her.

"Mom!"

There was no response.

What if she opened it and her parents were like Beth? The image of her mother and father as white, frozen statues—dead things—paralyzed her. Her hand had almost reached the doorknob, but she couldn't bring her fingers to close on it.

"Mommy?" she called softly.

No sound came from inside the room.

Jess backed away from the door, suddenly terrified that it would open, that something might come out. This nightmare might have anything in store for her. The unfamiliar house seemed completely alien now, blue and cold and empty of anything alive.

She turned and ran back toward her own room. Halfway there, she passed Beth's door, still open wide. Jessica turned her eyes away too late and saw in a terrible flash the exposed, lifeless white shape of her sister on the bed.

Jessica bolted into her room and shut the door tightly behind her, collapsing in a sobbing heap onto the floor. The first dream had been so beautiful, but this nightmare was completely awful. She just wanted to wake up.

Fighting back her terror, she tried to think through what the dream must mean. Jessica had been so wrapped up in her own problems, she hadn't seen the obvious. Beth needed her. She had to stop acting as if her sister's anger were just an inconvenience.

She hugged her knees to her chest, her back to the door, promising she'd be nicer to Beth tomorrow.

Jessica waited for the dream to end.

Hopefully this time there would be nothing left of it in the real world. No frozen Beth, no soggy sweatshirts. Just morning sun and the weekend.

Slowly, gradually, Jessica's tears ran out, and the blue dream wrapped itself around her. Nothing changed or moved.

The still, cold light shone from everywhere and nowhere; the silence lay total and absolute. Not even the whispering creaks and groans of a house at night could be heard.

So when the scratching came, Jessica lifted her head at once.

There was a shape in the window, a small dark form silhouetted against the even glow from the street. It moved smoothly and sinuously, taking catlike steps back and forth across the window frame, then paused to scratch against the glass.

"Kitty?" Jessica said, her voice rough from crying.

The animal's eyes caught the light for a moment, flashing deep purple.

Jessica stood shakily, her legs all pins and needles. She moved slowly, trying not to scare the cat away. At least something else was alive here in this hideous nightmare. At least she was no longer alone with the lifeless shape in Beth's room. She crossed to the window and peered out.

It was sleek and thin, glossy and black. Muscles rippled under its midnight fur; the animal seemed as strong as a wild cat of some kind, almost like a miniature black cheetah. She wondered for a moment if it was even a pet cat at all. Her dad had said that there were bobcats and other small wild felines in the countryside around Bixby. But the beast looked very tame as it paced impatiently on the window ledge, gazing up at her with pleading indigo eyes.

"Okay, okay," she said.

She pulled open the window, giving up on what this part of the dream meant. The cat bumped heavily against her as it leapt into the room, its corded muscles solid against her thigh.

"You're a real bruiser," she muttered, wondering what breed it was. She'd never seen any cat this strong.

It jumped up onto her bed, sniffing her pillow, ran in a small circle on the rumpled covers, then jumped into one of her boxes. She heard it rummaging through the stuff in the box.

"Hey, you."

The cat sprang from the box and peered up at her, suddenly cautious. It backed away slowly, muscles tense and quivering as if it were ready to spring away.

"It's okay, kitty." Jessica began to wonder if it wasn't a wild cat after all. It wasn't acting like any domestic cat she'd ever met.

She knelt and offered one hand. The cat came closer and sniffed.

"It's all right." Jessica reached out one finger and scratched lightly at the top of its head.

"Rrrrrrr." The low, terrible noise welled up from the creature, as deep as a tiger's growl, and it backed away with its belly pressed to the floor.

"Hey, relax," Jessica said, pulling her hand back to a safe distance.

The black cat's eyes were filled with terror. It turned and ran to the bedroom door, scratching plaintively. Jessica stood and took a few careful steps toward it, reaching out to open the door.

The cat bounded down the hall and disappeared around the corner. She heard it complaining at the front door. It didn't howl like a normal cat. The high-pitched cries sounded more like those of a wounded bird.

Jessica looked back at her open window in puzzlement. "Why didn't you just . . . ?" she started, then shook her head. Wild or not, this cat was nutty.

Careful not to look into Beth's room, she followed the creature's anguished noises down the hall and to the front door. The cat cringed as she approached but didn't bolt. Jessica gingerly reached out and turned the knob. The second the door was open a crack, the cat squeezed itself through and took off.

"See you later," she said softly, sighing. This was perfect. The only other living thing in this nightmare was terrified of her.

Jessica pulled the door the rest of the way open and went out onto the porch. The old wood creaked under her feet, the sound reassuring in this silent world. She took a deep breath, then stepped onto the walk, glad to leave the lifeless, alien house behind her. The blue light seemed cleaner, somehow healthier out here. She missed the diamonds, though. She looked around for anything—a falling leaf, a drop of rain—suspended in the air. Nothing. She glanced up to the sky to check for clouds.

A giant moon was rising.

Jessica swallowed, her mind spinning as she tried to make sense of the awesome sight. The huge half orb consumed almost a quarter of the sky, stretching across the horizon as big as a sunset. But it wasn't red or yellow or any other hue Jessica could name. It felt like a dark spot burned into her vision, as if she had looked at the sun too long. It hung colorlessly in the sky, coal black and blindingly bright at the same time, merciless against her eyes.

She shielded her face, then looked down toward the ground, head aching and eyes watering fiercely. As she blinked away the tears, Jessica saw that the normal color of the grass had returned. For a few seconds the lawn looked green and alive, but then the cold blue rushed back into it, like a drop of dark ink spreading through a glass of water.

Her head still pounded, and Jessica thought of eclipses, in which the sun was darkened but still powerful, blinding people who unknowingly stared at it. An afterimage of the huge moon still burned in her eyes, changing the hues of the whole street. Glimpses of normal colors—greens, yellows, red—flickered in the corners of her vision. Then slowly her headache subsided, and calm blue tones settled over the street again.

Jessica glanced up at the moon again and with a flash of realization saw its true color: a bright darkness, a hungry blankness, a sucking up of light. The blue light in this dream didn't come from objects themselves, as she'd thought at first. And it didn't come directly from the giant moon above. Rather, the cold, lifeless blue was a leftover, the last remnant of light that remained after the dark moon had leached all the other colors from the spectrum.

She wondered if the moon—or dark sun, or star, or whatever it was—had been in the sky in her last dream, hidden behind the clouds. And what did it mean? So far, Jessica had thought these dreams were adding up to something. But this was just bizarre.

A howl came from down the street.

Jessica whirled toward the sound. It was the cat again, this time screeching the high-pitched call of a monkey. It stood at the end of the street, glaring back at her.

"You again?" she said, shivering at the sound. "You're pretty loud for such a little kitty."

The cat yowled once more, almost sounding like a cat now. An unhappy one. Outside in the moonlight its eyes flashed indigo and its fur was even blacker, as rich and dark as an empty night sky.

It yowled again.

"All right, I'm coming," Jessica muttered. "Don't get all psychosomatic on me."

She walked after the creature. It waited until it was sure she was following, then padded away. As they walked, it kept looking over its shoulder at her, making shrieking or barking or growling noises in turn. It stayed well ahead, too scared of Jessica to let her get close but taking care not to lose sight of her.

The cat led her through an otherwise empty world. There were no clouds in the sky, no cars or people, just the vast moon slowly rising. The streetlights were dark, except for the uniform blue glow that came from everything. The houses looked abandoned and still, dead silence hovering over them, pierced only by the weird menagerie of noises from the anxious cat.

At first Jessica recognized some of the houses from her route to school, but the neighborhood looked alien in this light, and she quickly forgot how many turns she and the cat had taken.

"I hope you know where you're going," she called to the animal.

As if in answer, it stopped and sniffed at the air, making a gurgling sound almost like that of a small human child. Its tail was high in the air, flicking nervously from side to side.

Jessica approached the cat slowly. It sat in the middle of the street, shivering, the muscles under its fur twitching with tiny spasms.

"Are you okay?" Jess asked.

She knelt next to it and put one hand out carefully. It turned to her with wide, frantic eyes, and Jessica pulled away.

"Okay. No touching."

Its fur was rippling now, as if there were snakes crawling under its skin. The cat's legs curled up tightly against its shivering body, its tail sticking out stiffly behind.

"Oh, you poor thing." She looked around, instinctively searching for help. But of course there was no one.

Then the change began in earnest.

As Jessica watched in transfixed horror, the cat's body grew longer and thinner, the tail thicker, as if the cat were being squeezed into its own tail. Its legs were absorbed into the body. The head began to shrink and flatten, teeth protruding from its mouth as if they couldn't fit inside its head anymore. It stretched and stretched, until finally the creature was one long column of muscle.

It twisted around to face her, long fangs glistening in the dark moon's light.

It had become a snake. Its sleek black fur still shone, and it still possessed the large, expressive eyes of a mammal, but that was all that was left of the cat she had trustingly followed here.

It blinked its cat eyes at her and hissed, and Jess was finally released from her paralyzing terror. She cried out and scrabbled away backward on hands and bare feet. The thing was still shivering, as if not yet fully in control of its new body, but its gaze followed her.

Jessica leapt to her feet and backed away further. The creature began to writhe now, twisting around in circles and making horrible noises that sounded halfway between a hiss and the noise of a cat being strangled. It sounded as if the cat were inside the snake, trying to fight its way out.

A chill passed through Jessica's whole body. She hated snakes. Tearing her gaze from the creature, she frantically scanned the surrounding houses, trying to remember where she was. She had to get home and back into bed. She'd had enough of this dream. Everything in it transformed into something horrible and foul. She had to end the night-mare before it got any worse.

Then another hiss came from behind her, and Jessica's heart began to pound.

Black, almost invisible shapes slithered from the grass onto the street around her. More snakes, dozens of them, all like the creature she had followed here. They took up positions in a circle around her.

In moments she was surrounded.

"I don't believe this," she said aloud slowly and clearly, trying to make the words true. She took a few steps toward where she thought home was, trying not to look at the slithering forms on the street in her path. The snakes hissed and backed away nervously. Like the cat, they were wary of her.

For a crazy moment Jessica remembered her mom's lecture about wild animals before they'd left the city. "Remember, they're more scared of you than you are of them."

"Yeah, right," she muttered. There wasn't room in a snake's brain for how scared she was.

But she kept walking, taking slow, deliberate steps, and the snakes parted for her. Maybe they really were more scared than she was.

A few more steps and she was out of the circle. She walked away quickly, until she had left the snakes half a block behind.

She turned and called, "No wonder you taste like chicken. You *are* chicken."

The new sound came from behind her.

It was a deep rumble, like the elevated train that had passed a block away from their old house. Jessica didn't so much hear it as feel it through the soles of her feet. The sound seemed to travel up her spine before it broke into an audible growl.

"What now?" she said, turning around.

She froze when she saw it at the end of the street.

It looked like the cat but much larger, its shoulders almost at Jessica's eye level. Its black fur rippled with huge muscles, as if a hundred crawling snakes lived under the midnight coat.

A black panther. She remembered Jen's story in the library, but this creature didn't look as if it had escaped from any circus.

Jessica heard the snakes behind her, a growing chorus of hisses. She turned to glance back at them. The wriggling black forms were fanning out, as if herding her toward the cat.

They didn't look afraid of her anymore.

8

12:00 A.M.

SEARCH PARTY

"Something bad is happening."

Melissa's words were spoken softly and filled the silence of the blue time like an urgent whisper. Dess looked to the edge of the junkyard lot where her friends stood. Melissa's upturned eyes caught the light of the midnight moon. Rex, as usual, hovered close to her, focused on every word.

Dess waited for more, but Melissa just stared into the sky, listening with her whole being, tasting the motionless air.

Dess shrugged and returned her gaze to the ground, scanning the pile of metal bits that Rex had picked for her. According to him, all of them were untouched by inhuman hands. If he was right about tonight, there was the possibility of a serious rumble, and she was going to need clean steel to work with.

Of course, Rex could be wrong. It didn't feel like a bad night to Dess. Friday, September 5, the fifth day of the ninth month. The combination of nine and five wasn't particularly nasty: the numbers made four, fourteen, or forty-five (when subtracted, added, or multiplied), which was kind of a cute pattern if you liked fours, which Dess did, but hardly dangerous. On top of that, *"S-e-p-t-e-m-b-e-r f-i-v-e"* spelled out had thirteen letters, which was as safe as any number could be. What was to complain about?

But Rex was worried.

Dess looked up. The dark moon looked normal, rising at its usual stately pace and resplendent with its usual gorgeous, pale blue light. So far, Dess hadn't heard the sounds of anything big roaming. Nor had she seen too many slithers. Not a single one, in fact, not even out of the corner of her eye.

That was weird, actually. She looked around the junkyard. There were rusted-out cars, a corrugated iron shack flattened by some ancient tornado, and a jumbled tire pile—plenty of places to slither under and peer out from, but not a flicker of movement anywhere. And even when they couldn't be seen, the chirps and calls of slithers were usually audible. But none of the little guys were watching tonight.

"Almost too quiet," she said to herself in a bad-guy accent.

Across the junkyard Melissa moaned, and despite the constant warmth of the blue time a shiver passed through Dess.

It was time to get started.

She squatted and began to sort through the pieces of metal, looking for bright steel uncorrupted by rust. Stainless was best, unpainted and shiny. The twisted, uneven shapes of the metal also played a part in her selection process. The long trip from factory to junkyard had weathered some pieces to certain proportions, small rods with elegant ratios of length and width, scarred old bolts with harmonious spacings between their dents. Dess arranged her finds happily. Steel came alive here in the blue time. She saw iridescent veins of moonlight streak across the metal and then fade, as if the steel were reflecting a fireworks show in the pale sky above.

As she chose from the bits of metal, Dess brought each to her mouth and blew a name into it.

"Deliciousness."

Some of the big pieces were beautiful, but she needed to be able to carry all of them easily, possibly while running for her life. She selected a small but perfect washer, rejecting a heavy length of pipe.

"Overzealously," she whispered to it.

Words tumbled through her head, some of which she didn't even know the meanings of, scraps of language that had stuck in her mind because of the number or arrangement of their letters. Words weren't really her thing, except when they collided with numbers and patterns, like stretching across a Scrabble board to grab a triple-word score.

What she wanted tonight was pretty straightforward: thirteen-letter words to boost the power of these pieces of steel.

"Fossilization," she named a long, thin screw, the thread of which wound exactly thirty-nine times around its shaft.

The crunch of Rex's boots came from right behind her. She hadn't heard him approach, lost as she was in the pleasures of steel.

"If you were a slither, you'd've bit me," she murmured. The foul little things didn't exactly *bite*, of course, but close enough.

"Melissa's found her," Rex said.

Dess lifted an old hubcap up to the light. Trapped blue fire coursed around its rim.

"About time."

"But she says we have to hurry. There's trouble. Something big out there, or just nasty. Whatever it is, it's giving Melissa a *serious* headache."

Dess brought the hubcap close to her lips.

"Hypochondriac," she whispered to it.

"You ready?" Rex asked.

"Yeah. This stuff's all weaponized."

"Let's go, then."

She stood up, clutching the hubcap in one hand and dropping the smaller bits of metal into her pockets. Rex turned and jogged to the edge of the junkyard where their bikes were stashed. He jumped on his and rode after Melissa, who was already headed down the road toward downtown. Of course, Dess thought. Jessica Day was a city girl. Her parents could afford to live close in, away from the badlands and the smells of oil rigs and roadkill.

Dess walked over calmly and pulled up her bike, mounted it, and began to pedal after the two. She didn't rush. Melissa could only move so fast without losing her way as she cautiously felt for the trembling threads in the tenuous psychic spiderweb of midnight. And even with her crappy one-speed, Dess could beat either of them in a race. It would be no problem to catch up before the fireworks started.

She just hoped this wasn't a wild-goose chase, a symptom of Rex's beginning-of-the-school-year paranoia. Sure, there was a new midnighter in town, but that had happened once before, and the consequences hadn't exactly been earth-shattering.

Rex had sounded pretty scared on the phone, though. So Dess had worn her sensible shoes. Running shoes.

The hubcap rattled happily in the basket on Dess's bike. She smiled. Whatever was out there, she wouldn't have to run right away. The comforting weight of metal clinked heavily in her pockets, and Dess knew without counting how many weapons she had made tonight.

"Lucky thirteen," she said.

They drew closer to the city, the wide, blank spaces of vacant lots and new developments giving way to strip malls and gas stations and, of course, her favorite store: 7-Eleven, a fraction also known as point-six-three-six-three-repeat-to-infinity.

Up ahead Melissa was going faster now, no longer feeling her way, apparently certain of the direction. Something was really giving off bad vibes tonight. Dess pedaled a little harder, swerving her bike around the occasional motionless cars that hogged the road.

Rex was right behind Melissa, making sure she didn't crash into a car while she had her nose in the air. Melissa was a lot more functional here in the blue time, but Rex still hovered. Eight years of baby-sitting was a hard habit to break.

Dess saw a shape in the sky. Silent and gliding—a winged slither. Against the almost fully risen moon she could see the fingers in the wing. Like a bat's, the slither's wing was really a hand: four long, jointed finger bones spread out like kite struts, with paper-thin skin webbed between them.

The slither made a chirping call, a strangled little noise that sounded like the last cry of a stomped-on rat.

Answers sounded. There were more of them up there, a full flock of twelve. They were headed in the same direction as Dess and her friends.

Dess swallowed. It was probably a coincidence. Or maybe the little guys were just coming along for the ride. There were always some around, curious about the little tribe of humans who visited the blue time. They didn't usually make trouble.

She looked up. Another flock had swept in to join the first group. She counted the dark, translucent shapes at a glance: twenty-four of them now.

Dess started counting aloud to calm her nerves. "*Uno, dos, tres . . .*" She knew how to count in twenty-six languages and was working on a few more. The rhythmic sounds of number-words soothed her, and she always found the different ways of dealing with the tricky teens amusing.

She switched nervously to Old English. *"Ane, twa, thri, feower, fif . . ."*

September the fifth. Nothing big was happening tonight, she was positive. Nine plus five was fourteen. And it was the 248th day of the year, and two plus four plus eight also made fourteen. Not as good as thirteen, but no bad karma there.

There were still more shapes in the sky. Their calls came mockingly from every direction.

"Un, deux, trois, quatre." She switched to French, counting louder to drown out the slithers. Dess decided to go all the way to eighty, which was "four twenties" in French. *"Cinq, six, sept . . ."*

"Sept!" she said aloud, skidding her bike to a halt.

Sept meant seven in French and in a bunch of other languages too. (A septagon has seven sides, her brain uselessly informed her.) *Sept* as in September. She remembered now—way back in the old days, a thousand years ago, September had been the seventh month, not the ninth.

September fifth had once been the fifth day of the seventh month.

And seven plus five was twelve.

"Oh, crap," Dess said.

She lifted from her bicycle seat, thrusting her right foot down hard against its pedal as she pulled up on the handles, straining to get the bike moving again. Melissa and Rex had gotten way too far ahead. On a night this serious, she and her weapons should be leading the pack.

A long, piercing cry sounded above her, and another thirteen-letter word came unbidden into Dess's head.

"Bloodcurdling," she whispered, and kept on pedaling.

9

RUMBLE

The black panther roared again.

The sound felt loud enough to knock Jessica backward, but her feet were frozen in place. She wanted to turn away, to run, but some ancient terror had taken hold of her muscles, leaving them paralyzed. It was fear of the huge cat's fangs, of its hungry roar, of the thin, cruel line of pink tongue that flickered out from its maw.

"Dreaming or not," Jessica said softly, "getting eaten would suck."

The beast's eyes flashed bright purple in the moonlight. Its mouth began to twist and change shape, the two longest fangs stretching out until they were as long as knives. It crouched, gathering itself into a bundle of muscle, head lowered and tail raised high like a sprinter setting up to start a race. Its muscles quivered, the huge paws kneading the ground. The grating sound of claws scraping asphalt reached Jessica's ears, sending shivers up her spine. When the cat sprang toward her, it became suddenly as long and swift as an arrow.

The moment it moved, Jessica was released from its spell. She turned and ran back toward the snakes.

Her bare feet slapped painfully against the asphalt, and the arc of snakes was arrayed across the street directly in front of her, so she veered off to one side, onto the softer strip of lawn. The snakes moved to cut her off, slithering into the high, uncut grass in front of a ramshackle old house. Jessica gritted her teeth as she ran, imagining sharp fangs piercing the soles of her feet with every step. When she reached the spot where she guessed the snakes were, Jessica launched herself into a long jump. The air rushed around her, and the leap seemed to carry her incredibly far. She leapt twice more, taking bounding steps until she reached the edge of the next driveway.

Jessica stumbled painfully on the concrete as she landed, but she managed to keep running. The snakes were definitely behind her now, and she realized with relief that she hadn't been bitten. But the footfalls of the black panther were still closing in. She might be fast in this dream, but the creature behind her was faster.

Images from a million nature specials flashed through her head: big cats taking down their prey, grabbing hold of gazelles with their teeth and disemboweling them with hind claws that spun like the blades of a blender. Cheetahs were the fastest animals in the world; panthers probably weren't that far behind. There was no way she could beat the beast in a straight line. But she recalled how antelope escaped cheetahs: by twisting and turning, so that the heavier, less agile cats shot past and tumbled to the ground before they could right themselves for another attack.

The problem was, Jessica was no antelope.

She risked a glance over her shoulder. The panther was only a few bounds behind, terrifyingly huge this close. Jessica angled toward a willow in front of the next house, a wide old tree that sheltered the entire yard. She counted down from five as she ran toward it, hearing the cat's footfalls tearing into the grass closer and closer. At *one*, Jessica threw herself to the ground behind the wide trunk.

The panther's leap took it over her, a dark shadow blotting out the giant moon for a split second. A ripping sound came with the wind of the creature's passage, as if the air itself were splitting.

Jessica raised her head. The big cat was scrambling to a stop in the next driveway, its claws drawing a spine-chilling screech from the asphalt. Then she spotted the marks inches from her face and swallowed. The tree trunk bore three long, cruel gouges just above where her head had been, the freshly exposed wood white for a moment before the moon leached it blue.

She stood and ran.

There was a narrow gap between two houses, an overgrown channel of grass and dark shapes. Jessica dashed instinctively for the narrow space. She crashed through the high grass, jumping the rusting shape of an old push mower leaning against one wall, then stumbled to an abrupt halt.

At the other end of the gap was a chain-link fence.

Jessica ran toward it. There was nowhere else to go.

She leapt as high as she could, fingers hooking into the weave of metal, pulling herself up. Her feet scrambled for purchase, toes gripping better than shoes but much more painfully. At least the fence was new, the metal smooth and rust-free.

As Jess climbed, she could hear the rumbling breath of the giant panther behind her reverberating between the two houses. The creature pushed through the high grass with a rushing noise like wind in leaves. She reached the top of the fence and swung over, coming suddenly face-to-face with her pursuer.

The beast was only a few yards away. Its eyes locked with hers. In those deep pools of indigo Jessica thought she recognized an ancient intelligence, remote and cruel. She knew absolutely, beyond any argument, that this wasn't a mere animal; it was something much, much worse.

Except, of course, that this had to be a dream: that pure evil staring back at her was all in her head.

"Psychosomatic," she whispered softly.

The creature raised a huge paw to swipe at Jessica's clinging fingers, still exposed through the holes of the fence. She released her grip and pushed herself backward. As she fell, a shower of blue sparks exploded in front of her, lighting the big cat's gleaming fangs and the houses rising on either side. The whole fence seemed to ignite, blue fire running along every inch of metal. The fire seemed to be drawn to the paw of the beast, spiraling inward toward the long claws entangled for a moment among the chain links.

Then the creature must have freed itself; the world went dark.

Jessica hit the ground softly, her fall broken by the unkempt grass. She blinked blindly; the weave of the fence was burned into her vision, dazzling blue diamond shapes overlaying everything she saw. The smell of singed fur almost made her choke.

She gazed at her own hands wonderingly. They were unhurt, except for triangular red marks from hoisting herself over. If the fence had been electrified, why hadn't it burned her as it had the cat? There were no sparks now except for the echoes in her vision, and the fence was whole before her. She was surprised that the panther hadn't ripped it down with a single swipe of its paw.

Jessica peered through the metal at her pursuer, blinking to clear her vision. The panther was shaking its head in confusion, backing away to the far end of the gap, limping slightly. It held up one paw and licked it, the pink tongue snaking out between the two long teeth. Then the cold indigo eyes locked onto Jessica. The cool intelligence was still there. The cat turned and padded out of sight.

It was looking for another way around.

Whatever the fence had done to the panther, she was grateful. The beast could've jumped the fence, which wasn't more than eight feet high, but the blue sparks had spooked it.

Her respite wouldn't last long, though. She had to get moving. Jessica rolled over onto her hands and knees and started to stand.

A hissing sound came from the ground in front of her. Through the high grass she glimpsed two purple eyes flashing in the moonlight.

Her hand darted in front of her face just in time. Cold shot through her from palm to elbow, as if long, icy needles had been thrust deep into her arm. Jessica leapt to her feet and stumbled away from where the snake had been hidden.

Her eyes widened with fear as she looked down at her hand.

The snake was attached by black filaments that wrapped around her fingers and wrist, her hand grasped by a spreading cold. The filaments came from the snake's mouth, as if its tongue had split into a hundred black threads and twisted itself tightly around her. The cold was moving slowly up her arm toward her shoulder.

Without thinking, Jessica swung the snake against the fence. The chain links lit up again, though much less explosively than when the cat had struck it. Blue fire shot toward her hand, then ran down the length of the writhing snake. The creature puffed up for a moment, its sleek black fur standing on end. The filaments unraveled, and the snake dropped lifeless to the ground.

Jessica leaned against the fence, exhausted.

The metal was warm and pulsing against her back, as if the steel had become alive. Feeling rushed back into her arm painfully, along with imaginary pins and needles, like blood returning after she'd slept on it all night long.

Jessica sagged with relief, letting the metal hold her weight for a moment.

Then, from the corner of her eye, she spotted movement. There was a narrow gap under the fence, like a dog would dig. More of the snakes were coming through.

Jessica turned and ran.

The backyard of this house was small, bounded by high fences. She might be safe from the panther within them, but in the uncut grass the snakes could hide anywhere. She climbed over the locked gate in the back, dropping to the ground in a narrow, paved alleyway.

The big cat had headed back the way Jessica had come, so she ran down the alley in the opposite direction. She wondered how she would ever get home.

"Just a dream," Jess reminded herself. The words brought her no comfort at all. The adrenaline in her blood, the sharp pain in her fingers from climbing the chain-link fence, her heart pounding in her chest—the whole experience seemed absolutely real.

The alley led out onto a wide road. A street sign stood at the next corner, and Jess ran toward it, casting her eyes around for the panther.

"Kerr and Division," she read. That was on the way to school. She wasn't so far from home. "If I can just make it past the hairy snakes and the giant predator, I'll be fine," she mumbled. "No problem."

The moon was fully risen now. It was moving much faster than the sun did during the day, Jessica realized. It hardly felt like half an hour since the dream had started. She saw how gigantic the moon was now. It filled so much of the sky that only a strip of horizon remained visible around it. The huge bulk hanging overhead made the world seem smaller, as if someone had put a roof on the sky.

Then Jessica saw shapes against the moon.

"Great," she said. "Just what I need."

They were flying creatures of some kind. They looked like bats, their wings fleshy and translucent, slowly gliding rather than flapping their wings. They were larger than bats, though, their bodies longer, as if a pack of rats had sprung wings. Several of them wheeled above her, making low chirping sounds.

Had they spotted her? Were they, like everything else in this dream, hunting Jessica Day?

Staring into the dark orb was giving Jessica a headache again, making her feel trapped under its light-sucking gaze. She turned her eyes back down to earth, watching for the panther as she jogged toward home.

The flying shapes stayed overhead, following her.

It wasn't long before she felt the rumble of the panther's growl again.

The black shape slid into sight in front of her a few blocks away, directly between Jessica and home. She remembered the intelligence in the panther's eyes when they had faced each other through the fence. The cat seemed to know where she lived and how to stop her from getting there. And its little slithering friends were probably already in formation to prevent any escape.

This was hopeless.

The creature started padding toward her, not breaking into its full stride this time. It knew now how fast she could run and understood that it only had to go a little bit faster to catch her. It wouldn't overshoot this prey again.

Jessica looked around for a place to hide, somewhere to escape to. But the houses here on the main roads were farther apart, with big wide strips of grass on every side. There were no tight spaces to crawl into, no fences to climb.

Then she spotted her salvation, one block in the opposite direction from the panther. A car.

It was sitting motionless right in the middle of the street, its lights off, but she could see that someone was inside it.

Jessica ran toward it. Maybe whoever was at the wheel could drive her to safety, or maybe the panther couldn't get inside the car. It was the only hope she had.

She looked over her shoulder at the cat. It was running now, still not at full speed, but fast enough to close the distance with every bound. Jessica ran as fast as she could. Her bare feet ached from pounding the concrete, but she ignored the pain. She knew she could make it to the car.

She had to.

The cat's raspy breathing and padded footfalls reached

her ears, the sounds carrying like whispers through the silent blue world, closer and closer.

Jessica dashed the last few yards, reached the passenger side door, and yanked at the handle.

It was locked.

"You've got to help me!" she cried. "Let me in!"

Then Jessica saw the face of the driver. The woman was about her mom's age, with blond hair and a slight frown on her face, as if she were concentrating on the road ahead. But her skin was as white as paper. Her fingers gripped the wheel motionlessly. Like Beth, she was frozen, lifeless.

"No!" Jessica shouted.

A hissing came from below. Snakes under the car.

Without thinking, Jessica leapt up onto the hood. She wound up facing the driver through the windshield, the blank eyes staring back at her like a statue's.

"No," Jessica sobbed, pounding the hood of the car.

She rolled over to face the panther, exhausted, defeated.

The beast was only a few strides away. It paused, growling, and the two long fangs glinted in the dark moonlight. Jessica knew that she was dead meat.

Then something happened.

A tiny flying saucer came screaming past Jessica, headed toward the panther. The object left a wake of blue sparks and electrified air. Jessica felt her hair stand on end, as if lightning had struck close by. The panther's eyes flashed, wide and panicked, reflecting gold instead of indigo.

The projectile burst into a blue flame that wrapped itself

around the giant cat. The creature spun around and leapt away, the fire clinging to its fur. It bounded farther down the street, howling a menagerie of pain—lions' roars and stricken birds, cats being tortured. The beast passed from sight around a corner, its cries finally fading into a hideous, tormented laugh like that of a wounded hyena.

"Wow," came a familiar voice, "Hypochondriac killed the cat." The nonsense words were followed by a giggle.

Jessica turned to face the voice, blinking away tears and disbelief. A few yards away, somehow invading her dream, was Dess.

"Hey, Jess," she called. "How's it going?"

Jessica opened her mouth, but no sound came out.

Dess was astride a rickety old bike, one foot resting on the pavement, the other on a pedal. She wore a leather jacket over her usual black dress and was flipping what looked like a coin in the air.

Jessica heard a hissing noise from below. A few dark squiggles were wriggling their way toward Dess.

"Snakes," she managed to croak.

"Slithers, actually," Dess said, and flipped the coin into the dark shapes.

It pinged against the ground among them, raising a single bright blue spark, and, with a chorus of thin screeching noises, the snakes scuttled back under the car.

Two more bikes rolled into view.

They were ridden by Dess's friends from the cafeteria. The boy with the thick glasses pulled up first, only he wasn't wearing glasses now. His long coat billowed around him as he halted, and he was breathing hard. Then the other girl who'd been at Dess's table, whom Jessica had never met, pulled up.

Jessica looked at the three of them blankly. This dream was getting weirder and weirder.

"You're *welcome*," said Dess.

"Be quiet," the boy said breathlessly. "Are you okay?"

It took a moment for Jessica to realize that the question was directed at her. She blinked again and nodded dumbly. Her feet hurt and she was out of breath, but she was okay. Physically, anyway.

"Sure, I'm fine. I guess."

"Don't worry about psychokitty; it's gone for the night," Dess said, looking after the departed panther. She turned to the boy. "What was it, Rex?"

"Some kind of darkling," he said.

"Well, duh," Dess said.

Both of them looked at the other girl. She shook her head, rubbing her eyes with one hand. "It tasted very old, maybe even from before the Split."

Rex whistled. "That's old, all right. It must be insane by now."

The girl nodded. "A few fries short of a Happy Meal. But still crafty."

Dess dropped her bike to the ground and walked over to where the cat had stood. "Whatever it was, it turned out to be no match for the mighty power of Hypochondriac."

She knelt and plucked a dark disk of metal from the ground.

"Ouch!" Dess passed it from hand to hand, grinning. "Still sparky."

It looked like an old hubcap, blackened by fire. Was that the dazzling flying saucer of a minute ago?

Jessica shook her head, dazed but slowly calming down. She was breathing evenly now. Everything was moving into more familiar dream territory: total craziness.

Rex rested his bike on the street and walked to the side of the car. Jessica shrank from him a little, and he put up both palms.

"It's okay," he said softly, "but you should probably get off the car. It looks like it's going pretty fast."

"Come on," Dess said, looking up at the sky. "It's like a quarter till."

"It's still not a good habit, Dess," he said. "Especially when you're new."

He offered his hand. Jessica looked down suspiciously at the ground, but there were no snakes apparent. She saw the same shiny ankle bracelets that Dess wore looped around Rex's boots. The other girl had them too, rings of metal piled up around her black sneakers.

She looked at her own bare feet.

"Don't worry, the slithers are gone."

"They departed somewhat overzealously," Dess said, giggling. Her eyes were wide, as if the encounter with the panther had been some exciting fairground ride.

Jessica ignored Rex's hand and slid off the car hood toward the front. She pushed off from the bumper and took a few quick steps away, peering into the shadows beneath it. But the snakes did seem to have disappeared.

"I wouldn't stand in front of it either," Rex suggested mildly. He looked at the tires. "It's probably going about fifty miles an hour."

Jessica followed his gaze and saw that the tires weren't actually round. They were oval, compressed out of shape and tipped slightly forward. They looked how wheels in motion were drawn in cartoons. But the car was absolutely still. The driver still wore the exact same expression, oblivious to the strange events going on around her.

Rex pointed up at the dark moon. "And when that bad boy goes down, it'll jump back into regular motion. No hurry, like Dess said, but good to keep in mind."

Something about Rex's calm voice annoyed Jessica. Possibly the fact that nothing he said made any sense whatsoever.

She looked up at the moon. It was still moving across the sky quickly, almost half set.

A gasp came from the other three. She dropped her gaze to them. They stared back at her.

"What is it?" Jessica asked sharply. She'd had enough of their weirdness.

The girl whose name she didn't know took a step closer to Jess, peering closely at her face with an appalled expression.

"Your eyes are wrong," the girl said.

10
MIDNIGHTERS

"My eyes are *what*?"

"They're . . ." The girl took a step closer, peering into Jessica's eyes. Jessica raised a hand to her own face, and the girl flinched as if afraid of being touched, then looked up at the sky with a puzzled expression.

As her eyes met the moon, Jessica cried out. They flashed a deep indigo, just like the panther's.

Jessica took a step back from the three of them. Those reflecting eyes belonged to cats or raccoons, owls or foxes—things that hunted in the dark. Not people. The girl's eyes looked normal now, but after that momentary reflection, she seemed less human.

"Melissa's right," Dess said.

Rex quieted the other two with a wave of his hand. He took a step closer, peering into Jessica's eyes with a calm intensity.

"Jessica," he said quietly, "look up at the moon, please."

She did so for a few seconds but dropped her eyes back to Rex suspiciously.

"What color is it?" he asked.

"It's . . ." She looked up again, shrugged. "No color. And it gives me a headache."

"Her eyes are wrong," repeated the other girl, whom Dess had called Melissa.

Dess piped up. "Today she said the sun doesn't bother her. I told you she was totally daylight. No dark glasses or anything."

"What on earth are you *talking about*?" Jessica suddenly cried, surprising herself. She hadn't meant to shout, but the words had launched themselves out of her.

The startled looks on the others' faces were somehow satisfying.

"I mean—," she sputtered. "What's going on? What are you talking about? And what are you doing in my *dream*?"

Rex stepped back and put up his hands. Dess giggled but half turned away as if embarrassed. Melissa cocked her head.

"Sorry," Rex said. "I should have told you: this isn't a dream."

"But—" Jessica started, but sighed, knowing suddenly that she believed him. The pain, the fear, the feel of her heart pumping in her chest had all been too real. This was not a dream. It was a relief not to pretend to herself anymore.

"What is it, then?"

"This is midnight."

"Say again?"

"Midnight," he repeated slowly. "It's 12 A.M. Since the

world changed color, this has all happened in a single moment."

"A single moment . . ."

"Time stops for us at midnight."

Jessica peered through the car windshield at the frozen woman at the wheel. The look of concentration on her face, the hands tight on the wheel . . . She did look as if she were driving but trapped in a frozen instant.

Dess spoke up next, her voice without its usual nasty edge. "There aren't really twenty-four hours in the day, Jessica. There are twenty-five. But one of them is rolled up too tight to see. For most people it flashes by in an instant. But we can see it, live in it."

"And 'we' includes 'me'?" Jessica said quietly.

"When were you born?" Rex asked.

"Huh? You mean this is because I'm a *Leo*?"

"Not your birthday, what time of day?"

Jessica pondered the question, remembering how many times Mom and Dad had told this story.

"My mom went into labor in the afternoon, but I wasn't born until thirty-something hours later. Not until late the next night."

Rex nodded. "Midnight, to be exact."

"Midnight?"

"Sure. One out of every 43,200 people is born within one second of midnight," Dess said, smiling happily. "Of course, we're not exactly sure how close you have to get. And we're talking *real* midnight here."

"Yeah. My birth certificate says 1 A.M.," Melissa said glumly. "Lousy daylight savings time."

Rex looked up at the moon, his eyes catching its nonlight with that inhuman flicker. "In a lot of cultures people believe that those born at the stroke of midnight can see ghosts."

Jessica nodded. That actually sounded familiar. One of those pirate books she'd read for English last year— *Kidnapped?* or *Treasure Island?*—had been about that. Some kid was supposed to find treasure by seeing the ghosts of dead men buried with the gold.

"The real story is a bit more complicated," Rex continued.

"I'll say," Jessica said. "If that panther was a ghost, we seriously need new Halloween decorations."

"Midnighters don't see ghosts, Jessica," Rex continued. "What we see is a whole secret hour, the blue time, that zooms right past everyone else."

"Midnighters," Jessica repeated.

"That's the word for us. Midnight is ours alone. We can walk around while everything else in the whole world is frozen."

"Not everything," Jessica said.

"True," Rex admitted. "The darklings and slithers, and some other stuff, live in the blue time. For them the blue time is like normal daylight and vice versa. They can't get into the other twenty-four hours, like most humans can't get into the twenty-fifth."

"Only us midnighters get to live in both," Dess said happily.

"Yay," Jess said. "I'm thrilled."

"Come on, haven't you ever wished for an extra hour in the day?" Rex asked.

"Not an extra totally *weird* hour! Not an extra hour where everything tries to kill me! No, I don't think I *ever* wished for that."

"Wow, you are *so* daylight," Melissa said.

"I've got to admit, things have been bad for you," Rex said, using his Mr. Calm voice again. "But it's usually not like this. Normally the slithers only watch us, and darklings don't care much about us at all. They're like wild animals. They can be dangerous if you do something stupid, but they don't go out of their way to mess with humans. A midnighter being attacked for no reason is new to me."

"It's pretty much new to me too!" Jessica said. "And I didn't do anything stupid, all right? One of those . . . *slithers* led me out here on purpose. Then the big cat thing tried to kill me. Twice."

"Yeah, we should try to figure this out," Rex said mildly, as if Jessica had been assigned a locker at school that wouldn't open. She guessed that none of those darklings had ever come after him.

"I knew you were different," Melissa said, "even before psychokitty tried to eat you." She closed her eyes, tipping back her head as if smelling the wind. "There's something funny about the way you taste."

Melissa's face went blank, almost as lifeless as Beth or

the woman driving the car. Jessica rolled her eyes. Melissa
was calling *her* different?

"But right now we should get you home," Rex said,
glancing up at the sky. "There's only about five minutes left."

Jessica started to speak, a million questions on her
tongue. But she just sighed. Nothing was getting explained.
Everything these people said confused her more.

"Fine." As she said the word, Jessica realized how good
home sounded. The panther must still be around somewhere.

Rex and Melissa pushed their bikes, walking next to
Jessica. Dess rode in slow circles around them, like a bored
kid forced to travel too slowly.

"Tomorrow we'll have time to tell you more," Rex said.
"Meet us at the Clovis Museum? Noon?"

"Um." Jessica thought about her plans to unpack
tomorrow. To finally get her life under control. Of course, it
didn't look as if it were going to be that simple anymore.
"Yeah, sure. Where's that?"

"It's close to the main library. Just follow Division." Rex
pointed toward downtown. "Meet us downstairs."

"Okay."

"And don't worry, Jessica. We'll figure out what happened tonight. We'll make sure you're safe here."

Jess looked into Rex's eyes, seeing the concern there.
He seemed confident that he could figure out whatever
had gone wrong. Or maybe he was just trying to make her
feel better. It was strange. Even though nothing he said

made sense, Rex managed to sound as if he knew what he was talking about. Here in the blue time he stood straighter and the thick glasses didn't hide his calm, serious eyes. The guy seemed like much less of a loser than he did in the daylight.

"So, you don't really need those glasses, do you? It's an act, like Clark Kent?"

"Afraid not. In daylight I'm blind as a bat. But here in the blue time I can see perfectly. Better than perfectly."

"That must be nice."

"Yeah. It's great. And I can see more than . . ." He paused. "We'll explain it all tomorrow."

"Okay."

Jessica looked at the three of them. Dess circling happily on her bike, Rex's eyes clear and confident, Melissa silent, but without her usual headphones and pained expression. They all seemed to actually *like* this midnight time.

Of course, why wouldn't they? It didn't seem like their lives were going so great during the "daylight" hours. Here there was no one to push them around or notice how weird they were. For this one hour a day the whole world was their private clubhouse.

And now she was in the club. Great.

They took Jessica right to her door. She realized that the light was slowly changing. The dark moon had almost set, now mostly hidden behind the houses across the street.

"So how are you guys getting home?" she asked.

"The usual way. During regular time," Rex said,

mounting his bike and reaching into his shirt pocket. He pulled out his glasses.

Jessica looked around, her eyes searching for any sign of the panther. "And you're sure this blue thing is almost over?"

"Happens every night, as regular as sundown," Rex said.

Jessica realized that they must be miles from home. "What about the curfew? I mean, everyone's going to wake back up, right? What if the police see you?"

Melissa rolled her eyes. "We've been dealing with curfew for years. Don't worry about us."

"But we should get going," Rex said. "You'll be okay here, Jessica. And it'll all make more sense in the morning." He pedaled down the walk and into the street. "See you at noon."

Dess's bike rattled across the lawn. "See you in 43,200 seconds, Jess," she called as she passed. "And wear shoes next time!" She laughed and pedaled to catch up with Rex. Jessica looked down at her bare feet and had to smile.

Melissa stayed a moment longer, her eyes narrowing.

"You don't belong," she said softly, her voice almost a whisper. "That's why the darkling wanted to kill you."

Jessica opened her mouth, then shrugged.

"I didn't ask to be a midnighter," she said.

"Maybe you're not," Melissa said. "Not a real one, anyway. Something about you is so . . . 11:59. You don't belong."

She turned and rode away without waiting for an answer.

Jessica shuddered. "Great, the biggest weirdo in the weirdo club says I don't belong."

She turned and went into the house. Even in the strange light of the dark moon it seemed welcoming as it never had before. Just like home.

But Jessica sighed as she walked down the hall toward her room. Melissa's words were still with her. The darkling hadn't seemed like a wild animal to her—more like something that hated her with all its heart. The slither had led her into a trap because it wanted her dead.

"Maybe Melissa's right."

This blue time didn't feel like a place she was meant to be. The alien light pulsed from every corner of the house, haunting and wrong. Her eyes stung from an hour of it, as if she were about to cry.

"Maybe I don't belong here."

Jessica paused at Beth's door. Her white shape was still there, unmoving, sprawled on the bed in its anxious pose.

She went in and sat next to her sister, forcing herself to look, to wait for the end of midnight. She had to know that Beth wasn't dead. If Rex had been telling the truth, she was only stuck for a moment in time.

Jessica pulled the sheet up around her sister's neck and reached out to touch the motionless cheek, shuddering as her fingers met its cool surface.

The moment ended.

The boxes and corners faded back into darkness, no longer lit by their own light. Dim streetlights slanted in through the windows, making zigzag shadows on the cluttered floor. The world felt right again.

Beth's cheek grew warm, and a muscle in it flicked under Jessica's hand.

Her eyes opened gummily.

"Jessica? What are you doing in here?"

Jessica pulled her hand away, suddenly remembering that an awake Beth could be just as scary as a frozen one.

"Hey, I, um, wanted to say something."

"What? I'm *asleep*, Jessica."

"I just had to say that I'm sorry for avoiding you. I mean, I know it's tough here," Jessica said. "But . . . I'm on your side, okay?"

"Oh, *Jessica*," Beth said, twisting away and winding herself further into the tangle of sheets. Then she turned her head to stare accusingly. "Did Mom tell you to do this? That is so lame."

"No. Of course not. I just wanted—"

"To be Miss Mature. To show how you've got time for me even though you're Miss Popular here. Whatever. Thanks for the pep talk, Jess. Maybe some sleep now?"

Jessica started to reply but stopped herself and then had to stifle a smile instead. Beth was back to normal. She had defrosted from the blue time without any visible damage.

"Sleep tight," Jessica said, crossing to the door.

"Yeah, no bedbugs and all that." Beth rolled over grumpily, pulling the sheet over her head.

Jessica closed the door. As she stood all alone in the

hall, her sister's last words rattled around in her head. *"Don't let the bedbugs bite,"* she whispered.

She went to her own room and closed the door tightly, suddenly feeling as if the blue time hadn't really ended. The light was back to normal, and the sound of the constant Oklahoma wind had returned, but everything looked different to her now. The world Jessica had known—the world of night and day, of certainty and reason—had been completely erased.

In another twenty-four hours the blue time would come again. If Rex had been telling the truth, it would come every night.

Jessica Day lay down in her bed and pulled the covers up all the way to her nose. She tried to go to sleep, but with her eyes shut, Jess felt as if something else were in the room. She sat up and peered into every corner, making sure again and again that no unfamiliar shapes lurked there.

It was like being little again, when night was a time of peril, when things lived under the bed, things that wanted to eat her.

There were worse things than bedbugs, and they did bite.

11

MARKS OF MIDNIGHT

Beth was in fine form the next morning at breakfast.

"Mom, Jessica was sleepstalking last night."

"Sleepwalking?" Mom asked.

"No. Sleep*stalking*. She was creeping around my bedroom, stalking me while I was asleep."

Jessica's parents looked at her, raising their eyebrows.

"I was not stalking you," Jessica said. She dug her fork into the *huevos rancheros*—cheese and eggs—that Dad had made, wishing this topic of conversation would just go away. She should have known that Beth wouldn't keep quiet about her visit last night.

When Jessica looked up, everyone was still staring at her. She shrugged. "I couldn't sleep, so I went in to see if Beth was awake."

"And to give a little speech," Beth said.

Jessica felt her face flush. Her little sister always instinctively found the route to maximum embarrassment. She wanted every uncomfortable fact out in the open. Every awkward moment desperately needed her commentary.

"A speech?" Dad asked. He sat across the table in one of his sleeping T-shirts. The shirt was emblazoned with the logo of some software company he used to work for, the once bright colors faded. His hair was scruffy, and he hadn't shaved for a couple of days.

Mom was eating standing up, already dressed for work in a two-piece suit, the collar of her blouse blindingly white in the sunlit kitchen. She'd never dressed up this much for work in Chicago, but Jessica guessed she was trying to impress her new bosses. Mom had never worked on Saturday before, either. "Why couldn't you sleep?"

Jessica realized that there was no way to tell the truth on that one. Before she'd showered this morning, the soles of her feet had been almost black, a lot like the feet of someone who had walked a mile on asphalt barefoot. Her hands still had faint red marks on the palms, and she had a bruise on the hand the slither had bitten.

Of course, there was still the barest chance that it had all been a dream, complete with sleepwalking and sleep-fence-climbing. She would be checking that possibility in a couple of hours.

"Jessica?"

"Oh, sorry. I guess I'm kind of tired today. I've been having these weird dreams since we moved. They wake me up."

"Me too," Dad said.

"Yeah, Dad," Beth said, "but you don't come into my room and make little speeches."

All three of them looked at Jessica expectantly, Beth smiling cruelly.

Normally Jessica would have made a joke or left the room, anything to escape embarrassment. But she had already fibbed about why she couldn't sleep. She decided to make amends in the truth department.

"I just thought that I'd tell Beth," she said haltingly, "that I knew moving was tough on her. And that I was here for her."

"That is so *lame*," Beth said. "Mom, tell Jessica not to be so lame."

Jessica felt her mom's fingers lightly on the back of her head. "I think that was really sweet, Jessica."

Beth made an *ugh* noise and fled from the kitchen with her breakfast. The sound of cartoons came on in the living room.

"That was very mature of you, Jess," Dad said.

"I didn't do it to be *mature*."

"I know, Jessica," Mom said. "But you're right—Beth needs our support right now. Keep trying."

Jessica shrugged, still a little embarrassed. "Sure."

"Anyway, I've got to go," Mom said. "I get to try out the wind tunnel this afternoon."

"Good luck, Mom."

"Bye, sweethearts."

"Bye," Jessica and her father said together. The moment the front door had closed, they took their breakfasts in front of the TV. Beth scooted aside on the couch for Jessica but didn't say a word.

At the first break between cartoons, however, Beth picked up her empty plate to take it away, hesitated, and looked down at Jessica's dish.

"You done?"

Jessica looked up. "Yeah . . ."

Beth bent down and stacked up Jess's plate on her own, then carried them both back, rattling in her hands, to the kitchen.

Jessica and her father exchanged surprised glances.

He smiled. "Being lame does work sometimes, I guess."

An hour later Dad decided to be Mr. Responsible. He stood up and stretched, then muted the TV. "So, you guys are going to finish unpacking today, right?"

"Yeah, sure," Beth said. "Got all day."

"We really should get some work done before your mother gets home," Dad said.

"Actually," Jessica said, "I have to go to this museum downtown. The Clovis Museum or something. For homework."

"Homework already?" Dad asked. "Back in my day you didn't get any homework the first week. You were just supposed to hang out for a while, then they'd slowly reintroduce the concept of work."

"So not much has changed for you, has it, Dad?" said Beth.

Dad gave his new, defeated sigh. He didn't put up much of a fight against Beth anymore.

Jessica ignored her. "Anyway, Dad, it's not that far away. I think I'll just bike it."

The streets and houses from the night before were still there, recognizable in the daylight. She checked her watch. No chance of being late—she still had an hour to get to the Clovis Museum.

There were so many questions in her mind. What were darklings and slithers, and where did they come from? How had Dess scared off the giant panther with a hubcap? Why hadn't Jessica ever seen the blue time before coming to Bixby? And how did Rex and his friends know any of this stuff, anyway?

Jessica rode slowly, retracing her steps to piece together where everything had happened the night before. The route from her house to the street where she'd first seen the panther was the fuzziest part of her memory. She'd been following the kitty-slither, dreamily looking around and not paying attention. But it was easy to find the corner of Kerr and Division and, from there, the spot where the frozen car had stood.

Of course, it was gone now. Jessica tried to imagine it jumping suddenly into motion as the secret hour ended, the driver calmly continuing down the road as though nothing had happened. There were no marks in the street, no burned hubcap, nothing to show that a battle had taken place there just eleven hours ago.

From there she traced her path backward, remembering

all too clearly the way she had run while the panther was tracking her. She found the narrow alley and followed it to the backyard fence she had climbed over to escape it. Jessica wasn't about to climb back over during daylight, and the thought of standing in that high grass still made her nervous, so she circled around to the street side of the house.

The old willow dominated the block, like a huge umbrella blotting out the hot sun. Jessica dismounted and walked her bike over the unkempt lawn to the tree. In the darkness below its shade she spotted the three gouges in the trunk, the claw marks of the giant panther.

Her skin crawled as she traced one of the cuts with a quivering finger. It was more than an inch deep, as wide as her thumb. Her finger came out sticky. She teased the trace of sap between her fingers, realizing that the tree had bled instead of her.

"Sorry about that," she said softly to the willow.

"Hey!"

Jessica jumped, looking around for the voice.

"What're you doing on my lawn?"

She spotted a face in the window of the ramshackle house, barely visible through the sunlight reflected from the mosquito screen.

"Sorry," she called. "Just looking at your tree." Okay, Jessica thought, *that* sounded weird.

She pulled her bike back to the main street and climbed onto it, shading her eyes with one hand for a moment as she looked back. The face had disappeared, but Jess recognized the thirteen-pointed star on a plaque mounted next to the door. Dess had been right: they were everywhere in Bixby.

An old woman emerged from the house, wearing only a wispy nightgown that clung to her frail frame in the light breeze. She was clutching something to her chest, a long, thin object that glimmered in the sun.

"Get away from my house," the woman shouted in a voice that was bigger than her tiny body.

"Okay, sorry." Jess started to pedal away.

"And don't come back tonight either," a final shout followed her down the street.

Come back tonight? Jessica wondered as she rode. What had the old woman meant by that?

Jessica shook her head, checking her watch. The marks on the tree proved that the secret hour was real. She had to face the fact that something really had tried to kill her last night. And she had to find out how to protect herself before the blue time came again.

Jessica rode fast toward downtown.

She hated being late.

12

ARROWHEADS

As they drew closer to downtown Bixby, Rex could feel the car slowing. He glanced at Melissa, whose hands gripped the steering wheel.

"It's okay, Cowgirl," he murmured. He tried to think calm thoughts, hoping it would help.

It wasn't a real downtown, like Tulsa or Dallas had, just a handful of five- and six-story buildings that included the town hall, the library, and a couple of office buildings. On a Saturday the workplaces were empty. There would be a few people at the expensive shops on Main and lining up for the first shows at the restored 1950s cinema. That was about it.

But crowded or not, downtown sat right in the center of Bixby, surrounded by rings of housing developments. As they drew closer, the densest part of the city's population encircled them. It wasn't nearly as bad as school, but it always took Melissa a minute or so to adjust to the accumulated weight of those minds.

Soon her knuckles relaxed on the wheel.

Rex took a deep breath and leaned back into his seat.

He stared out the window, pulling off his glasses to look for signs.

They were out there. Lots of them.

Usually it was pretty clean this far from the badlands. With his glasses off, the city should have been one big reassuring blur. But Rex could see marks of visitation everywhere—a house that stood out with strange clarity from its neighbors, a street sign that he could easily read with unaided eyes, a slithering path across the road that shimmered with Focus, the sharp edges that revealed the touch of inhuman hands.

Or claws, or wriggling bellies.

The signs of midnight were here, where they shouldn't be, creeping closer toward the bright lights of downtown. Rex wondered what the darklings and their little friends were up to. Were they testing their limits? Growing in number? Showing a sudden interest in humanity?

Or were they searching for something?

"What do you think she is, Rex?" Dess asked from the backseat.

"Talentwise?" He shrugged. "Could be anything. Could be another polymath."

"Nah," Dess said. "I'm in trig with her, remember? She's hopeless. Sanchez had to explain radian measures to her three times this week."

Rex wondered what radian measures were. "Trigonometry isn't really part of the lore, Dess."

"It will be one day," Dess said. "Sooner or later arithmetic has to run out of steam. Like obsidian did."

"That'll be a long time from now," Rex answered. He hoped it would, anyway. Trig was beyond him too. "Anyway, Jessica only just got here. She could take a while to find her talent."

"Come on," Dess said. "You guys tracked me down when I was eleven, right? By that time my mom and dad were letting me do their taxes for them. Jessica's fifteen, and she can't handle high school trig? She's no polymath."

"She isn't a mindcaster either," Melissa said.

Rex glanced over at his old friend. Unlike the blurry dashboard and passing background, Melissa's face was in perfect midnighter Focus. Her expression was grim, and her hands gripped the wheel hard again, as if the old Ford were passing a busload of brawling five-year-olds.

"Probably not," he said mildly.

"*Definitely* not. I could taste it if she was."

Rex sighed. "There's no point arguing about it now. We'll find out what she is soon enough. She could be a seer for all I know."

"Hey, Rex, maybe she's an acrobat," Dess said.

"Yeah, a replacement," Melissa joined in.

Rex glared at her, then put his glasses back on. Melissa's face went a little blurry as the rest of the world sharpened, and he turned away to stare out the car window.

"We don't need an acrobat."

"Sure, Rex," Dess said. "But wouldn't a full set be better?"

He shrugged, not taking the bait.

"Collect 'em all," Melissa added.

"Listen," Rex said sharply, "there's lots more talents than the four we've seen, okay? I've read about all kinds of stuff, going back as far as the Split. She could be anything."

"She could be nothing," Melissa said.

Rex shrugged again and didn't say another word until they reached the museum.

The Clovis Period Excavation Museum was a long, low building. Most of the museum was underground, sunk into the cool, dark shelter of the red Oklahoma clay. With its single row of tiny windows it looked to Rex like one of those bunkers that rocket scientists cowered in while they tested some new missile that might explode on the launchpad.

This was the first weekend of the school year, so the parking lot was almost empty. Later in the day there might be a trickle of tourists, and in a month or so the school trips would start. Every student within a hundred miles of Bixby made the visit at least three times during their school career. It had been on a fifth-grade trip that Melissa and Rex had first come here and begun the process of discovering who and what they were.

Anita wasn't at the ticket and info desk. The woman sitting there was new and looked up suspiciously as the three of them walked through the door.

"Can I help you?"

Rex fumbled in his pocket, hoping he'd remembered to bring his membership card. He found it after a few anxious moments. "Three, please."

The woman took the crumpled card from him and eyed it closely, one eyebrow raised. There was the usual wait as she looked them over, her eyes tracing his black coat and the girls' clothes, trying to think of a reason to keep them out.

"Anytime this year," Dess said.

"Pardon me?"

"She said that the membership should be good throughout this year, ma'am," Rex offered.

The woman nodded, lips pursed as if all her suspicions had been confirmed, and said, "Well, then, I see."

She punched a key, and three tickets emerged from a slot in the desk. "But you-all watch yourselves, y'hear?"

Dess snatched the tickets and was about to say something, but an older man in a tweed suit came through the staff door behind the desk, interrupting her just in time.

"Ah, it's the Arrowheads," Dr. Anton Sherwood said with a chuckle.

Rex felt the tension leave him. He grinned at the museum's director. "Good to see you, Dr. Sherwood."

"Got anything for me today, Rex?"

Rex shook his head, taking a moment to enjoy the confusion on the ticket woman's face. "Sorry, we're just here for a quick visit. Anything new to look at?"

"Mmm. We got a new biface point in from Cactus Hill,

Virginia. Looks like a good candidate for a Solutrean link. It's in the pre-Clovis case on this floor. Let me know what you think."

"I'd be happy to," Rex said. He smiled politely at the baffled woman behind the ticket desk and led Dess and Melissa into the museum.

"Psych-out," Dess said softly. Even Melissa was smiling. Rex allowed himself a few moments of pride. At least his two friends weren't ragging him about acrobats anymore.

The museum's low lighting settled around them, relief from the blinding noonday sun. Rex breathed in the cool, comforting smell of exposed red clay. One wall of the museum was open to the original Bixby excavation, the walkways suspended a few feet from the raw earth. Set into the hard clay, as if never fully excavated, were tools made of bone, fossilized wooden implements, obsidian flakes in the shape of arrowheads, and the skeleton of a saber-toothed tiger. (Saber-Toothed Tiger was what the label said, anyway. Rex was certain that his own theories and Dr. Sherwood's differed on exactly what the beast had been.)

As they headed for the sloping ramp that led down to the basement floors, Rex checked his watch. It was a few minutes past noon; Jessica might already be waiting. But on the way he paused for a quick glance into a glass case of pre-Clovis finds.

The case was full of crude arrowheads ranging from a half inch to five inches in length. Some were long and thin, others wide and barely pointed, like the end of a shovel. Most were spear points rather than true arrowheads. The makers had attached throwing shafts to them, but the wood had rotted away twelve thousand years ago. The newly arrived point was easy to spot. It was almost eight inches long, wafer thin and proportioned like a narrow leaf. It bore the telltale marks of a hammer made of soft stone and all the signs of a skilled workman. He propped up his glasses.

It dissolved into a blur; no Focus clung to it at all. Rex's face twisted with disappointment, and he continued down the ramp. So far he hadn't seen anything from outside Bixby that showed signs of the blue time.

In the whole world, were he and his friends really alone?

Jessica Day was already there, waiting on the lowest level, her gaze lost in a model of a mastodon hunt. Tiny Stone Age figures surrounded the elephantine animal, hurling spears into its thick hide from every direction. One of the little guys was about to be impaled on a long, twisted tusk.

"Pretty brave, huh?" Rex said.

Jessica started, as if she hadn't heard them approach. She recovered, then shrugged.

"Actually, I was thinking twenty against one."

"Nineteen," said Dess. Jessica raised an eyebrow.

This is going well already, Rex thought. He'd had a whole speech planned, a regular show-and-tell. He had rehearsed it in his mind again and again before going to sleep the night before. But Jessica looked exhausted. Even with his glasses making her a bit fuzzy, her green eyes bore the marks of a sleepless night. He decided to throw out the speech.

"You must have a lot of questions," he said.

"Yeah, I do."

"This way." They led Jessica to a small cluster of tables against one wall. This was where school groups ate their bag lunches. The four of them sat, Melissa pulling out her headphones, Dess leaning back precariously in her plastic chair.

"Ask away," Rex said, folding his hands on the table.

Jessica took a deep breath, as if about to speak, but then a helpless expression came across her face. Rex could read it even with his glasses on. It was the look of someone with too many questions to know where to start. Rex forced himself to be patient as Jessica collected her thoughts.

"A *hubcap*?" she finally blurted out.

Rex smiled.

"Not just any hubcap," Dess said. "That was from a 1967 Mercury."

"Is 1967 a multiple of thirteen?" Rex asked.

"Not hardly," Dess scoffed. "But they made hubcaps out of real steel back then. None of this aluminum crap."

"Time-out," Jessica called.

"Oh, sorry," Rex said sheepishly. "Explain, Dess, but keep it simple."

Dess pulled her necklace out of her shirtfront. A thirteen-pointed star dangled from its chain. In the dim light of the museum it caught the spotlights on the exhibits, twinkling as if with its own light.

"Remember this?"

"Yeah, I've noticed those all over Bixby since you told me about them."

"Well," Dess said, "this necklace is Darkling Protection 101. There are three things the darklings don't like. One is steel." She pinged the star with one fingernail. "The newer a type of metal is, the more it freaks darklings out."

"Steel," Jessica said quietly to herself, as if this made sense to her.

"Basically, darklings are really old," Dess explained. "And like a lot of old people, they don't like stuff that's changed since they were born."

"They used to be afraid of cut stone," Rex said. "Then forged metals: bronze and iron. But gradually they got used to them. Steel is newer."

"Hasn't steel been around a long time?" Jessica asked. "Like swords and stuff?"

"Yeah, but we're talking stainless steel, a modern invention," Dess said. "Of course, one day I'd like to get my hands on some electrolytic titanium or—"

"Okay," Jessica interrupted. "So they don't like new metals."

"Especially alloys," Dess said, "which means a mix of metals. Gold and silver are elements. They come straight up from the ground. The darklings aren't scared of them at all."

"But they're scared of alloys. So they couldn't get through something made of steel?" Jessica asked.

"It's not that simple," Dess said. "Thing number two that darklings are afraid of is . . . math."

"Math?"

"Well, a certain kind of math," Dess explained. "There are certain numbers and patterns and ratios that freak them out, basically."

Jessica's expression remained one of disbelief.

Rex had prepared for this. "Jess, have you heard of epilepsy?"

"Uh, sure. It's a disease, right? You fall down and start foaming at the mouth."

"And bite your own tongue off," added Dess.

"It's a brain thing," Rex said. "The seizures are usually triggered by a blinking light."

"It doesn't matter how strong or fit you are," Dess said. "A blinking light and you're suddenly helpless. Like Superman and kryptonite. But the thing is, the light has to be flashing at a certain speed. Numbers work that way on the darklings."

"And that's why Bixby has this thing about thirteen?" Jessica asked.

"You got it. Guaranteed protection against darklings and their little friends. Something about that number drives them totally crazy. They can't stand symbols that mean thirteen or groups of thirteen things. Even thirteen-letter words fry their heads."

Jessica let out a low whistle. "Psychosomatic."

"Yeah, that's a good one," Dess said. "So I gave that old hubcap a thirteen-letter name, Hypochondriac, and psychokitty got burned."

"Sure," Jessica said.

"Just remember to always keep a fresh tridecalogism in your mind."

"A fresh *what*?"

"*Tridecalogism* is a thirteen-letter word that means 'thirteen-letter word,'" Dess said, grinning happily.

"Really?"

"Well, I kind of made it up myself. So don't try to use it to protect yourself. And remember, when you actually use a tridecalogism on a darkling, make sure you come up with a fresh one for the next night."

"They get used to words faster than they do metals," Rex said.

"Who knows?" Dess continued. "Maybe one day they'll get used to the number thirteen. Then we'll be looking for thirty-nine-letter words."

Rex flinched at the idea. "That's not going to happen anytime soon."

"So all I have to do is carry a piece of metal with a thirteen-letter name around with me," Jessica asked with disbelief in her voice, "and I'll be fine?"

"Well, there's a lot more to it," Dess said. "For one thing, the metal should be clean."

"What, they're afraid of soap too?"

"Not that kind of clean," Rex said. "Untouched by midnight. You see, when something from the daylight world is disturbed during the blue time, it becomes part of their world. That changes it forever."

"So how can you tell what's clean?"

Rex took a deep breath. It was time to take over from Dess. "Haven't you wondered how we knew you were a midnighter, Jessica?"

She thought hard for a second, then gave a defeated sigh. "I can't keep track of all the stuff I've been wondering lately. But yeah, Dess seemed to know something from the moment we met. I just figured she was psychic."

Melissa snorted quietly, her fingers drumming along with her music.

"Well, when things have been changed by the secret hour, they look different. To me, anyway. And you're a midnighter, so you always look different. You're naturally part of that world." Rex pulled off his glasses.

Jessica's face became completely clear to him. Rex could see the lines of exhaustion below her eyes and her alert, questioning expression, ready to absorb whatever they could tell her.

"I can also read the lore, marks left behind by other midnighters. There are signs all over Bixby, some of them left thousands of years ago."

Jessica looked at him closely, possibly wondering if he was crazy. "And only you can see them?"

"So far." He swallowed. "Can we try something, Jessica?"

"Sure."

He led her to a museum case by the excavated wall. Under the glass was a collection of Clovis points, all from the Bixby area and all about ten thousand years old.

Although the label didn't say so, one of the points had been retrieved from inside the rib cage of the "saber-tooth" skeleton embedded in the wall. The rest had been found in ancient campsites, burial mounds, and the snake pit. With his glasses off, Rex could instantly spot the difference.

That one spearhead stood out from the rest with burning clarity, every facet so distinct that he could envision how the ancient hammer had struck off each flake of stone. The Focus had clung to this piece of obsidian for millennia, and from his first glimpse of it Rex had known instinctively that it had pierced the heart of the beast on the wall.

This point had killed a darkling.

Rex's naked eyes could also see subtle differences in the way it had been crafted—the meridian groove where the shaft had once been attached was deeper and sturdier, the edge much sharper. Ten thousand years ago this spearhead had been a piece of high technology, as advanced as some futuristic jet fighter. It might have been made of rock, but it had been the electrolytic titanium of its day.

"Do any of these . . . jump out at you?" he asked.

Jessica looked over the points carefully, her brow furrowed in concentration. Rex felt his breath catch. Last night he had allowed himself to wonder what it would be like if Jessica were another seer, someone else who could see the signs and read the lore. At last Rex would have someone to help him sift through the endless troves of midnighter knowledge, to compare interpretations of confusing and contradictory tales, to read alongside him.

Someone to share responsibility when things went wrong.

"This one's kind of different."

Jessica was pointing at a digging trowel, a stubby hand tool that wasn't a spearhead at all. Rex let his breath out slowly, not wanting his disappointment to show, not wanting to feel the entire weight of it yet.

"Yeah, it is different. They used it to dig for root vegetables."

"Root vegetables?"

"Big fans of yams, Stone Agers." He put his glasses back on.

"So it's a yam digger. That's not what you brought me over here for, is it?"

"No," he admitted. "I wanted to know if you could see something."

"You mean, see the secret hour like you can?"

Rex nodded. "I can tell which of these spearheads killed a darkling. The touch lingers. I can see it."

Jessica stared into the case and frowned. "Maybe my eyes *are* wrong."

"No, Jessica. Different midnighters have different talents. We just don't know what yours is yet."

She shrugged, then pointed. "That's a darkling skeleton up there, isn't it?"

He was surprised for a moment, then nodded, realizing that she'd seen a creature like it in the flesh.

"Wow. So these things really were around ten thousand years ago," she said. "Shouldn't they be extinct by now or something? Like dinosaurs?"

"Not in Bixby."

One of her eyebrows raised. "Rex, there aren't any dinosaurs in Bixby, are there?"

He had to smile. "Not that I've seen."

"Well, that's something."

Rex silently led her back toward the table. It could have changed everything if Jessica had turned out to be a seer. He swallowed, unable to speak for a moment, then found part of last night's speech on the tip of his tongue.

"Darklings almost went extinct, Jessica, but instead they hid themselves in the blue time. It's been a long time since they lived in the world with the rest of us."

"That must have been exciting, being chased around by those things twenty-four seven."

"Twenty-*five* seven," Rex corrected her. "Humans weren't the top of the food chain back then. People had to deal with tigers and bears and dire wolves. But the darklings were the worst. They weren't just stronger and faster, they were *smarter* than us. For a long time we were completely defenseless."

They sat back down at the table, the darkness of the unused corner of the museum surrounding them. Melissa looked up at Rex, her satisfied expression showing that she could taste his disappointment.

"How did anyone survive?" Jessica asked.

Dess leaned forward. "The darklings are predators, Jessica. They didn't want to wipe human beings out, just take enough to keep themselves fed."

Jessica shivered. "What a nightmare."

"Exactly," Rex said. A small group of tourists was descending the ramp, and he lowered his voice. "Imagine wondering every night if they would be coming to feed. Imagine having no way to stop them. They were the original nightmares, Jessica. Every monster in folklore, every mythological monster, even our instinctive fear of the darkness, they're all based on ancient memories of darklings."

Dess's eyes narrowed as she leaned forward, also lowering her voice. "Not all darklings look like panthers, Jessica. You haven't even met the *really* scary ones yet."

"Oh, wonderful," Jessica said. "And they all live in Bixby now?"

"We're not sure about that," Dess said. "But Bixby's the only place with midnight that we know of. Even up in Tulsa, twenty miles from here, the blue time doesn't come."

"For some reason, Bixby's special," Rex said.

"Great," Jessica said. "Mom wasn't kidding when she said moving here would require some adjustments."

She slumped in her chair.

Rex tried to remember the threads of his speech. "But don't forget, we humans won. Gradually we discovered ways to protect ourselves. It turned out that new ideas scared the darklings."

"Ideas? Scared *that* thing?" She looked across the room at the darkling skeleton.

"New tools, like forged metal and alloys," Dess said. "And new concepts, like mathematics. And the darklings were always afraid of the light."

"Fire was the first defense," Rex said. "They've never gotten used to it."

"Well, that's a relief," Jessica said. "I'll make sure I've got a flamethrower next time the secret hour comes around."

Dess shook her head. "It won't help you. Fire, electronic stuff, car engines, none of those technologies works in the midnight hour. You think we rode bicycles halfway across Bixby last night for the exercise?"

"That's why the blue time was created," Rex said. "A few thousand years ago, when the darklings were being pushed into the deepest forest by steel weapons and fire, they created it as a sanctuary for themselves."

"They *made* the blue time?" Jessica asked.

Rex nodded. "The lore says that they took one hour from the day and collapsed it down to an instant so that human beings couldn't see it anymore."

Jessica said softly, "Except those who were born at exactly that instant."

"You got it," Dess said. "It has to happen to some people, you know? Only so many seconds in the day."

Dess was looking at Jessica expectantly.

"What?" Jess asked.

Rex sighed. "She wants you to tell her how many seconds are in a day."

Jessica shrugged. "A lot?"

"Sixty seconds per minute," Dess supplied. "Sixty minutes per hour. Twenty-four hours per day."

"That would be . . ." Jessica looked up at the ceiling in rapt concentration. "A *whole* lot?"

"Eighty-six thousand, four hundred," Dess said quietly. "I thought maybe you were, you know, really good at math. You are in trig, after all."

Jessica snorted. "That was my mom's idea. When we changed schools, she decided to promote me to misunderstood genius."

"Tough luck," said Dess. She shrugged at Rex.

Melissa giggled again, singing along softly with her headphones. Rex barely caught the words.

"Tastes like . . . vanilla."

13

ACROBAT

Last year at PS 141 there'd been this really gross experiment in biology. . . .

Jessica's class had raised two bunches of flatworms in terrariums, which were basically aquariums but full of dirt instead of water. The flatworms really were flat, with little triangular heads kind of like the spear points that Rex was so fond of. They had two little spots that looked like eyes but weren't. They could detect light, though.

In one terrarium the class always put the worm food in the same corner, under a little light that they switched on at feeding time. The light was like a restaurant sign: Come In, We're Open.

In the other terrarium the class just sprinkled the food randomly on top of the dirt.

The flatworms in the first terrarium weren't stupid. Pretty soon they figured out what the light meant. You could point a flashlight at any side of that terrarium, and the worms would come looking for food. They would even follow the light around in circles, if worm racing was what you were into.

Then, as it did in every biology class, the time came for the gross part.

Using the flashlight as bait, the class collected all the clever light-loving worms from the first terrarium. Then the teacher, Mrs. Hardaway, put them into a bowl and squished them into worm paste. Nobody was forced to watch, but a few kids did. Not Jessica.

In case that wasn't gross enough, Mrs. Hardaway then fed the squished worms to the other worms. Apparently flatworms would eat anything, even other worms.

The next day the class gathered around, and for the first time ever Mrs. Hardaway moved the little restaurant light to the second terrarium. She let Jessica herself switch on the light. One by one the worms popped their little flat heads up, hungry for food. They had learned about the restaurant light by eating the worms from the other terrarium, like learning French by eating french fries, except infinitely grosser.

Tonight, sitting on her bed, waiting for midnight, surrounded by unpacked boxes, Jessica Day had the aftertaste of midnighter in her mouth.

Rex and Dess had kept her at the museum for hours, cramming her brain with everything they knew about the darklings, the blue time, midnighters and their talents, and the secret history of Bixby, Oklahoma. They'd ground up years of incredible experiences and unbelievable discoveries and served them all as one gigantic meal. And of course Jessica had no choice but to eat every bite. The secret hour was dangerous. What she didn't know could really hurt her.

In the end, even Melissa had taken off her headphones to join in, explaining her own weird talent. It turned out that she, not Dess, was the psychic—a *real* psychic, not the psychosomatic kind—but in a way that sounded completely awful. She'd described it as being in a room with fifty radios blasting, all tuned to different stations. And Rex had warned Jessica not to touch her; physical contact turned the volume up way too high.

No wonder Melissa was so much fun to be around.

As Jessica watched the clock's second hand slowly sweep out the remaining minutes, she rested one hand on her churning stomach. She had the feeling she always got before a test. This was quite a test. It included math, mythology, metallurgy, science, and ancient history. And getting a single question wrong could mean becoming worm food herself.

The day had probably been a lot more fun for Rex, Dess, and Melissa. For years the three of them had kept an entire world secret. They'd had to face the terrors and joys of midnight alone. So of course they'd been anxious to share them with someone new.

Jessica just wished she could remember more of what they'd said. After the first hour or three her sleepless night had started to take its toll, their voices turning into competing drones. Finally she'd told them she was going home.

It was amazing how quickly a new and mysterious world could go from totally unbelievable to completely unbearable.

She'd gotten back home just in time for dinner. Jessica could tell that Mom had been all ready to yell at her about the still unpacked boxes. But one look at Jessica's exhausted face and her mother had instantly switched gears.

"Oh, sweetheart. You've been doing homework all day, haven't you? This is my fault for putting you in all those advanced classes, isn't it?"

Jessica hadn't bothered to disagree. She'd half dozed through dinner and then gone straight to sleep. But she'd set her alarm for eleven-thirty. Tonight she wanted to be completely awake and dressed when the blue time came.

Although she couldn't remember half of what the other midnighters had tried to teach her, she hadn't forgotten the important stuff. Jessica was armed with three new weapons: Deliciousness, Fossilization, and Jurisprudence, which were a coil of wire, a long screw, and a broken car-radio antenna. They weren't much to look at, and Dess had said that none was as formidable as the mighty Hypochondriac, but she had guaranteed they would light a fire under a darkling's tail. Or at least a sparky blue fireworks show. Jessica had also borrowed a few recipes of Dess's to create her own traps. Her bedroom was slitherproof now.

In addition, there was no way she was going outside tonight.

The other three midnighters were headed for what Rex had called a "lore site." Apparently there had been midnighters in Bixby for as long as there had been a secret hour, some born here and some, like Jessica, who'd stumbled into town. Generations of seers like Rex had slowly collected knowledge about the blue time and the darklings and recorded their discoveries where only other seers could find them. Out in the unchanging badlands huge, ancient rocks were marked with invisible runes that told the ancient stories.

Rex said that he would search until he discovered why the darklings were so interested in Jessica. "But maybe last night was a coincidence," he'd said unconvincingly.

"Maybe they just like you," Melissa had said, smacking her lips. "As in, 'I like pizza.'"

Two minutes to go.

Jessica swallowed and lifted her feet off the floor. The slithers couldn't possibly be here yet, but last night had brought all her childhood fears back to her. There were things under the bed. Maybe at the moment they were psychosomatic things, but she could still feel them down there.

She looked at her clock, which was set to Bixby time now. Dess had explained that "real midnight" happened at a different moment in every city. Time zones just kind of faked it. But now when her clock hit twelve, Jessica Day would be as far away from the sun as you could get.

One minute to go.

Jessica picked up Jurisprudence and pulled it out to its full length. She swished it through the air like a sword. The radio antenna was from a Chevy made in 1976, a year that apparently *was* a multiple of thirteen. Dess had been saving it for something special.

Jessica smiled. It was the oddest gift she'd ever gotten, but she had to admit it felt good in her hand.

The secret hour arrived.

The overhead light seemed to wink out, replaced by the familiar blue glow from every corner of the room. The sound of wind among the trees ceased abruptly. Her first time completely awake for the change, Jessica could *feel* as well as see and hear it. Something invisible seemed to pull at her, tugging her forward, as if she were finishing a roller-coaster ride, the car gradually coming to a halt. A sense of lightness came over her, and she felt a subtle flutter of arrested motion throughout her body.

The tingle of the whole world, stopping around her.

"Okay," Jessica said to herself. "Here we go again."

However real she knew it was, the blue time still seemed like a dream.

She walked around her room, touching things to reassure herself. The rough edges of cardboard boxes felt the same, the pinewood boards of the floor were as smooth and cool as always.

"Real, real, and real," she affirmed quietly as her fingers brushed clothing, desk, the spines of books.

Now that midnight was here, Jessica found herself wondering what she was going to *do* with this extra hour. A few minutes ago she had heard her parents talking in the kitchen. But she didn't want to see them pale and frozen; she was staying in her own room.

There was plenty of unpacking to do. She opened a few of the boxes and looked into their chaotic depths. But the blue, shadowless light seemed too alien for anything so mundane. She sat on her bed, picked up the dictionary she'd unpacked when she got home, and opened it to look for tridecalogisms.

She'd found only one—*splendiferous*—when her head started to hurt from the light. The other midnighters could probably read in the blue time just fine. Maybe Melissa was right; Jessica's eyes did feel wrong, at least here in the secret hour.

She glanced out the window at the motionless world but shivered and looked away. The thought of something looking back in at her was too frightening.

She picked her feet up off the floor, lay back, and stared at the ceiling.

Jessica sighed. This could get very boring.

Not much later, she heard the noise.

It was a very soft thud, barely audible even in the absolute silence. Jessica immediately thought of panther paws and jumped off her bed.

She picked up Jurisprudence and jingled Fossilization and Deliciousness to check that they were still in her pocket. From the end of the bed Jessica couldn't see very much of the street, but she was too scared to get any closer to the windows. She maneuvered around her bedroom, trying to catch a glimpse of whatever was outside.

A dark shape moved on the front walk. Jessica backed out of its view and gripped the car antenna tighter. Rex and Dess had promised she would be safe here. They had said she knew enough to defend herself.

What if they were wrong?

Her back was pressed against the door now. She imagined the great cat squeezing through the front door and down the halls of the house, stealing up behind her. It seemed incredibly unlikely that the thirteen thumbtacks stuck into the wood of her door would be a match for its powerful muscles.

No more sound came from outside. Was whatever it was still out there?

She had to take a look.

Jessica sank to her hands and knees and crept along the floor against the wall until she was just below the window. She sat there, listening as hard as she could. The total silence seemed to roar quietly, like the sound of the ocean trapped in a shell.

She inched her head up to peer over the windowsill.

A face looked back at her.

Jessica jumped away, swinging Jurisprudence in an arc before her so that it cracked against the glass. She scrambled backward until she bumped against her bed. The window began to slide open.

"It's okay, Jessica. It's just me," a voice called through the gap.

Her car-radio antenna thrust out before her like a

sword, Jessica blinked, forcing her brain to put together the familiar voice and the face she had glimpsed. After a few seconds of fear, recognition came, along with a wave of relief and surprise.

It was Jonathan.

Jonathan perched at the window, evidently a bit reluctant to come inside. He seemed to think that Jessica was going to take another swing at him. Jurisprudence was still in her grip, passed nervously from hand to hand.

Jonathan sat with one leg folded under him, his other knee drawn up under his chin. He certainly didn't seem very scary now.

He hadn't said much since arriving at the window. He seemed to be waiting for her to calm down. Unlike in the lunchroom at school, Jonathan's eyes were open wide. He didn't look sleepy at all. Maybe he was photophobic in the daylight too.

She was glad he didn't hide his eyes behind dark glasses, though. They were very pretty eyes.

He watched as Jessica slowly gained control of her breathing, his gaze intent but silent.

"I didn't know you were a midnighter," she finally managed.

"They didn't tell you?" He laughed. "That figures."

"They know about you?"

"Sure. Since the day I moved here."

Jessica shook her head in disbelief. Six hours of

midnighter lore and neither Rex, Dess, nor Melissa had bothered to mention the fifth midnighter in town.

"Wait a second," Jess said as something occurred to her. "Are you the only one they didn't tell me about? How many of you *are* there?"

Jonathan grinned. "Just one of me," he said.

She stared back at him, still too overwhelmed to make sense of anything.

"No, there aren't any others," he said, more seriously. "I'm the only person they didn't mention."

"What, don't they like you?"

He shrugged. "I'm not in the club, you know? I mean, Rex is okay, I guess, and Dess is actually pretty cool." He paused, obviously not wanting to get started on Melissa. "But they take the whole thing way too seriously."

"Too *seriously*?"

"Yeah. They act like they're on a mission from the Midnighters World Council or something."

"There's a Midnighters World Council?" Jessica asked.

He laughed. "No, but I bet Rex wishes there was. He thinks this whole midnight thing has some deep and mysterious meaning."

Jessica blinked. It had never occurred to her to doubt that there were deep and mysterious forces at work. It all seemed pretty deep and mysterious to her.

"So what do you think, Jonathan?"

"I think we're lucky to have a whole world to ourselves.

To play in, explore, do whatever we want. Why mess it up with some big purpose?"

Jessica nodded. Since the darkling had attacked her, the secret hour had become a crisis, a deadly challenge. But that first, beautiful dream had been something else entirely. Something . . . easy.

"For Rex," Jonathan continued, "the blue time is like some big textbook, and he's always studying for the final exam. For me, it's recess."

She gave him a sour look. "There are some pretty big bullies on the playground."

He shrugged. "I'm faster than the bullies. Always have been."

Jessica wondered how that could be true. But Jonathan seemed perfectly at ease. He dangled his foot outside the window, never checking over his shoulder, unafraid.

"You guys all seem to enjoy the secret hour," she said sadly. "You all think it's exciting, for one reason or another. For me, it's just been a nightmare. This thing—these *things*—tried to kill me last night."

"That's what Dess told me."

"She told you about me?"

"Yeah, back when Rex first spotted you. And this morning she gave me your address. What, did you think I used superpowers to find you?"

"The phone book, actually."

He smiled. "You're not in information yet. I checked.

But Melissa got the psychic 411 on you last night, so Dess called me."

"Dess gave you my address, but she didn't tell me about you?"

"She would have, but not in front of Rex. He and I have this . . . personality conflict. Namely, I think he should get a new one. But Dess prefers to stay out of it."

"Oh." Jessica leaned back against the wall. "This gets more complicated every minute."

"Yeah, it's awful that you ran into a darkling so soon," Jonathan said. "But last night was weird all over town. It was probably just darkling New Year's Eve or something. Was that your first time out?"

She started to nod, then shook her head. She'd almost forgotten the first night. With Rex and Dess cramming her head with midnighter lore and history all day, she'd only thought about the dangers of the blue time, not the splendor of the frozen storm.

"It must be nice," she said quietly, "being happy to be a midnighter."

"Quit calling me that," he softly chided. "I'm not a 'midnighter.' That's Rex's word."

Jessica frowned. "It seems pretty appropriate to me. Kind of makes the point and sounds better than 'twelve o'clocker.'"

"I guess it does," Jonathan admitted with a smile. "And I do like the word *midnight*. Since I moved to Bixby, anyway."

Jessica took a breath and dared to look past him to the blue-lit street. Even before the secret hour had come, it had been a beautiful night, gusty and dramatic. She could see falling autumn leaves trailing from the giant oak trees like flocks of dark and frozen birds. Their brilliant reds and yellows had turned black in the blue light.

She remembered the raindrops that first night, how her fingertips had released them from midnight's hold. Would the leaves also fall at her touch? She wanted to run through them, knocking handfuls out of the air. Back in Chicago she had never been able to resist snapping off icicles, breaking winter's spell.

But among the black leaves Jessica could still imagine the darkling that had attacked her. Its cruel form might be lurking anywhere among the frozen shapes outside. She shuddered and turned away from the window.

Her bedroom still seemed alien. It looked wan in the blue light, like a fading memory. Motionless dust hung in the air.

"Midnight is beautiful," she said. "But cold, too."

Jonathan frowned. "It never feels cold to me. Or hot, either. It's more like a perfect summer night."

Jessica shook her head. "I didn't mean that kind of cold."

"Oh, I see," Jonathan said. "Yeah. It feels kind of empty sometimes. Like we're the last people on earth."

"Thanks. That makes me feel much better."

"You shouldn't be scared of midnight, Jessica."

"I'm only scared of being eaten."

"That was just bad luck."

"But Rex said—"

"Don't worry about what Rex says," Jonathan interrupted. "He's way too paranoid. He thinks no one should explore the blue time until they know all ten thousand years of midnighter lore. That's like reading a whole VCR manual just to watch a movie. Which I've seen Rex actually do, by the way."

"You should've seen the darkling that attacked me," Jessica said.

"I've seen darklings. Lots of them."

"But—"

Jonathan disappeared from the window, and Jessica's breath caught short. He had slipped out of sight so quickly, so gracefully, rolling backward like a scuba diver off a boat. A moment later his head and shoulders reappeared.

He extended his hand through the window. "Come on. Let me unscare you."

Jessica hesitated. She looked at the row of thirteen thumbtacks that Dess had told her to line up under the window. As Jessica had stuck them into the window frames and door of her bedroom, she'd felt incredibly stupid. *Thumbtacks* were supposed to protect her from the forces of evil?

But the kind of object didn't matter, Dess had explained, only the number.

Jonathan saw where she was looking. "Let me guess.

You're protected by the mighty power of paper clips?"

"Uh, no. Mighty power of thumbtacks, actually." Jessica felt herself starting to blush and hoped it wouldn't show in the blue light.

Jonathan nodded. "Dess does know some pretty cool stuff. But I know a few tricks too. You'll be safe with me, I promise."

He was smiling again. Jessica decided that she liked Jonathan's smile.

And she realized that he was totally unafraid. She considered his offer. He had lived here in Bixby for more than two years and had managed to survive, even to enjoy himself. Surely he must understand midnight as well as Rex or Dess.

And before he had appeared, she'd been afraid just sitting here in her room. Now she felt secure. She was probably safer with an experienced midnighter—or whatever he called himself—than on her own.

Jessica telescoped Jurisprudence down to its shortest length, put it into her pocket, then pulled on her sneakers.

"Okay, unscare me."

She put one foot up on the windowsill and reached for Jonathan's hand.

As his palm pressed against hers, Jessica's breath caught short. She felt suddenly light-headed . . . light-*bodied*, as if her whole bedroom had turned into an elevator and headed for the basement.

"What—," she started.

Jonathan didn't answer, just pulled Jessica gently out the window. She floated up and out easily, as if she were full of helium. Her feet landed softly, bouncing a little before settling softly onto the ground.

"What's going on?" she finished.

"Midnight gravity," Jonathan said.

"Uh, this is new," she said. "How come I never—"

Jonathan let go of her hand, and weight returned. Her sneakers pushed into the soft dirt.

Jessica reached for Jonathan's hand again. When she took it, the buoyant feeling returned.

"*You're* making this happen?" she said.

Jonathan nodded. "Rex does lore. Dess does numbers. Melissa does . . . her stuff." He faced the house across the street. "And I do this."

He jumped. Jessica was pulled after him, like a kid's balloon tied to a bike. But she didn't feel as if she were being dragged. It hardly seemed as if they were moving at all. The world dropped softly away, the ground rolling beneath them. The road passed by below, frozen leaves brushing against them, the neighbor's house sliding closer like some big, stately ship pulling into dock.

"You . . . *fly*," Jessica managed.

They settled on the neighbor's roof, still featherlight. She could see the whole motionless street now, two parallel rows of roofs stretching away in either direction. But strangely there was no sense of height, no fear of falling. It was as if her body didn't believe in gravity anymore.

Jessica found a leaf clutched in her free hand. She must have grabbed it out of the air as they'd passed through the frozen swirl of leaves.

"It's okay," Jonathan said. "I've got you."

"I know," she whispered. "But . . . who's got *you*?" The soles of Jonathan's shoes barely brushed the slate roof, as if he were a hot-air balloon anxious to get off the ground.

In response he took the leaf from her hand. He held it with two fingers and released it. It didn't fall, just stayed where Jonathan had placed it in the air.

Jessica reached out her hand. When her fingertips brushed the leaf, it fell softly to the roof, then skittered down the steep angle. Just as it had the raindrops, her touch released it. But Jonathan's was different.

"Gravity stops when time does," Jonathan said. "Time has to pass for something to fall."

"I guess so."

"Remember the intro chapter to our physics book? Gravity is just a warp in space-time."

Jessica sighed. Another advanced class she was already behind in.

"So," Jonathan continued, "I guess I'm a little bit more out of time than the rest of you. Midnight gravity doesn't have a real hold on me. I weigh something but not much."

Jessica tried to get her head around his words. She supposed that if raindrops could hover in the air, it made sense that a person could too. *Why should any of the midnighters fall?* she wondered.

"So you can fly."

"Not Superman fly," Jonathan said. "But I can jump a long way and fall any dista—*hey*!"

Without thinking, Jessica had let go of his hand. Normal weight hit her all at once, as if someone had suddenly dropped a necklace of bricks around her head. The house reared up under her, and she collapsed onto its instantly treacherous slope. She was no longer made of feathers but solid bone and flesh. A sudden terror of heights struck her like a punch in the stomach.

Her hands reached out instinctively as she slid downward, fingernails grasping at the slate roof tiles. She half rolled and half skidded toward the edge of the roof.

"Jonathan!"

The edge loomed up toward her. One foot went off into space. The toe of her other sneaker caught in the rain gutter, and she halted for a second. But she had only a tenuous grasp on the roof tiles. Her fingers, her foot, everything was slipping. . . .

Then gravity let go again.

Jessica felt Jonathan's hands gently grasping both shoulders. The two of them floated down to the ground together.

"I'm so sorry," he said.

Her heart still pounded, but she wasn't scared anymore. The featherlight feeling had returned so quickly, like a wave of relief when some horrible test was over.

Their feet settled onto the ground.

"Are you okay?" Jonathan said. "I should have warned you."

"It's all right," she said, shaking her head. "I should have realized. I was just thinking that it's too bad we can't all fly."

"No, just me. Although when you turned up, I was kind of hoping."

She looked at Jonathan. His eyes were still wide with alarm. And Jessica could also see his disappointment that she had fallen, that she wasn't like him.

"Yeah, I was kind of hoping too, I guess." She took his hand firmly. "But take me up again. Please?"

"You're not scared?"

"Kind of," she admitted. "So unscare me."

They flew.

It was true, Jonathan wasn't Superman. Flying was hard work. Jessica found that they went much higher if she jumped with him, pushing off as hard as she could. The timing was tricky—if one of them pushed too soon and too hard, they would fly apart and be jerked to a halt at arm's length, then spin helplessly around each other, laughing until the ground caught them again. But they got better with every jump, coordinating their leaps to soar higher and higher.

She gripped Jonathan's hand hard, nervous and excited, terrified of darklings and thrilled to be in the sky.

Flying was beautiful. The pale blue streets glinted like rivers beneath them as they crashed through high, wind-borne columns of autumn leaves. There were birds up here, too, their wings outstretched in arrested flight and angled to catch the frozen winds. The dark moon glowered over them, almost risen all the way, but it didn't seem to crowd the sky as oppressively as it had last night. From up here Jessica could see the band of stars that stretched around the horizon, bright pinpoints whose white light hadn't been leached blue by the moon.

The layout of Bixby was still unfamiliar to her, but now that Jessica could see the town from above, laid out like a map, it started to make sense. From the highest jumps the houses and trees looked small and perfect, a city of dollhouses. Jonathan must see the world completely differently from everyone else, she realized.

They drew closer to the edge of town, where the houses thinned and wilderness encroached on the city. It was easier going out here, not having to negotiate houses, stores, and tree-lined streets. Soon Jessica could see all the way out to where low, scrubby trees dotted the rough, low hills.

The badlands.

As they got closer to the desert, her eyes nervously scanned the ground for any movement, imagining the skulking shapes of darklings under every tree. But everything below seemed motionless, tiny and insignificant as they soared over it. She realized that they were moving much more quickly than the panther could even at full speed, taking leaps a hundred times as great as the giant cat's.

Jonathan really was faster than the bullies.

He took her to one of the big water towers outside of

town. They alighted on it, the city on one side, the black badlands on the other. It was flat on top, with a low guardrail around the edge.

"Okay, hand-rest time," he said.

They let go of each other. Jessica was prepared this time, bending her knees as normal weight settled back onto her.

"Ow," she said, rubbing her fingers. She realized that every muscle in her hand was sore. Jonathan stretched his own hand with a pained expression. "Oops, sorry. Didn't mean to be all clingy."

He laughed. "Better clingy than splatty."

"Yeah, totally." She stepped carefully to the edge of the tower, keeping one hand on the rail. As she looked down, her stomach did a back flip. "Okay, fear of heights still in working order."

"Good," Jonathan said. "I worry that one day I'll forget that it's not midnight and jump off a roof or something. Or I'll forget what time it is and still be flying around when gravity comes back."

Jessica turned toward him, put one hand on his shoulder, and the lightness returned. "Please don't."

She blushed and let go. Her voice had sounded so serious.

He smiled. "I won't, Jessica. Really."

"Call me Jess."

"Sure. Jess." His smile grew broader.

"Thanks for taking me flying."

"You're welcome."

Jessica turned away shyly.

She heard a crunch. Jonathan was eating an apple.

"Want one?"

"Uh, that's okay."

"I've got four."

She blinked. "Do you ever stop eating?"

Jonathan shrugged. "Like I said, I've got to eat my own body weight every day."

"Really?"

"No. But flying makes me hungry."

Jessica smiled and looked out over the town, feeling secure for the first time since last night's "dream" had gone all wrong.

Her eyes followed a bird flying along the horizon, backlit by the moon, which had just begun to set. She was so happy, still featherlight inside, that it took a moment for her stomach to sink.

The bird was *moving*.

"Jonathan, what's wrong with this picture?"

He followed her gaze. "Oh, that. It's just a flying slither."

She nodded, swallowing. "I saw some last night."

"That's what Dess calls them, anyway," Jonathan said. "Although 'flying slither' kind of sounds like a contradiction to me. But the winged ones and the crawly ones are the same creature. They change their shape, did you know?"

"Yeah, I know." She remembered the kitty-shaped slither that had led her so far from home before turning into a snake. The flying slither was circling them slowly, its leathery wings transparent against the cold moon. "It's creeping me out."

"Don't worry. Those things never bother anyone." He reached into his shirt and pulled up a necklace of thick steel links. "And if that one decides to, I've got all thirty-nine links of Obstructively to protect us."

Jessica shivered. "A slither bit me last night. Or whatever you'd call it. Tongued me."

"Ouch. Were you messing with a nest or something?"

She looked at Jonathan sourly. "No, I wasn't doing anything stupid. A bunch of them were helping the darkling hunt me. It snuck up on me in the grass and gave me this slither hickey." She showed him the mark.

"Yuck. They are nasty little creatures. But it won't bother us, I promise, Jess."

"I hope not." She hugged herself. Somehow it felt colder up here, as if the suspended desert wind blowing off the badlands had left a trace of itself. Jessica wished she had brought a sweatshirt.

Jonathan put a hand on her shoulder. The lightness returned, the feeling of safety and warmth. Her feet disconnected for a moment from the tower, as buoyant as a cork on water. She shivered again, but not with the cold this time.

"Jessica?" Jonathan said.

"Call me Jess, I said."

"Jess!" His voice sounded wrong. He was staring the other way, toward the badlands outside of town. She followed his gaze.

A darkling was coming.

It wasn't at all like the one from the night before. It shifted as it flew, muscles rippling as it transformed from one shape to another—first a snake, then a tiger, then a bird of prey, scales and fur and feathers all blurring together on its crawling skin, the huge wings beating with the sound of a flag whipping in the wind.

It could fly too, and quickly. It was headed straight toward them.

But Jonathan had seen lots of darklings before, Jessica reminded herself. He had been out in midnight hundreds of times. He was faster than the bullies.

She looked back at his face. Jonathan's mouth had dropped open.

Jessica knew instantly that he'd never seen a darkling like this one.

14

BEASTS OF PREY

Along with a flood of terror, a few morsels of Jessica's day-long cram session trickled into her mind.

"Jonathan, this tower's made of steel, isn't it?"

He shook his head. "It's not clean. Nothing this far out of town is."

"Oh, right. So we . . ."

"Jump."

They locked hands and stepped to the edge of the water tower. Jonathan placed one foot squarely on the guardrail and pulled lightly upward. They floated up to a precarious balance on the thin rail.

"One, two . . ."

Even though she was nearly weightless, Jessica's sneakers were unsteady. She bent her knees as she and Jonathan slowly listed forward, seeing nothing below but the hard ground.

". . . *three.*"

They pushed off, almost straight out from the tower. Jessica realized that Jonathan had meant it to work exactly this way. The scrubby earth zoomed by under them faster than ever, their momentum carrying them forward rather than up. They descended toward the ground quickly.

"That parking lot," Jonathan said, pointing with his free hand. "Keep jumping, low and fast."

The huge factory lot was perfect for landing. A few long trucks were crowded in the middle, but otherwise it was clear. As they arced down to it, Jess dared a glance over her shoulder. The darkling still pursued them.

They touched down on the asphalt and took one bounding step that carried them over the trucks and almost to the other end of the parking lot.

"This way," Jonathan shouted as they flew, tugging her hand in the direction he intended. They jumped again, launching themselves toward an empty expanse of highway that led past the factory. Following Jonathan's lead, Jessica kept their trajectory low. They didn't want to waste effort soaring high into the sky. Only speed mattered.

They descended toward the highway, heading for a spot that was clear of cars. They were still well ahead of the darkling.

"Which way?" Jessica shouted.

"Down the highway!"

As they landed, Jonathan's hand clenched, letting her know exactly when to push off again.

They took two more bounds down the highway, the four-lane width making it an easy target. They were moving fast. Jess glanced over her shoulder again; the darkling actually seemed to be falling behind.

But as the road led them farther into Bixby, it narrowed to two lanes, and more late-driving cars began to appear on it. Jonathan was hesitant with their jumps now as he frantically calculated how to come down in a clear spot.

Their leaps grew timid. They were moving slower and slower.

An errant jump carried them toward a house and onto its treacherously sloped roof. Jonathan slipped as they pushed off, and they went spinning. When they landed, the darkling was closer.

They leapt again, trying to get back onto the road.

"It's too crowded here," he cried. "We have to get farther out of town."

"Toward the badlands?"

"Yes. The open desert's perfect."

"Isn't that where the bad guys *come from*?" she asked.

"Yeah. But we're too slow here."

Jessica checked the beast behind them. It had stopped changing shape, settling on a thin, snakelike form with a beaked head. The creature's wingspan had grown, as if the thing's bulk had been transferred from its body to its wings. It looked faster now, and it was getting closer.

"Okay."

At the next landing they turned, angling back toward the edge of town. Suddenly Jessica recognized where they were.

"My mom works near here. Next jump: that way!"

"What? Your mom can't help us, Jessica."

"Shut up and follow me."

Jessica felt Jonathan's hand tighten, resisting her for a moment, but when the next leap came, he followed her lead. As they reached the top of their arc, they found themselves soaring over a high fence and onto the grounds of Aerospace Oklahoma. Mom had driven Jessica past here on the first day of school, almost making her late. The complex was huge, dotted with wide airplane hangars and low office buildings, mostly runways and vast empty spaces. They tested new wings, landing gear, and jet engines here, and Jessica's mom had said they even had an old Boeing 747 that they would occasionally set aflame to practice fire fighting.

It all required a lot of open space.

They jumped three times long and fast, eating up the entire length of a runway with the speed of a jet aircraft. Then they soared over a huge hangar and found another long runway. The darkling fell farther behind.

The beast's cry reached their ears. Unlike the bellow of the panther, its scream was high and reedy, torturing Jessica's ears like the shriek of a boiling teakettle.

A chorus of cries came in answer, piercingly high chirps from somewhere in front of them.

"The badlands are up ahead," Jonathan said.

Jessica nodded and said softly, "They're waiting for us."

The setting moon filled the horizon now, and she could see a cloud of flying slithers against its lightless but blinding face. There were hundreds of them, wheeling in a chaotic mass, and two larger shapes, darklings on the wing.

"This is too weird," said Jonathan. "I've never seen—"

"This way," Jessica interrupted as they struck the ground. She pulled him to one side, angling away from the armada of creatures ahead. But her decision had come too late. Their hands jerked taut against each other, and she felt her fingers slipping. She reached out with her other hand for him, but their momentum carried them apart.

"Jess!" she heard Jonathan shout.

As they tugged free, she felt gravity take a brutal hold upon her body. They had just left the ground, and there wasn't far to fall, but the asphalt was moving past under her quickly. It was like looking down at the street through the window of a speeding car. She rolled into a ball.

Just before Jessica hit the ground, the asphalt seemed to change texture, suddenly dark and uneven. When she struck the earth, it was covered with something unexpectedly soft. She rolled and rolled, the ground pummeling her from every direction.

Jessica finally came to a stop, bruised and breathless. She lay there for a second, feeling terribly heavy. When she could breathe, the smell of grass filled her nose. That was what had broken her fall.

Jessica sat up slowly. She looked around.

She had just missed the runway, landing where thick Oklahoma scrub grass led up to its edge. There was the metallic taste of blood in her mouth, and she was dizzy, but her arms and legs all seemed able to move.

The sounds of slithers came from in front and behind,

closing in on her. In the distance their shapes moved against the vast, dark moon like a haze of gnats. Jonathan was nowhere to be seen.

Her normal weight felt as heavy as lead now that she could only run, not fly.

She stood slowly. Started painfully to walk.

"Jess!"

Jonathan was skimming across the ground toward her, one hand extended.

She thrust out her right hand. As he flew past, Jonathan grasped her wrist, and she was transformed into a toy balloon again, pulled in his wake. The bruises on her hands complained, and she cried out.

"Are you okay?"

"Yeah. Just banged up."

"I thought you were dead!"

She giggled, a little hysterically. "I thought you were halfway to Texas."

Jonathan didn't say anything, just grasped her wrist tighter.

"Thanks for coming back," Jessica said. She could hear the crazed sound of her own voice and wondered if she'd bumped her head. It was hard to tell if her light-headedness was brain damage or the effect of Jonathan's touch.

"They're on three sides of us now," he said.

Jessica blinked, trying to clear her mind. She could see a cloud of slithers to their right and a lone darkling to their left and assumed there were more of each behind. On the open ground they were moving quickly again, one of her ankles twinging with pain whenever they jumped. Eventually, though, they would be driven out over the badlands, and if another group of pursuers appeared in front of them, they would have nowhere left to go.

Suddenly Jessica spotted a mesh of girders off to the right. Rising into the sky a few stories, a brand-new building was going up at the edge of the complex.

"Steel," she said.

"What?"

She pointed. "New steel, untouched by midnight."

"Let's hope so."

The sounds of their pursuers came from all around now. Chirps and squeaks and caws, like being trapped inside some insane bird sanctuary. As they angled toward the new building, a flock of flying slithers drew closer.

Jessica pulled out Jurisprudence with her free hand and used her teeth to pull the antenna out to its full length. The building was only a few jumps away.

She spotted the slither just before it hit.

The leathery wings struck first, wrapping themselves around her face. Jessica flailed away with Jurisprudence, and blue sparks filled her vision. Then the creature was gone.

"They're trying to separate us," Jonathan shouted.

Jess felt a creeping cold in her shoulder. The thing had struck for their interlocked hands. It knew she couldn't fly on her own.

Another slither approached, but she swiped at it with the still sparking antenna, and it flapped away.

One last jump took them into the mesh of steel girders. They landed hard on a metal beam strung with cables.

"I'm letting go," Jonathan warned.

Jessica gained her footing with only a second to spare. Weight crashed back onto her, and she knelt, clinging to the beam.

Jonathan pulled the necklace over his head, wrapping it around his fist.

"Splendiferous," Jessica whispered to the steel.

"If we can just hold out a few more—," Jonathan started, but his voice choked off in confusion. "What in the—"

The forest of steel around them bloomed with light—white, not blue. The world shifted into full color, the metal beams suddenly a dusty red. Jessica's face and hands turned pink, Jonathan's light brown.

Suddenly there were panicked shapes all around them, screaming past like angry rockets. Slithers were flying into the building site, screeching and leaving a trail of sparks as they struck the white light, retreating back to the edge of the steel girders.

The cloud of slithers regrouped and wrapped itself around the building, circling as if Jessica and Jonathan were caught in the eye of a tornado. Wounded sounds came from all around them, but nothing dared enter the grid of steel.

Jessica could see three darklings together at the edge of

the light, their silhouettes pulsing through horrible, half-glimpsed shapes. Their eyes flashed a deep indigo.

A low growl came from one of them, long and full of varied sounds, as if it were trying to make words and meaning. But it was no more understandable than fingernails on a chalkboard.

Then the three darklings turned and flew away. The flying slithers slowly gathered themselves up into a ragged cloud, the whole mass heading back out toward the badlands.

"The moon's setting," Jonathan said.

Jessica nodded, unable to speak.

"We'd better get down."

Of course, Jessica thought. In a few minutes Jonathan wouldn't be able to fly anymore. They'd be stuck up here.

She held out her hand, and he took it. They jumped from the steel beam, falling softly to the ground. The white light around them slowly faded, returning to the placid blue light of the secret hour.

"What was that?" she said. "What saved us?"

"I'm not sure," he said. "Maybe the steel?"

"I gave it a thirteen-letter name," she suggested.

Jonathan let out a short laugh. "The whole *building*?"

"I guess. The part we were standing on, at least."

He shook his head. "You can charge up a ring or a necklace, and Dess can do bigger stuff if it's the right shape, but not a whole building. Maybe this place is made of some kind of crazy new metal. What does your mom do here?"

"Aircraft research."

"Hmm." Jonathan nodded. "We should look into it. That was totally cool." He looked up at the building over their heads. "Wouldn't mind some brass knuckles made of that stuff. Or maybe it was just the end of the blue time coming on. Lots of steel in conjunction with moonset."

Jessica shrugged. This was another mystery for Rex, it sounded like.

Then a terrible thought struck her.

"How long do we have?" she asked.

Jonathan glanced at the moon. "Only a minute or so until the blue time runs out. I guess we'll be walking home tonight."

"Not unless we get out of here."

"What?"

"They do classified defense work here, Jonathan," she said hurriedly. "My mom got background-checked, interviewed by the FBI, and fingerprinted twice. There are security guards all over and a big fence all around."

"Great," he said, scanning the horizon. He pointed and grabbed her hand. "Bixby-side fence, now!"

She nodded. "Three, two . . ."

They jumped, heading back toward the city.

It took several bounds just to carry them to within sight of the fence. It was at least thirty feet high.

"Oh boy," Jonathan said.

"What? We can clear that easy."

He swallowed, clenching her hand hard. "I usually don't

jump at all this close to moonset. It's not fun getting a face full of gravity when you're up high."

"Tell me about it," Jessica said.

"Oh, yeah."

They neared the fence. Jessica could see the coil of razor wire that capped it now, like a long, vicious Slinky stretched along its top. The light was changing slowly, a bit of color coming back into the world.

"Not long now," Jonathan said.

Jessica swallowed. If she were caught trespassing in here, they'd blame her mother. The new job would be in the toaster.

"Just one more jump," she cried. "Go!"

They soared into the air and over the fence, clearing the razor wire by at least twenty feet.

"Oh no," said Jonathan. "I think that was maybe a little . . ."

"Too hard?" she asked.

They continued to sail upward.

The moon was slipping behind the hills. In the distance ahead the trees were turning green. Jessica realized that it was like sunset, right on the edge of day and night, when the light moved from east to west across the planet. Moonset and normal time—and gravity—were rushing toward them.

"This is not good," Jonathan said.

They soared helplessly farther into the sky.

Jessica thought furiously. They just needed something to

pull them downward. If only they had something heavy. . . .

Then she realized. They did have something heavy: her.

"Give me your chain," she ordered.

"What?"

"Do it!" she yelled.

Jonathan unwound Obstructively from his fist. She snatched it from him. The stainless steel links looked strong enough. She held one end in her free hand. "Grab the other end. Tight."

He grabbed it.

With her other hand, she let go of Jonathan.

"Jess, no!"

She fell, yanking the chain taut and pulling Jonathan downward after her.

"Jess!" His eyes were full of terror.

In a few seconds they were falling fast enough, and she yanked on the chain to bring him close to her again. They frantically grabbed for each other's hands, and with the warmth of his flesh, weightlessness wrapped itself around Jessica again.

Momentum carried them down toward the ground quickly, but with the soft pressure of midnight gravity.

Jonathan wrapped his arms around her. Jessica realized she was shaking.

"I never dropped anyone before," he said quietly. "And now I've dropped you twice in one night."

The grass below them was turning green. They were at treetop level, and then their feet touched the ground lightly.

Normal weight settled onto them a few seconds later.

"Well, the third time's a charm," Jessica said. She was still shaking.

They stood there, looking at each other.

Finally they let go of each other's hands.

"Ouch," he said softly.

Jessica giggled, rubbing her hand. "*Ouch* is right."

Jonathan laughed out loud. "You've got one hell of a grip, Jess. My hand feels it got slammed in a door. Talk about clingy."

"Me?" she retorted, laughing too. "*My* hand feels like a truck ran over it."

They were both still laughing when the police car pulled up.

15

CURFEW

The police car crunched onto the roadside, gravel popping out from under its tires as it slid to a stop.

Jonathan clutched Jessica's hand and instinctively bent his knees to leap, seeing in his mind's eye the precise jump that would take them safely over the car and onto the roof of the house across the street. He could see the proper angle of landing and how the next leap would take them over to the next block and out of sight. Away to freedom.

But his legs crumpled under him, and Jonathan remembered that he was heavy, leaden, earthbound. Flying time was over.

Jonathan's exhausted leg muscles could barely push him back to standing again. He doubted he could even make a run for it. For the next few minutes his body would feel like stone as it slowly readjusted to normal weight. Even breathing took effort in these horrible moments after the secret hour ended.

A familiar claustrophobic feeling settled over him. He was trapped here in normal time. Trapped by the cops, by the Bixby curfew, by the suffocating, inescapable blanket that was gravity. Stuck like an insect drowning in glue.

All Jonathan could do was squeeze Jessica's hand.

The police car's doors opened, and a spotlight popped on, ripping into his eyes. He spun away, covering his face with his hands.

"Think you can hide, Martinez?" a deep voice called, laughing. "I recognize your pretty face."

Jonathan's heart sank, but he tried to make his answer sound brave. "Turn that thing off, St. Claire. We're not going anywhere."

He heard the crunch of boots, then felt Sheriff Clancy St. Claire's hand fall onto his shoulder. It felt like a hairy lump of lead clamping itself onto Jonathan, pushing him down into the quicksand that the ground had become.

"Jonathan Martinez, you have never spoken truer words."

"Hey, Clancy, where do you suppose Martinez got himself a girlfriend?" another voice called from the car.

"Hmm. Now, that is a puzzle." Then St. Claire's voice softened. "Man alive! What happened to you, girl?"

Jonathan managed to open his eyes, squinting against the glare. Jessica looked dazed and battered, her face deathly pale in the spotlight. The knees of her jeans were stained with grass and blood, her hair wild from an hour of flying.

"I fell down," she said feebly.

"You fell down? Sure, you did." Jonathan felt the

sheriff's hand tighten on his shoulder. "I don't believe I know you, honey."

"Jessica Day."

"And how old are you?"

"Fifteen."

"So, Jessica Day, I don't suppose your parents know where you are?"

The spotlight went dark, and Jonathan was blind for a moment in the sudden blackness. He heard Jessica's breath catch as she tried to think of a way around the question. There was defeat in her voice when she finally answered.

"No. They think I'm home in bed."

"Well, honey, that's probably where you should be."

They sat Jessica down in the back of the police car while St. Claire talked on the radio for a while, waiting for more cops to arrive. The police in Bixby always liked to do things in overwhelming numbers.

Jonathan wished he could talk to Jessica, even for a few moments. He wanted to explain that this was no big deal, really. The cops just took you home and woke your parents up. He'd been through the procedure seven times in the last two years, and it didn't seem to get any worse than that. His dad would be grumpier than usual for a couple of days, but he'd told too many stories about his own wild days to stay angry at his son.

"I've never been arrested, Dad, only detained and

transported to parental custody." Those were the magic words. Dad couldn't say the same.

Jonathan had a feeling, however, that Jessica had never taken a ride in a police car before. She sat in the backseat with her head in her hands, forlorn and unmoving, not looking over at him.

It was horrible, being trapped here on the ground, unable to whisk her away. They'd survived being chased by the three biggest darklings he'd ever seen, only to be caught by a doofus like St. Claire. He felt helpless. And worse, he felt guilty, as if he'd dropped Jessica again. Three times in one night.

It had been so wonderful before the darklings had appeared. He'd never had that much fun flying with anyone else. Jessica seemed to know instinctively how to jump, as if she were an acrobat herself, as if they were connected. The thought of them never flying together again felt like ice in his stomach. He doubted that Jessica would even want to talk to him after tonight.

He took a deep breath, telling himself to be calm. He would go to her tomorrow midnight and make sure she was all right.

Finally another pair of headlights crawled up. Two deputies drove Jessica home, and St. Claire pushed Jonathan into the back of the second car, squeezing in beside him.

The weight of the large man flattened the springs of the backseat. Jonathan felt puny next to him. The deputy up front started the engine, and the car jolted onto the road.

"You and me are going to have a talk, Jonathan."

"Yeah, it's been too long, St. Claire."

The sheriff sighed, adjusting his bulk. He clapped and looked at Jonathan intently.

"Now, boy, it's one thing when you go wandering around all night by yourself. I don't care much if anything happens to you out here."

"That's fine with me."

"But getting a little girl like that into trouble is serious business."

Jonathan sighed with frustration. "I was just walking her home. We were okay until you showed up."

The sheriff's meaty hand clamped onto his shoulder again, pushing him into the seat like extra gravity. The claustrophobic feeling built inside Jonathan.

"She didn't look fine, Jonathan."

"That was an accident, like she told you."

"Well, if she says any different, or her parents do, you are going to be one unhappy hombre, Martinez."

Jonathan turned away and stared out the window. The first time he'd taken Jessica flying, and they'd wound up going home in police cars. He couldn't imagine being unhappier than he already was.

His usual postmidnight hunger descended on him. Jonathan checked his jacket pockets, but the apples were gone. They must have fallen out during the chase. He decided to eat a whole jar of peanut butter when he got home.

The fence around Aerospace Oklahoma was traveling past the police car window, the coiled razor wire pulsing in the passing streetlights. If they'd only jumped a little farther or come down quicker, they would have landed on some other street. The police car would never have seen them.

He saw a street sign and started.

"Hey, which way are we going?"

St. Claire chuckled. "Glad you noticed, Jonathan. See, I already had my little chat with your father, and he and I have come to an agreement."

A sickening feeling began to come over Jonathan. Breathing became harder, as if the pull of gravity were steadily increasing.

"You see, in the state of Oklahoma, if a parent feels unable to take charge of their delinquent child, they can request that the child remain in police custody."

"What?" Jonathan cried. "But my dad—"

"Can't seem to make it down here tonight. Previous engagement, I think."

"For how long?"

"Don't worry. It's just until a judicial hearing officer listens to the particulars of the case. Your dad has to show up for that, and I'm sure he'll take you home as soon as you've met the JHO and promised to be good."

"Are you kidding?"

The man laughed sharply, the sound as loud as a dog's bark in the cramped backseat. "Martinez, I never kid. It's time you learned a little lesson about the perils of breaking curfew."

The claustrophobic feeling began to overwhelm Jonathan. The car felt tiny and overheated, the barred partition between the front and back seats turning it into a cage. His stomach churned with nerves and hunger. "You mean I'm spending the night in jail?" he asked softly.

"The night? Not just one, Jonathan. You see, unlike your friendly sheriff's department, judicial hearing officers don't work on the weekend."

"What?"

"Your butt is mine until Monday morning."

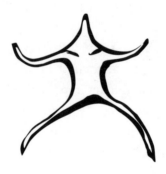

16

GROUNDED

The strange thing was, Jessica's dad was a lot more upset than her mom.

Mom had answered the door in her unpacking clothes—she must have still been working on the kitchen. She had talked to the police quietly and thanked them for bringing her daughter home. Never raising her voice, she'd told Jessica to wait in the kitchen while she woke Dad up.

Dad had flipped.

He was still wide-eyed, his hair standing on end from frantically running his hands through it. Mom had repeatedly told him not to wake Beth up, but Jessica couldn't imagine her little sister sleeping through his yelling. What freaked him out the most was the bruise on her face, which she could feel was just starting to show.

There were times, though, when it was good to have an engineer for a mother. Mom had quickly noticed that every bang and bump on Jessica was accompanied by a grass stain. Even the skinned patch on her bare elbow was marked by a circle of green. There was still grass in her hair.

She looked like a ten-year-old after a long summer day.

"So, you really did fall, didn't you, sweetheart?"

Jessica nodded. She didn't trust herself to speak yet. She'd already been such a wimp when the police had come, bawling her eyes out in the back of the car. Jonathan had been totally calm.

She'd messed everything up. Being the world's worst darkling magnet, not hanging on to Jonathan's hand and falling from their jump, looking like this when the cops showed up.

"You look like you rolled down a hill, Jessica."

"Yeah," she managed. "Just playing."

"Just *playing*!" Dad repeated loudly. He started up again every time she said anything, as if he couldn't bear to hear her voice.

"Don." Mom's voice sometimes had an edge with Dad that she never used on Jessica or Beth. He didn't say another word but sat there pulling on his hair.

Jessica took a breath, looking down at her knees. They hurt. The overall ache of her body was dividing up now into individual pains. One of the bumps would hurt for a while, then take a rest while another took over, like a bunch of smaller tag-team wrestlers whaling away on one of the big guys. Right now the bruise on her cheek was throbbing with her heartbeat, making her face feel lopsided and grotesque. She touched it gently.

Mom sprayed some ouchy stuff on a washcloth and rubbed it again.

"Jessica, tell me what happened. When did you leave?"

Jessica swallowed. The last time she'd seen her parents was right after dinner. "Jonathan came by about ten. I thought we were just going for a short walk."

"But the police said you were over by Aerospace around midnight. People can't walk more than a couple of miles an hour."

Jessica sighed. There were other times when having an engineer for a mom could be a pain. Bixby wasn't that big, but Mom worked on the other side of town. Jessica didn't know exactly how many miles away.

She shrugged. "I don't know, it was right after I went to bed."

"That was way before ten, Jessica. Right after dinner," her father said. "I thought it was weird how early you went to bed. Did you know he was coming over?"

"No. He just came by."

"And you just went for a walk with him?"

"He's in my physics class."

"The police said he's a year older than you," Mom said.

"My *advanced* physics class."

That shut her up. But Dad was going again.

"Why did you go to bed so early?"

"I was tired from working today."

"Were you really at the museum all day? Or with him?"

"I was at the museum. He wasn't there."

He nodded. "Doing a whole day's worth of homework in the first week of school? Can we *see* this homework?"

She swallowed. There was nothing to show them. She'd taken a few notes but had solemnly promised Rex never to show them to anyone. When had she started lying to her parents? When the world had stopped making sense, maybe.

"I was doing research."

"On what?"

"On the possible connection between the tool-making techniques of Solutrean Stone Age culture in southern Spain and certain pre-Clovis spear points found in Cactus Hill, Virginia," she blurted.

Dad's mouth dropped open.

Jessica blinked, surprised at her own words. Apparently some of her crash diet of midnighter lore had managed to stick in her head. She remembered Rex showing her the long case of gradually evolving spear points and the gap in the middle where everything had changed at once.

"There was a technological leap in New World spear points around twelve thousand years ago," she said with quiet focus. At least talking about this stuff didn't make her want to cry. It made her feel in control. "An improved meridian groove and a sharper edge. Some people think that the advanced technique somehow came over from Europe."

"It's okay, honey. We believe you," Mom said, patting her hand. "You're sure Jonathan didn't take you anywhere in a car?"

"I'm positive. We just wound up walking much farther than I thought we would. Really."

"You know this boy's been in trouble with the police before."

Jessica shook her head. "I didn't know that."

"Well, you do now. And you are never going to leave this house again without telling us, okay?"

"Okay."

"And you're not going *anywhere* except school for the next month," Dad added.

Mom looked unhappy with this for a split second, but she nodded.

"I'd like to go to bed now," Jessica said.

"Okay, sweetie."

Mom led her back to her bedroom and kissed her good night.

"I'm just glad you're okay. It's dangerous out there, Jessica."

"I know."

17

REVELATIONS

The walls were painted a deep purple that turned black during the secret hour. A blackboard hung on one, where Dess did her calculations in red chalk on those rare occasions when she couldn't do them in her head. On another wall was a self-portrait Dess had made out of Legos by fitting gray, black, and white elements together, like the pixels on a computer screen. She had been meaning to do an updated picture, now that she had dyed her hair and cut it shorter, but the thought of breaking up all those Legos and starting over was too daunting. Besides, unlike a computer image, there was no way to save the original.

In the center of the room was a music box, on which a motionless ballerina stood. The ballerina's pink tutu had long been replaced by dark purple gauze, her blond hair inked black, and tiny metal jewelry added to complete the outfit, which Dess had made out of soldered paper clips. The ballerina's name was Ada Lovelace. The guts of the music box were open so that Dess could change Ada's movements by switching around the gears. She had also filed off some of the tiny studs on the rotating drum that played the music, making it a little less sweet and predictable. The altered tune had no beginning or end, just a random series of pings to match any choreography.

Tonight the room smelled of burning metal.

Dess had been working all day on a weapon. It had started life as a microphone stand, which she'd found at a music store. She had stopped by to get steel guitar strings for tracing out protective patterns on her doors and windows. But when she saw the stand, Dess had decided to blow all her summer-job savings. Buying the metal brand-new guaranteed that it was clean, untouched by inhuman hands, although a lot of thirteen-year-olds had probably played rock star with it. (Dess herself had mimed exactly one song in front of her mirror with it before starting work.)

The stand could be adjusted for short and tall singers, from six feet long down to three, and it was very light with the heavy round base removed. Dess had never named anything this big before, but its proportions were mathematically perfect. Extended to its full length, it felt more like a real weapon than anything she'd ever made before.

She wondered if the darklings still had nightmares about spears, the weapons that Stone Age humans had used against them. Melissa always said the darklings had very long memories.

Dess had spent all Sunday adding small symbols to the shaft of the stand, mathematical glyphs and clusters of carefully patterned dots. She had even copied a few shapes from the local cave scratchings, supposedly created to memorialize a successful hunt ten thousand years ago. She'd worked until she had completed thirty-nine little pictures altogether, the ultimate antidarkling number.

Her soldering iron still smoldered in one corner, a white sliver of smoke winding up to the ceiling from its tip. As the candlelight in her room faded to midnight blue around her, Dess watched the smoke freeze into place, its snakelike undulations suddenly arrested. In the blue light it glowed against the black walls, as delicate and luminescent as a strand of spiderweb caught by sunlight.

Dess reached out one finger to touch it. A finger-width segment of the smoke detached itself and traveled upward to the ceiling.

"Hmm," she said. "Makes sense."

Just like anything caught in the midnight freeze, the smoke particles were released by her touch. But the hot smoke was lighter than air, so it rose instead of falling.

She hefted the stand. In the blue light it looked like a fine weapon.

If tonight's secret hour was anything like last night's, she was going to need it.

Only one more step: Dess wanted to give the spear a thirty-nine-letter name, but one that worked. A single word wasn't going to cut it. She'd only ever found a few chemical names that length, words used only by scientists, and they didn't seem to have much kick in the blue time. Not even slithers were afraid of names like benzohydroxypentalaminatriconihexadrene, possibly because they were generally found among the ingredients of Twinkies. But maybe a phrase made up of three thirteen-letter words would do the trick. Dess sat gazing into the tiny pictures along the microphone stand's length for a few minutes, letting words roll through her mind.

The other midnighters had to use dictionaries, but for a polymath it was automatic. For her, thirteen-letter words had their own smell, their own color, and stood out like ALL CAPITALS in her head. It was only a few moments before the perfect trio of tridecalogisms came into her mind.

She held the weapon close and whispered to it, "Resplendently Scintillating Illustrations."

As agreed, Dess rode to meet Rex at his house. He lived closer to Jess, and if one of them was going to be caught alone, she could handle it best. Melissa was staying home tonight, scanning the psychic landscape to try to get a feel for what was happening out in the badlands.

"You okay?" Rex said as Dess pulled up onto his threadbare lawn. He'd been waiting outside in a small circle of thirteen-rock piles.

"Yeah. Tonight's not as bad as last. At least, not here in town."

The lore site they'd been to the night before was very old, far out in the badlands. The slithers had followed them from the beginning, in the air and on the ground. They'd seemed to grow in number every time Dess looked up. All kinds of flying darklings had made appearances, their hideous and unfamiliar silhouettes crowding the moon. Two darklings had even tried to mess with them, probing the defenses she'd set up around the lore site. Things might have gotten ugly, but about fifteen minutes before moonset they had all left, as if suddenly remembering an appointment. It had all been very strange and unsettling.

"Let's get going," she urged Rex. Dess didn't like the idea of Jessica all alone. Thumbtacks might not cut it tonight.

Of course, she might not be alone, Dess thought with a quiet smile. Wouldn't *that* be a nice little surprise for Rex.

Rex took a good look around before getting on his bike. "I just hope it stays quiet. I wonder where all those darklings came from. I had no idea there were so many big ones."

Dess nodded. "I've been thinking about that. Want to hear a theory?"

"Sure."

"Okay. Darklings look like panthers or tigers, right? Except when they get all freaky like they were last night."

"Yeah. The lore says they're related to the big cats—lions and tigers—like we are to apes."

"Okay," Dess continued. "Well, *my* lore, which would be the Discovery Channel, says that cats spend a big percentage of the day sleeping. Take lions. They sleep twenty-two hours a day, lolling around, tails twitching to keep away flies, maybe yawning out the occasional territorial roar, but basically semiconscious."

"Twenty-two hours of sleep a day? That sounds like my dad's cat."

"So that leaves just two hours awake, right? For one of those hours they do kitty maintenance: lick themselves, play-fight other members of the pride, whatever. They hunt for only one hour out of twenty-four."

Rex whistled. "That's the life. A five-hour workweek."

"Seven," Dess corrected. "They don't get weekends."

"Harsh." ·

"So here's the thing. If darklings are like big cats, then they probably only hunt for one hour a day."

"Sure," Rex agreed.

"But what's a day for a darkling?"

Rex pondered as he rode, recalling his precious lore. "Well, the darklings only live one hour in twenty-five, the secret hour. They're frozen for the rest, like regular people are frozen during the blue time. So it takes them twenty-five of our days to live a single day in their life. That's part of why they live so long."

"Right," Dess said. "So, a darkling probably sleeps for *twenty-three* of our days in a row."

Rex's bike wobbled. She could tell he hadn't thought this through before. She shook her head. People's lives would be so much simpler if every once in a while they bothered to do the math.

"And that means," he said slowly, "that they only hunt about once a month. Like a werewolf in mythology."

"Exactly. That must be where the whole full-moon thing comes from. Except darklings hunt once every 3.571429 weeks, not every four. But who's counting? In any case, this means that there's a lot more darklings than we thought, because most of them are sleeping most of the time. We've only seen the tip of the iceberg. For every one hunting, another twenty-three are asleep."

Dess let Rex soak in this information for a while.

Finally he said, "So the question isn't, 'Where did they all come from?'"

"Right," she answered. "The question is, 'Why did they all wake up?'"

When Jessica answered the knock on her window, she looked disappointed to see them.

"Expecting someone else?" Dess asked.

"Kind of," Jessica said quietly.

Rex didn't notice or thought she and Jess were kidding. Dess wondered exactly what had happened last night.

She had called Jonathan's house today to see if he'd followed through on his threat to visit Jess during the blue time. But no one had answered the phone all day. She wasn't worried—Jonathan could take care of himself better than any of them—but Dess wanted to hear the scoop.

"Well, we've got big news for you," she said.

"Come on in," Jessica said, sliding the window open. Dess jumped through and reached back to give Rex a hand up. It occurred to her that they could just use the front door, but something about the blue time made everyone want to whisper, plot, and sneak.

Jessica sat slumped on her bed. She looked tired and

bummed. Apparently it hadn't been the best first date ever. Maybe darklings had crashed the party.

Dess noticed that Jess was rubbing her right hand, as if it was a bit sore. She knew from experience what *that* meant: things couldn't have gone completely wrong.

Dess put her questions aside. She could ask Jess in study period tomorrow, when Rex wasn't around to go ballistic.

"We went to a lore site last night," he said.

"It was a pretty hairy trip," Dess said. "Darkling city out there."

"But we may have found out what's going on."

Jessica looked up. "It's all my fault, isn't it?"

Rex look surprised for a moment, then shrugged. "It's not your *fault*, exactly."

"But it's *because of me*. Those things didn't used to bother you guys. Since I showed up, they're everywhere. Right?"

"That's true," Rex admitted. "The heavy darkling action could be related to you coming to Bixby. But only maybe."

"Maybe definitely," Jessica said. "You had a private world, a secret time all your own, and I messed it all up."

"You didn't mess it up. The darklings were already there, and we've tangled with them before," Rex said. "But it's possible you've got them scared."

"Scared?"

Dess sat down next to Jessica. "Every midnighter has his or her own talent, Jessica."

"So I noticed. Everyone but me, that is."

Rex paced the room. "The lore says that darklings can taste it when new midnighters arrive in their territory, like Melissa can. They can feel our talents, and they know when someone new is a danger to them."

"Me, a danger to *them*?" Jessica laughed. "You've got to be kidding. So far, my major talent seems to be disaster magnet. A walking bad-luck charm."

"That's because they're scared," Dess said. "They're still animals, in a way—wild cats."

"And you're stirring up their nest."

Dess rolled her eyes. "Cats don't have nests, Rex."

"Well, you're stirring up their . . . cathouse. But whatever your talent turns out to be, Jessica, it must be important. For us."

She looked up at him. "Are you sure?"

"If they want you, we need you," Dess said.

"But they want me *dead*."

"That's why we have to find out exactly what you are," Rex said. "Will you help us do that?"

Jessica looked at them both, then stared glumly out the window at the blue time. Dess saw the careful rows of thumbtacks lining each window and wondered what it would be like to be trapped in your room for the secret hour, with the whole world waiting empty for you outside.

Jessica's room had a crazed neatness to it, as if she'd been cleaning all day. As Dess had figured, her parents weren't poor. Jessica had a real stereo and a ton of CDs. But the room hardly looked lived in at all. It felt like a lonely room.

Jessica sighed before she answered. "Sure. What do I have to do?"

Rex smiled. "We have to take you to a certain lore site during the secret hour. There are ways of reading your talent there, testing you to find out what you are."

"Okay, except what happens when the darklings butt in?"

"They'll try," Dess said. "But I can set up defenses in advance, get everything ready in daylight. It'll be totally safe by the time midnight rolls around. Safer than this room, at least."

Jessica looked around, clearly unhappy with the idea that her room wasn't totally secure. "So the only problem is getting there," she said.

"We've got that covered too," Rex said. "You can tell your parents that you're spending the night with Dess. She lives out closer to the badlands. You can slip out and get there before—"

"Forget it."

"Why?" Rex asked.

"I can't spend the night with anyone, not for the next month, anyway. I'm grounded. Very."

"Oh." Rex looked as if he hadn't expected anything so mundane to mess up his plans. "Well, if you slip out on your own, Melissa can pick you up and drive—"

"No." Jessica said the word without hesitation. "I've lied to my parents enough. I've snuck around enough. Forget it."

Rex opened his mouth, then closed it.

Dess was dying to talk to Jessica away from Rex. What

had happened last night? She wondered if Jess's grounding had anything to do with Jonathan.

"I mean," Jessica continued, "I don't mind going out in
the secret hour, but I'm not leaving this house during regular time. If my parents found out, they'd be really upset. I
don't want to do that to them again."

"Do you want to wait a whole month?" Rex argued. "If
they're as scared as they seem, the darklings might try
something really serious soon."

"How far away is this place?" Jessica asked.

"Pretty far out," Rex said. "Even from Dess's, you can
barely make it there and back in an hour on a bike."

"What about flying?"

Rex's jaw dropped, and then his eyes turned coldly
toward Dess. She sighed and spread her hands with a little
shrug. There was no hope of avoiding blame. Rex knew
that Melissa would never have told Jonathan where Jess
lived. For that matter, if Dess hadn't blabbed, Jonathan
might not even have guessed that there was a new midnighter in town. She tried to look sheepish.

But inwardly Dess smiled. Occasionally Rex needed to
be reminded that nobody had elected him seer.

He gathered himself and turned back toward Jessica.

"It's too dangerous. You two alone, out in the badlands—
you'd be flying right into a death trap."

"Yeah," Jessica admitted, "it was pretty bad last night.
And we barely went past the edge of town."

"You went past—?" Rex bristled again but kept himself

in check. "We'll think of something else," he said. "Some way to get you there *before* midnight."

"Exactly where is this lore site, anyway?" Jessica asked.

Dess watched Rex carefully and thought she saw a moment of pleasure as he answered, now that he had another reason for Jessica Day to be scared of midnight.

"It's called the snake pit."

18

NOTORIOUS

On Monday morning it didn't take long to find out where Jonathan had spent the rest of the weekend. Jessica didn't believe it at first—it sounded too much like a rumor to be the truth—but his empty desk and the stares in second-period physics said it all.

It was true. He was in jail, and it was all her fault.

There were a lot of versions circulating, but everyone seemed to know that Jonathan had been busted in the company of Jessica Day. She had gone from new girl to bad girl in record time. Most people seemed surprised to see Jessica here in school, as if they expected her to be rotting away in her own jail cell. She caused a stir everywhere she went, with everyone (except those few clueless teachers who were eternally immune to gossip) wanting to know what had happened.

Thankfully, Constanza came to her rescue, shepherding Jessica between her morning classes and filling her in.

"It's like this: Someone's aunt, or mother, works as a dispatcher, or deputy, in the sheriff's department and was there on Saturday night when Jonathan was brought in. News travels fast in Bixby. What were you guys doing, anyway?"

"Just walking."

Constanza nodded. "Breaking curfew. That's what I figured. But some people are saying that you got busted for breaking into a car, or a drugstore, or both."

"None of the above. But why did they take me home and him to jail?"

"Well, everyone knows—at least as of this morning— that Jonathan has been in trouble with the police before. Like a million times. His father has too. In fact, I heard that Jonathan, or his father, maybe, was wanted for armed robbery back in Philadelphia, or maybe manslaughter, which is why the two of them had to move here in the first place."

"Are you absolutely sure about all this?"

"Absolutely not. But you have to know what people are saying, Jessica."

"Yeah, of course. Sorry."

A few freshman girls were standing near Jessica's locker, and Constanza shooed them away while Jess got her books for study hall. Jessica picked through her locker, feeling the stares of people passing by, trying to decide if she was more behind in trig or physics.

She could still see Jonathan's empty desk, the final confirmation that he hadn't made it home that night. Jessica couldn't believe how things kept getting worse. Everything that could have gone wrong, with the possible exception of being eaten, had.

Jessica Day: darkling magnet, police magnet, shady character.

She grabbed her trig book and slammed the locker closed.

"I heard you two were kissing when the cops showed up," Constanza said.

"No, we weren't."

"What, you were out there just to hold hands?"

"No." Jessica paused. "Well, actually, we were kind of holding hands." She rubbed her wrist, which was *still* sore. Hanging on for dear life required muscles that normally didn't get much exercise.

"So you and Jonathan are an item?"

Jessica felt her face heat up. "No. I don't know. Maybe . . ." She barely knew Jonathan, but she'd never felt a connection with any guy the way she had with him Saturday night. Of course, after the way the night had ended . . . "Probably not, after what happened," she finished.

Constanza put her arm around Jess, leading her toward the library.

"Me, I think that the curfew is a stupid law. I think I'm going to write an article about it for the school paper, maybe even the *Register*. 'Young lovers busted for holding hands.'"

"Just leave me out of it, please."

"I wouldn't use your real name, of course."

Jessica had to laugh. "Great idea, Constanza. No one will ever figure it out. Just change my name to Jess Shady."

Constanza smiled. "Not bad. I like it."

They entered the library as the late bell rang. Ms. Thomas looked up from her computer.

"Good morning," she said, one eyebrow raised. She looked as if she expected a good session of gossip to animate today's study period.

"Morning," Jessica said, then groaned inwardly as she saw the long table. The rest of Constanza's crew were already settled in, ready to hear the scoop.

She turned to Constanza and said, "I really have to study trig. What with my criminal career, I didn't get anything done this weekend."

Constanza smiled. "Oh, I wouldn't say *that*, Jess Shady. Sounds like you had fun. But don't worry. You get your studying done and I'll work on setting the record straight."

"Thanks, Constanza. I really appreciate it. But, um, which record are you going to use?"

"How about a medium one? Hand holding but no kissing? And no previous criminal record?"

"Well, thanks, I guess. Try not to make me sound too evil, though? I could be living here in Bixby for a while."

"Not a problem, Jess. A little drama wins more friends than boring. Which is not to say that you were . . . boring."

"Thanks."

"In fact, what are you doing this Friday?"

"Being grounded."

"That's too bad. Some friends of mine, of the senior persuasion, are having a party out at Rustle's Bottom."

"Rustle's what?" Jessica said.

"It's a dried-out lake bed. A good place to park a keg, you know? It's over in Broken Arrow County, officially outside the dreaded curfew zone. I'm not sure if Jessica Day would have wanted to come, but Jess Shady would have a great time."

"Sorry. Both of us are grounded until October."

"Too bad. Anyway, see you at lunch." Constanza hugged her. "And don't worry, this story's only prime-time news for a week, tops."

She swept back to the long table, and Jessica sank into the corner chair, grateful that Constanza would be filling in for her on the gossip circuit. At least someone was on her side.

Jess realized that Dess was in her usual place across the table.

"Oh, good. I was hoping you'd be here."

"I wouldn't miss my favorite period," Dess said.

"What, the tutor-Jessica-in-trig period?" Jessica asked hopefully.

Dess smiled. "Today, any tutoring will cost you."

Jessica groaned. "Not you too."

"Don't worry, I don't want to hear how you got busted. Your lame criminal record is uninteresting to me. All I want to know is, did you fly?"

Jess glanced at the long table. Constanza had them all spellbound.

She turned back to Dess and nodded.

"Isn't it excellent?" Dess said.

A tiny and unexpected stab of annoyance went through Jessica. Almost jealousy. But of course Jonathan had taken at least one of the other midnighters flying. How else would he know how it worked? Still, flying had felt like a private thing between the two of them.

"Yeah. It's great."

"I thought you'd like it. That's why I told Jonathan where you lived."

Jessica nodded and smiled at Dess. "I'm glad you did."

"Someone had to."

"You're sort of not taking sides in this Rex and Jonathan thing, are you?"

Dess sighed. "It's kind of pointless, really. Rex is okay. I wouldn't know half what I do without him. But he gets this seer-knows-best attitude sometimes. And Jonathan's great, but he can be all 'Freebird', not that I blame him. The thing between them goes back to the beginning, more than two years ago."

"So all four of you have never worked together?"

"For about two weeks. When Jonathan arrived, he was just starting to discover his power, his dream come true, when Rex and Melissa show up. Rex, of course, wants to spend every night checking out lore."

Jessica nodded. It must have been a lot easier for Rex to get out to his precious lore sites with Jonathan's help. It still would be.

"But Melissa and Jonathan *never* got along," Dess added. "She's never even flown with him."

"Really?"

"She couldn't stand it. She has this thing about . . . holding hands."

Jessica blinked. She'd been jealous of Dess a moment ago, but now she couldn't help feeling sorry for Melissa. Flying with Jonathan was the best part of midnight.

"So Melissa gets left out of all these trips to the badlands, Jonathan gets tired of being Rex's personal flying chauffeur, and all hell breaks loose."

Jessica swallowed. "I guess I can see where there might be a personality conflict or two there."

"Everything's been messed up since then, really." Dess looked down at the floor. "Well, maybe it's always been messed up."

"So, Dess, why didn't *you* tell me about Jonathan if Rex wasn't going to?"

"I didn't want to say anything in front of Rex. The mere thought of Jonathan makes him all snitty."

"You could have called me."

Dess shrugged, smiled. "I wanted it to be a surprise, maybe."

Jessica peered through the dark glasses and into Dess's eyes and realized she was telling the truth. However weird she might seem, Dess had always been honest with her. She'd tried to make it clear from the beginning that things were going to be different here in Bixby. Of course, Dess had never been able to just come out and explain everything, but that wasn't exactly her fault. Things had always been too complicated for that.

Jessica smiled. Even though Saturday night had wound up horribly, she was glad that Dess had told Jonathan about her.

"I guess it was pretty surprising. And yeah, excellent." Jessica sighed. "Until a load of darklings showed up, courtesy of me. And five minutes after we gave them the slip, the police were there. He probably thinks I'm a walking disaster."

"Don't worry too much about Jonathan, Jess. We've all been in the back of Clancy St. Claire's car. It goes with the territory."

"Oh, that makes me feel much better. My parents are already pretty upset. If I get brought home by the cops again, I'm toast. Blackened, charred, lever-got-stuck-down toast."

"We'll have to make sure that doesn't happen," Dess said.

"So I'm afraid to ask, but do you guys have a plan yet? To get me out to the snake pit?"

"Just can't wait, can you?" Dess said, smiling. "We're still working on that. It's too bad you can't go to that party at Rustle's Bottom."

Jessica frowned. As much as she liked Constanza, it hadn't sounded like her kind of party. "Why?"

"The snake pit is the name for the deepest part of the Bottom. You'd be five minutes' walk away. And I have a feeling this party's going at least until midnight. Are you sure there's no way to talk your parents into making an exception to this grounding thing?"

"Very sure."

"Too bad." Dess leaned back into her chair. "Well, on to more pleasant subjects."

"Like what, root canal surgery?"

"No, like trigonometry."

After school Jessica waited for her father in front. Dad was picking her up until further notice, his theory being that she might end up lost and/or arrested on the way home. As the unemployed member of the family, he had nothing better to do than worry and overreact. Of course, he was going to be late from having to stop off at Bixby Junior High halfway across town. Beth wasn't about to ride the bus if her crime-lord sister was getting chauffeured.

Crowds of students spilled out of the high school, all of them taking one last look. Jessica was thrilled that everyone was getting another chance to gawk at the new bad girl in town. It might be a while before they could stare at her again. Like tomorrow morning.

She glared back at a couple of freshman boys, and they flinched and ran to their waiting bus. One day into her grounding and public humiliation, Jessica Day had had enough.

She hadn't asked to be a midnighter, hadn't tried to get into trouble. As far as she could tell, her big mistake had been not stopping to explain to the darklings that Bixby had a curfew.

For the thousandth time that day she replayed in her mind the fantasy where the darklings had caught her and her shredded body was presented to her parents with a final note:

> *Mom and Dad,*
> *Couldn't run for life because of curfew.*
> *Dead but ungrounded.*
>
> *—Jess*

She was composing an alternate, much more ironic note when a voice came from behind her.

"Jess?"

She turned around. It was Jonathan.

"You're . . . out?" She felt a huge grin growing on her face.

He laughed. "Yeah. Good behavior."

"I'm sorry. I mean, it's good to see you." She took a step forward.

"You too."

The school sounds around them seemed to vanish for a moment, as if the blue time had somehow arrived in the middle of the day. For once Jessica knew she wasn't dreaming.

She looked at Jonathan, trying to gauge what he was thinking. He seemed tired but relaxed, relieved to see her. His hair was a little damp, as if he'd just taken a shower. Jessica realized that he must have come out to school just to see her, and her smile broadened.

"What happened?"

"St. Claire, the sheriff here in Bixby, just wanted to make a point," Jonathan said. "It's no big deal. He talked my dad into this thing where they could lock me up all weekend until Dad picked me up this morning. But it was all a joke. I wasn't even arrested, not for real. Just detained in custody."

Jessica shivered. She had imagined him being "detained" all day. None of the images in her mind had been comforting.

"How was it?"

Jonathan shivered. "Completely skyless. And not enough to eat. Spent the secret hour bouncing off the ceiling. But the rest of the time it was mostly . . . smelly. I've been taking showers all day and listening to my dad apologize."

"But you're okay?"

"Sure. How are you?"

Jessica opened her mouth, wanting to tell Jonathan about Rex's plan, to ask him more about jail, about midnight gravity, about how they'd escaped the darklings. Then she saw her dad's car crawling through the buses and shouting kids and decided to summarize.

"Well, I'm wanting to go flying again." She grinned hopefully. He smiled back.

"Great. How's tonight?"

19

MINDCASTER

"Whizzway'stown?"

Melissa took one hand off the wheel and pointed to her right, toward the great mass of sleeping humanity. The center of town tasted bloated and sweet, pulsing with slow and vapid dream rhythms, laced with a few sharp nightmares like undissolved chunks of salt. One good thing about Bixby was that people went to bed early. On a Wednesday night the mind noise started to fade about ten, and by eleven-thirty the few waking thoughts were merely annoying, like mosquitoes at the edge of hearing.

Rex grunted, spreading out the map with both hands and clenching a small flashlight between his teeth. It had been his idea to take the car tonight.

"I *know* how to get there," Melissa complained. "Let's just get onto Division. We've only got ten minutes."

"Donwannagesstopped," he mumbled around the flashlight.

Melissa sighed.

At sixteen in Oklahoma, she was stuck with a hardship

license valid only for going to and from school. (And work, in the unlikely event that she ever found a job that wouldn't drive her insane.) It was also after eleven o'clock, so Rex was being ultracautious and guiding her through the back roads. He didn't want to meet any police, in case Sheriff St. Claire had decided to launch some sort of curfew crackdown.

Jonathan's trip to jail had spooked Rex. In a way, Clancy St. Claire scared him more than anything in the midnight hour. When it came to fat, nasty sheriffs, there was no lore to turn to.

Jonathan's weekend disappearance had been alarming for Melissa too, but for different reasons. All Sunday's secret hour she'd been casting on her roof, mostly watching the growing darkling activity but partly wondering why Jonathan had never appeared. Normally she could taste him shooting across the landscape. He was easy to spot, faster than anything else in the midnight psychic terrain, even a flying darkling.

His absence had worried her more than she would have thought. When she found out on Monday morning that he'd only been in jail, surrounded by opaque steel, it had been a relief. Rex might have sheriff-phobia, but there were worse things than getting busted.

She smirked. A night on the ground might even have done Jonathan some good. He'd tasted a little more humble this week.

"Tahnright."

Melissa turned right.

She was starting to recognize the neighborhood. "Okay, we're not far. I'll park somewhere."

Rex looked up at her, nodding agreement.

"Ow! Blind me, why don't you?"

Rex pulled the flashlight from his mouth. "Sorry." He began to fold the map.

Now that they were almost there, Melissa was glad they'd driven. Riding their bikes in the blue time wouldn't have taken that long, but they would be exposed to whatever the darklings threw at them. Without a stack of Dess-quality weapons it wouldn't have been safe, and this was one trip she and Rex wanted to keep secret.

They had never told Dess all of the lore about mind casting. It would be hard for anyone else to understand the mistakes they'd made when they were young. Dess always walked around thinking she'd been left out, never appreciating how much easier she'd had it. Back when it had been just Rex and Melissa, they'd had to learn the rules of midnight the hard way. Those years hadn't been all fun and games.

Melissa shivered and brought her mind back to the present.

She brought her old Ford to a stop a block or so away and pulled up her right sleeve to check her watch. Three minutes to spare.

Rex noticed her black-gloved hands. "You're looking very commando."

She smirked. "So what's this girl's name again?"

"Constanza Grayfoot. You haven't heard of her?"

Melissa sighed, shaking her head. Even Rex didn't completely understand how unbearable school was for her. Melissa didn't know the names of half her teachers, much less every social big wheel.

"Anyway, her name doesn't matter," he said. "Just as long as you get the general idea across. Clear the way, and it'll happen by itself."

"No problem."

Melissa looked at her watch again, calmed herself, and closed her eyes. The buzzing of a waking mind was close by, some brainless wonder soaking in late night TV. But sweet relief was coming in sixty seconds.

"Make sure to get both of them in sync. We don't want to miss Friday while they're doing parental negotiations."

"Rex, it's going to be easy. Just show me the stiffs." She felt a twinge from him. Rex hated when she used that word. "Sorry," she said sarcastically. "Just show me the midnight-impaired persons, and I'll get it done."

Rex turned away from her and stared out the window, giving off unhappy vibes.

She sighed and reached out to stroke one of his hands. He looked down in surprise, then remembered that her flesh was protected by the gloves. He smiled, but for a moment she caught a taste of his old bitterness. He shared every thought with her, along with terrible secrets and a hidden world, but they would never touch.

"Rex, really, this is simple. Nothing's going to go wrong."

"You always say that."

"The blue time is a breeze, Rex. It's the rest of reality that's hard."

He turned to her, reached across, his fingertips stopping just inches from her. "I know."

"I did the toughest thing I'll ever do eight years ago."

He laughed. "So you always tell me."

That search had been the hardest, finding Rex the first time. Melissa had felt him for as long as she could remember, since before she could talk. When the blue time came and the maddening noise would finally stop, only a single voice would remain. A lone taste out there in the suddenly empty world, as tenuous as an imaginary friend. The idea that he was a real person had taken years to form, another year to act on. Finally she had run the miles to his house in the secret hour, eight years old and wearing pajamas covered with pictures of cowgirls, half thinking it was a dream. But finding each other had made the whole thing real.

It had been a close call, she realized now. Much longer alone and she would have gone crazy.

Melissa tried to settle her mind, preparing for midnight, for the task ahead. Taking deep breaths, she waited for the moment when all the noise and clutter, restless dreams and nightmares, half-conscious anxieties and outright night terrors would finally be . . .

Silenced.

"Oh, yeah," she said. "That's the stuff."

She could taste Rex's smile.

All his thoughts were open to her now. His relief that they were safely in the blue time, out of the reach of the law, and his grim determination to get this job done. She could even taste the tiny, well-nibbled corner of guilt he felt for going to this extreme.

"Don't worry, Rex. What they don't know won't hurt 'em."

"Just tell me if you think you're pushing too hard."

"You'll be the first to know."

They got out of the car, Melissa performing a quick mental sweep. Nothing around yet, but it was early. No creature that lived in the blue time would have spent the daylight this far into town.

Rex's eyes flashed as he searched for signs.

"You should see this, Melissa. They've been creeping around everywhere. More every night."

"Good thing Jessica doesn't stay home much."

Rex's annoyance sizzled in the air, the predictable result of even the vaguest reference to Jonathan Martinez. At least it wasn't jealousy, which she tasted enough of at Bixby High. Just Rex's wounded seer's pride that he didn't control everything in the secret hour.

A moment later Melissa felt him squash the emotion. "Yeah, the guy's finally good for something," he muttered.

They crept through a backyard and then hid themselves in some bushes across the street.

"He coming?"

Melissa cast herself deeper into the night, and flavors came to her from every corner of midnight. Jessica was right there, waiting expectantly in her room. Dess was still at home, happily working on toys. The slithers were stirring at the edges of Bixby, more agitated every night these days.

And coming from the other side of town, a swift-moving presence.

"On his way."

They settled deeper into the bushes.

A few minutes later Jonathan landed.

It had been a year since she'd seen him in action, Melissa realized. She remembered his grace now as his body corkscrewed downward to land softly on one foot, soundless and in slow motion. She might not ever fly with Jonathan, but at least Melissa could taste his mind when it was filled with the simple pleasure of flight.

Next to her Rex allowed himself a moment of quiet amazement.

"Hey!" Jonathan called into Jessica's room.

"Hey, yourself." Jessica crawled out her window, ran to him, took both his hands.

Melissa couldn't hear what they said then, but she could taste what passed between them, clichéd and daylight: Jessica vanilla. The two spoke quietly, so focused on each other that a darkling could have easily flown down and taken them both. After a solid minute on the lawn they half turned to face the same direction. Side by side, holding hands, they bent their knees and jumped, effortlessly coordinated, almost a single creature.

Two seconds later they were gone over the trees.

"Cute couple," Melissa said, pulling herself out of the bush.

As they crossed the street, Rex glanced nervously skyward.

"Relax, they're halfway to downtown." The last two nights Melissa had felt them close to the center of Bixby, probably up on the tall buildings down there, well away from darkling country and with a clear view in every direction. Jessica was a lot safer with Jonathan than at home, even Rex had to admit.

The front door was locked.

"Damn city folk," Melissa said. They crossed to Jessica's open window.

"You're in an awfully good mood," Rex said.

She pulled herself in through the window, tasting left-over Jessica thoughts in the room. She extended a hand to help Rex pull himself up and saw him instinctively jerk away before he realized she was wearing gloves.

"I'm always in a good mood in the blue time," Melissa said when he was inside. "Especially when I get to do some serious casting."

Rex gave off a sharp flavor of anxiety.

She sighed. "Don't worry, I promise not to have too much fun."

"Just don't start to enjoy it too much. The lore is full of—"

"Stuff that bores me," she interrupted. "Speaking of which . . ." Melissa looked disdainfully around Jessica's room. "Wow, she is so *daylight*."

Rex frowned. "She's not that bad. Why do you hate her so much?"

"I don't hate her, Rex. She's just . . . she's nothing in particular. I think she got switched at birth with a real midnighter. Everything's so easy for her."

"I wouldn't say that."

They went through the door and faced a long hallway. Melissa pushed open the first door on her left.

"Smells like . . . little sister."

"You can taste that?"

"I can see it." Melissa gestured at the floor. It was cluttered with skirts, jeans, shirts, crumpled papers, and schoolbooks. Two walls were covered with boy-band posters, and on the bed a small form lay twisted among the sheets, clutching a stuffed animal.

Rex laughed. "Your psychic powers never cease to amaze me."

They closed the door and headed farther into the house. There was a bathroom on the right, and the hallway opened on one side onto a living room. At the far end of the hall was one more door.

"This looks promising," said Melissa as she pushed it open.

Jessica's parents lay there, frozen while asleep.

Melissa looked at them, pale and defenseless. Like all stiffs, they didn't seem quite human, more like department-store mannequins that someone had tried really hard to make realistic but had mistakenly taken a left turn at creepy.

Rex was poking around the room, peering into the moving boxes near the closet. Like the other midnighters, he was a little bit freaked out by stiffs.

Melissa didn't mind them at all. Cold and hard though they were, this was the only time she would ever willingly touch another human being. She pulled off her gloves.

"I think we'll start with Mom."

20

A CHANGE OF MIND

"Good morning, Beth."

"In what sense?"

"Sight, sound, smell, all the other senses. It's sunny, and the birds are chirpy, and I'm letting you have this toast that I just put in for myself."

Beth paused next to the table. "What's wrong with it?"

"Nothing. You are my sister, and I'm making you toast."

Beth plonked down at the kitchen table and looked at her big sister warily.

"Aren't you kind of happy for someone who's grounded?"

Jessica considered this for a moment, watching the elements inside the toaster warm to a red glow. The smell of toast came from the machine, drawing a deep breath from her.

"Toast is good," she answered.

Beth snorted. "If you're going to be all retarded, could you make me an omelette, too?"

"I'm not *that* happy, Beth." The toaster popped. "Here you go."

Jessica pulled the bread out with her fingertips and

dropped it onto the waiting plate, twirled around, and placed it before her sister.

Beth inspected it carefully, then shrugged and started to butter it.

Jessica dropped another pair of slices into the toaster, humming to herself.

She still felt light, as if midnight gravity hadn't completely faded with the blue time. Every step felt as if it would turn into a leap, carrying her across the room, out the window, into the air. All last night she had dreamed of flying. (Except for that hour when she *had* been flying.)

She and Jonathan had hung out on the big, crumbling Mobil Oil sign atop the highest office building in Bixby. It was a huge Pegasus, a flying horse. The unlit neon tubes that outlined its shape had shimmered with dark moonlight, the spread wings shining like those of some angel come to protect her from the darklings.

The steel framework that held the sign in place was rusty, but Jonathan was pretty sure it was clean. It was in the center of town, where darklings almost never went. He'd been going there for almost two years and had never seen so much as a slither.

For three nights in a row she had felt safe in the blue time. Safe and secure, weightless and . . .

The toaster popped again.

"Happy," she said quietly.

"Yeah, you're happy. Got it." Beth was spreading jam onto her remaining piece of toast. "Omelette-level happiness yet?"

Jess smiled. "Pretty darn close."

"Let me know. So, Jess?"

"Yeah?"

"This Jonathan guy you got busted with? You like him?"

Jessica looked closely at her little sister. Beth seemed genuinely interested. "Yeah, I do."

"How long have you guys known each other?"

"That night we got busted was the first time we hung out."

Beth smiled. "That's what you told Mom. But how come the night before, when you came to visit me and make that Ms. Mature speech, you were all dressed?"

Jessica swallowed. "I was?"

"Yeah. Jeans and, like, a sweatshirt. You were all sweaty and smelled like grass."

Jessica shrugged. "I was just . . . I couldn't sleep. I took a walk."

"Good morning."

Jessica started. "Good morning, Mom. Want my toast? I can make some more."

"Sure, Jess. Thanks."

"Looking good, Mom."

"Thanks." Her mother smiled, smoothing the lapel of her new suit with one hand as she took the toast from Jessica. She sat down at the table.

"Wow, you're allowed to eat breakfast with us?" Beth asked. "I thought Aerospace Oklahoma frowned on family time."

"Hush, Beth. I have something to say to your sister."

"Uh-oh. From the toaster into the frying pan."

"*Beth.*"

Beth stuffed toast into her mouth, shutting herself up. Jessica pushed down the toaster lever slowly, her mind racing. She turned and sat down across from her mom, trying to think of what could have given her away. They had left nothing to chance. She always left after the blue time started—it took Jonathan a few minutes to get here from his house, anyway—and was back in bed before it ended. Maybe Mom had found a dirty shoe, or an open window, or taken fingerprints from the tops of buildings downtown. . . .

Beth. Jessica glared at her little sister. She must have told Mom and Dad about Jessica being dressed on Friday night. Beth blinked innocently.

"Your father and I have been talking about your punishment this morning."

"He's awake already?" Beth asked.

"Beth—," Mom started, then paused. "Actually he was awake early, but he went straight back to sleep. We were both tossing and turning a lot last night. And we both agreed that we should have thought about your punishment a little longer before we decided on anything."

Jessica looked at her mother warily. "Does this mean worse punishment or less?"

"Yeah," Beth said. "Are you guys caving?"

"We're thinking that you're new to this town, and you probably feel a need to be accepted. What you did was wrong, Jess, but you weren't trying to hurt anyone."

"You *are* caving!"

"Beth, go get ready for school."

Beth didn't move, just sat there with her mouth wide open. Jessica couldn't quite believe what she was hearing. Dad was always the one who gave in, or tried to, but Mom always stopped him, explaining that any punishment open to negotiation was meaningless, which was something they apparently taught you in engineering school.

"We're also thinking that you need to make new friends now. You need stability and support. Keeping you locked up in your room isn't healthy. It could lead to more trouble later on."

"So, what's the deal? I'm not grounded?"

"You're still grounded, but you can go out to visit friends one night a week. As long as we know exactly where you are at all times."

Beth made a noise that was only half stifled by toast. Mom reached across the table and held Jessica's hand. "We want you to have friends, Jessica. We just want them to be the right friends and to make sure you're safe."

"Okay, Mom."

"Anyway, I'm late. I'll see you both tonight. Don't be late for school."

After she had left, Beth took the untouched toast from her mother's plate and started to butter it, shaking her head.

"I'm remembering this conversation next time I get in trouble. You got Mom to redefine grounding in a whole new way. Nice work, Jessica."

"*I* didn't do anything."

"'Have some toast, Mom.' 'Nice suit, Mom,'" Beth mimicked. "I'm surprised you didn't make *her* an omelette."

Jessica blinked, partly awestruck by what had just happened and partly confused by her own reaction. She'd been happy before her reprieve, but now she wasn't so sure. A trickle of nerves had started in her stomach. Flying to safety with Jonathan every night had been wonderful, like a dream. But now she had no excuse to delay Rex's plan, no good reason to put off going to the snake pit. She would have to face the darklings head-on.

"I'm not sure, Beth. I don't think it was the toast."

"Yeah, I bet Dad caved. He's cracking up."

Jess shook her head. "I don't know. Mom seemed pretty intense about it, like she's thought about it a lot." She turned toward Beth. "But thanks for not mentioning that . . . walk I took Friday night."

"Your secret is safe with me." Beth smiled. "Until I find out what your secret is, that is. Then you're dead."

Jessica reached out and squeezed her sister's hand. "I love you, Beth."

"Ewww, no fair! Mom being all flaky is bad enough."

Jessica frowned. "Maybe I just scared them, sneaking out like that."

"Maybe," Beth said, and shoved the last piece of bread into her mouth. "The whole thing's scaring me."

Later that morning, the library was dead quiet.

Jessica and Jonathan had been the big gossip for a couple

of days, but the story was getting old. Now that it was the second week of school, work was starting to pile up. Everyone was actually using study period for studying. Even Constanza was reading what looked suspiciously like a history book.

Jessica was buried in her physics textbook. The last few nights Jonathan had been helping her with the basics while they were together in the secret hour, and she was really starting to understand the equal and opposite reaction business. Bounding around mostly weightless every night had made the laws of motion much more interesting, and having to run for her own life had given her a very real appreciation of inertia. But all the formulas were still giving her trouble, so she'd decided to get some help from Dess.

It took most of the period for Jessica to get up the nerve to tell Dess what had happened at breakfast.

"So, you know the whole snake pit expedition?"

"Yeah, we're still working on it. Rex and I are trying to come up with a way to get you out there safely," Dess said. "Anyway, it sounds like you're having fun avoiding the baddies."

"That's true." Jessica smiled. The ever present danger made her secret hours with Jonathan much more exciting than regular hanging out would be. "But I've got news, Dess. I found out at breakfast that I'm not grounded anymore."

"Really? That's great."

"Yeah, I guess so. It was kind of weird, though. My parents were totally ready to lock me up for good. Then this morning my mom gives me this whole speech about making new friends."

Dess shrugged. "That happens. My parents do it all the time. Last spring, the first time I got busted with Rex and Melissa for breaking curfew, they said they were going to send me off to psycho camp once school was out."

"Where?"

"It's like a summer camp for juvenile delinquents. Run by the state and very jail-like. My dad works on oil rigs, and he's a big believer in hard work to purify the soul. But a couple of days after the bust they completely changed their minds. Since then they've been pretty cool. They've even started to like Rex and Melissa."

"Well, my parents weren't going to send me away, I don't think. But it was still weird to see Mom backing off like that." Jessica sighed, rubbing her hands nervously. "So I guess we should try to do that snake pit thing."

"The sooner the better," Dess said. "Once we know what your talent is, we can figure out why the darklings are so scared of you. Constanza's party is a perfect opportunity."

"I don't know," Jessica said. "Mom didn't say anything about late night parties."

Dess leaned closer. "It's the surest way to get you out there before midnight. We have to untangle ourselves from Rex's dad and my parents. We might have to fight our way out to the snake pit. With you along, that would get hairy. It's not that we don't like you, Jess. But you do attract a bad element."

"Oh, right," Jessica said glumly. "Jessica Day, disaster magnet."

"The darklings have been getting worse every night,

especially out in the badlands. It's not like downtown."

"But once the party freezes, I'll be *alone* out there."

"You'll practically be at the snake pit. It's right in the middle of the Bottom," Dess said. "Just take a walk five minutes before midnight, and you'll be inside my defenses. Melissa can drive me and Rex to the edge of the Bottom. We'll walk from there. Without you along, we won't get swarmed by darklings if we're late."

Jessica gulped. The thought of making her way to the infamous snake pit, all alone at midnight, didn't make her very happy. "We'll really be safe there?"

Dess nodded. "Absolutely. I've been working on protection all week. I've got a ton of metal ready to go. Rex and I can set it up after school tomorrow. The darklings won't be able to get within a hundred yards of the snake pit."

"Really?"

"We'll be perfectly safe. Of course, remember to watch out *before* midnight."

"For what?"

"The snakes."

Jessica blinked.

"You know," Dess said patiently, "in the snake pit."

"Oh. I thought maybe 'snake pit' was just a colorful nickname, not to be taken literally."

"Well, don't let the name fool you," Dess said. "It's more of a sinkhole than a pit. A sinkhole full of snakes."

"Great, I'll keep that in mind." Jessica shivered, remembering the slithers that second night. The idea of real snakes didn't make her much happier. "But maybe this party thing isn't going to happen. I don't even know if I'm still invited."

Dess looked across the library at the older girls' table. "There's only one way to find out."

A couple of Constanza's friends looked up when Jessica came over. She still drew some stares, especially in the lunchroom with Jonathan. Jessica ignored them and knelt next to Constanza.

"About the party this Friday?" she whispered.

Constanza looked down at her. "Yeah?"

"I kind of got, um, ungrounded."

"Really?" Constanza smiled broadly. "Wow. The police bring you home and you're partying a week later. Not too bad, Jess Shady."

"I guess not. So how about that party at Rustle's Bottom? I mean, I know you're probably—"

"Great."

"I mean, if there's already too many—"

"Sure. Come along."

Jessica swallowed. "I don't really know how to get there. And it's probably too far—"

"I'll drive you. You can sleep over. That way your parents won't be freaking when we get home super-late."

"Oh," Jessica said, "good idea." Excuses and bailout lines were still rolling around in her head, but Constanza's beaming smile silenced them all.

"Come home with me tomorrow from school? We'll have a great time."

"Cool," Jessica managed.

"I can't wait for you to meet some of the guys at this party. I know you like that Jonathan guy, but trust me, Broken Arrow men are much more fun than the boys from Bixby. Much more mature. You're going to have the night of your life, Jess."

21

PEGASUS

Jessica was scared. Jonathan could feel it.

They had made it up to Pegasus in record time, shooting down Division like a stone skipping on water, then gaining altitude from rooftop to rooftop, making a giant obstacle course out of the Bixby skyline. The Mobil Building was the tallest in town, and now they were high atop the winged horse with the darkened city spread out below them.

But Jess had seemed anxious the whole way. She kept looking over her shoulder, not trusting in their speed to keep them safe. Even up here, her green eyes still scanned the horizon. The muscles in her hand were tight, and the connection that Jonathan usually felt when they flew together was missing.

"Are you okay?"

"What?"

"You seem nervous."

She shrugged.

He smiled. "Like maybe you're worried about being seen with me."

Jess laughed, looking out over the dark, empty city. "Yeah, if any slithers tell my mom about us, I'm dead." She paused, then blurted, "Anyway, *you're* the one who's all antitouching during daylight."

Jonathan blinked. "Really?"

"Yeah." Jessica looked away. "I mean, it's no big deal, but it's not like you ever put your arm around me or grab my hand."

"We hold hands all the time!"

"At *midnight* we do. In school you get all anxious about it."

He frowned, annoyed and wondering if it was true. "Well, we've got to rest sometime. Or we'll wind up with Nintendo wrist."

Jess pulled away her flying hand and flexed it. "I guess so."

Jonathan gently took it back and started to massage the tendons. He felt her muscles begin to relax. "So what are you really nervous about?"

Her gaze swept the skyline. "How safe do you think we are up here?"

"We're in the middle of town, sitting on ten tons of clean steel. *Mobil Building* has thirteen letters in it. *And* we can fly if we need to. Pretty safe, I'd say."

Jess ran a finger along the rusty strut they were perched on. "How do you know this steel's clean? It's been here a long time, looks like."

"I asked Dess if Rex could take a look with his glasses off. When Pegasus is lit, you can see it from all over Bixby, you know. He said the horse doesn't show a bit of Focus. It's clean."

She smiled at him. "Thanks for doing that."

He shrugged. "Rex can be a pain, but the guy's good for some things." He concentrated on rubbing her hand.

Jonathan hadn't told Jess, but over the last week he had spotted a few slithers at the edges of downtown, daring to come closer to the tall steel buildings than he'd ever seen before. They were tentative, slithering across the low warehouses on the fringes, blurring them into the midnight world, laying claim to them. Since Jess had come to town, the midnight creatures were pushing their way in, a little closer every night. It might take months, but Jonathan had grown certain that eventually there wouldn't be any clean places left in Bixby. The slithers and their darkling masters would be able to claim even Pegasus.

Where would he and Jess go then?

"But we can't sit on top of this sign forever, Jonathan."

He looked up at her, wondering how she knew what he was thinking. He dreaded that Jess's mysterious talent might have something to do with mind casting. He hoped not. Jonathan had no idea how Rex could stand to hang out with Melissa. He shivered. No privacy, not even in your brain.

"We're safe for now, Jess. And maybe once you get ungrounded—"

"I got ungrounded today," she said.

"That's great! Why didn't you tell me?" he said. Then he saw her expression. "Jess, why isn't that great?"

"Well, because now I'm allowed to go to that party tomorrow night, out at Rustle's Bottom."

"Oh, the snake pit." Jess had told him about Rex's master plan a few days ago. The idea had sounded dangerous enough when it was way off in the future. Now that it was twenty-four hours away . . .

"You know that's out in the badlands."

"They kind of mentioned that. But Rex says it's the only way to find out what I am," Jessica said. "Dess can make it safe out there, and Rex says my talent could be important or maybe something I can protect myself with. In the museum he told me there's lots of kick-ass talents."

"If Rex told you to jump off a cliff—," he started.

"Jonathan," she said, laughing, "that would be *you* telling me to jump off a cliff."

Jonathan smiled. "Probably. But I'd jump with you."

She pulled him closer. "I've got to do *something*, Jonathan. I can't spend the rest of my life sitting up here."

"I know." He sighed. "So you've got to do what Rex says. He's the only one of us who's got the manual for midnight, after all."

Jess looked into his eyes. "That's why you don't like him, isn't it? Because he can read the lore and you can't."

Jonathan frowned at her. "It's more complicated than that." He swallowed, wondering how much he should say. "You don't know Rex and Melissa as well as I do. Let's just say I don't trust Rex. I don't think he tells everything he knows, even to Melissa."

"Why would he do that?"

"To keep control of the whole thing. If everyone else

knows what he knows, being a seer doesn't give him any power."

"Rex withhold information? Come on, Jonathan. Last weekend at the museum he told me stuff about the blue time for, like, six hours. I had to tell him to stop or my head was going to explode."

"Six hours, and he didn't tell you about me."

Jessica blinked. "Oh, right. He did kind of forget to mention you."

Jonathan smiled sourly. "He wanted you to be one of *his* midnighters."

She sighed and looked out again. He followed her gaze past the city to the horizon. From up here they could see all the way to the edge of Bixby, where dark clusters of houses faded away into the badlands. The low flat plains shone with dark moonlight, and the mountains beyond were black silhouettes against the stars.

"So what do I do?" she said softly.

"I guess you don't have a choice. You've got to do what Rex says." Jonathan sighed. "Sometimes I think the whole midnighter thing is rigged."

"Rigged?"

"Yeah. It's a setup. We've all got our own talents. Rex reads lore, I fly, Melissa casts, Dess does the math. You must do *something*. So we wind up all dependent on each other, like we're supposed to fit together into a team."

Jess squeezed his hand. "Jonathan, what's so bad about that?"

He scowled. "I didn't ask to be on a team. I don't even know who put the team together."

"Maybe fate put us together."

"I didn't ask to be on fate's team either." He pulled his hand away. "It all seems totally rigged, like we're stuck with each other."

Jess shook her head. "Jonathan, that's not rigged. That's just life."

"What's life? Having Rex tell you what to do?"

"No, needing help. Getting stuck with other people."

"Like being stuck up here with me?"

"Yeah, exactly. Like you being stuck protecting me." Jessica stood up on the narrow strut. She took a few steps away, glaring out over the dark city.

"I didn't mean—," he started, standing himself.

The two were silent. Jonathan took a deep breath, trying to figure out when this conversation had turned into a fight. He did feel trapped now. Not by Jess, or even the darklings who were after her, but by the words they'd said—by not knowing what to say to make it better.

It was strange not touching Jessica, not sharing his gravity with her. The midnight air seemed cold, as if the space between them had filled with ice. When they flew, everything was so easy. Over the last four nights they'd stopped saying out loud where their next jump would take them. They communicated through their hands much better than with words.

And now they were stuck up here—not flying, not

talking, not touching. It felt to Jonathan as if daylight gravity had come already and was crushing him.

He looked down through the rusty framework that held up the Pegasus sign to the rooftop of the Mobil Building forty feet below.

"Jess?"

She didn't reply.

He reached out. "You should hold my hand. It's dangerous up here."

"It's dangerous everywhere. For me."

The fear in her voice chilled him. Midnight should have been so beautiful for her, an infinite playground, but it seemed as if something—Rex and his lore, the curfew, the darklings—was always screwing it up.

"Jess," he said. "Just hold my . . ." He trailed off as something hit him—maybe the reason she was upset with him, the reason he'd been missing. "I'll be out there tomorrow night. At the snake pit. You know that, right?"

She turned to look at him, her green eyes softening. "You will?"

"Yeah, of course. I mean, I'm not going to let you guys have all the fun."

Her face broke into a smile.

"I'll even let Rex give the orders," he said. "This might be one of those things where you'd actually want to read the manual."

"Thanks, Jonathan." She finally took his hands again, and he could feel midnight gravity reconnect them.

Jonathan grinned back. "Jess, I wouldn't let you . . ."

But before he could finish the sentence, she leaned her head toward his and kissed him.

Jonathan blinked with surprise, then let his eyes close. Jessica was warm against him, even in the summer-night air of the secret hour. He put his arms around her, feeling her feet come lightly up off the ground in his embrace.

When they parted, he grinned. "Wow. I think we found your talent."

She laughed. "It's about time, Jonathan."

"That we kissed? Yeah, I was going—"

"No. That you said you were coming out to the snake pit."

"Jess, of course I'm coming. I'm not going to let Rex get you killed."

"You should have told me right away," she said.

"You should have asked me."

She groaned, pulling him against her again in a too tight hug. "You shouldn't be such an idiot," she whispered.

Jonathan frowned, afraid to say anything. Staying close to her, he reached up and undid the clasp of his necklace.

"Here, take this for tomorrow night."

"Your necklace?"

"It's called Obstructively: thirty-nine links. It'll take me about ten minutes to fly out to the Bottom from my house. You might need it before I get there."

Her fingers closed around the metal links. "But then you won't have anything to protect yourself."

"Maybe Dess will give me something. She's been making toys all week. I want you to have this, though."

"Thank you, Jonathan." Jess's face was lit up by her smile. "Tell me, have you ever kissed anyone be—"

"Duh." He saw her frown and swallowed. "I mean, yeah."

"As I was saying," she said, her eyes sparkling, "have you ever kissed anyone before *in the secret hour*?"

He blushed, then shook his head. "Not until now."

Jess's smile brightened. "Then you haven't done *this*."

She grabbed him around the waist and bent her legs. He barely had time to prepare before she jumped, carrying them both straight up into the sky.

"Oh," he said.

And then they were kissing again.

22

DRESSED TO KILL

"Well, what do you think, Jess? Are we ready to go?"

Jessica stared at herself in the mirror. She recognized the red hair and green eyes, but that was about it.

Constanza had spent the evening doing a makeover on them both. She'd taken one look at Jessica's party outfit and decided to lend her a jacket. Then some makeup. Then a dress.

Spending a few hours trying on Constanza's clothes had turned out to be a lot of fun. There were two closets full of them, and a whole wall of her bedroom was covered with mirrors. Most of her things seemed to fit Jessica, and everything was beautiful or at least expensive looking. Constanza absolutely *loved* every outfit Jessica had put together. It was like being a regular teenager again, getting ready to go to a normal party instead of a snake pit full of evil creatures. Constanza played CDs and Jessica played dress-up, and it had been the first night all week that she'd been able to forget what time it was and what would happen when the clock reached twelve.

Now, looking at the whole ensemble, Jessica was surprised

how little she looked like herself. In Constanza's thigh-length leather jacket, with just an inch of red dress visible below the hem, and the matching dark red lipstick, she looked more like Jess Shady than Jessica Day.

"Are you sure I don't look . . . too dressy?"

"*Too* dressy?" Constanza said. "As in too beautiful or too gorgeous?"

"As in too silly."

"Jessica, you don't look silly at all. You'll knock them dead."

"Who's them again?"

"The guys at the party. And these are Broken Arrow guys."

Broken Arrow was the next county over, where the boys were cuter, the grass greener, and curfew nonexistent, at least according to Constanza. And everyone was a senior, apparently.

Jessica felt weird dressing up like this. She never particularly thought about what she wore to school or even to go flying with Jonathan. She knew she didn't have to worry about that with him.

"So, do these guys have names?" Jessica asked. She was still a bit nervous about the regular-time dangers of a late night party full of strangers.

"I guess so."

"I mean, how well do you know them?" Jessica pushed.

"Rick, who invited me, is a friend of Liz, who'll be there."

Jessica sighed, reminding herself that the main point was getting out to Rustle's Bottom. Surviving the snake pit and finding out why the darklings were after her was the only thing that counted.

"Okay, I guess I'm ready. You look great too, by the way."

Constanza was wearing a houndstooth jacket and skirt with high-heeled boots. She clearly wasn't planning to run away from any darklings tonight.

"Yeah, not bad, if I do say so myself." Constanza swept her car keys from off the makeup table and headed out, calling good-bye to her mother.

Jessica dug into the pockets of the jacket she'd brought with her, fishing out a small flashlight, a compass, and a carefully folded piece of paper. Dess had given her the compass and drawn her a map of the Bottom to help her find the snake pit. After a second warning about stepping on snakes in the dark, the flashlight had been Jessica's idea. Around her neck she was wearing Obstructively, Jonathan's thirty-nine-link chain.

"Come on, Jess!"

She took a deep breath. Jessica hadn't mentioned the party to her parents and wasn't sure what would happen if Mom called after she and Constanza had left. Well, the worst they could do was reground her. Forever.

She looked at herself one last time in the mirror and practiced her tridecalogism of the night.

"Serendipitous."

On the way out to Rustle's Bottom, Jessica looked out of the car window to see a roll of razor wire passing by. She realized that they were driving along the fence around Aerospace Oklahoma.

"Hey, my mom works here," she said.

"You said she designs planes, right?"

"Just wings."

"That's so funny that your mom works and your dad doesn't."

Jessica shrugged. "Dad gave up his job in Chicago to come down here. He's always switching jobs anyway."

"That was pretty cool of him, though."

"Yeah, I guess. I think he's wishing he hadn't."

Jess sat up straight. A tall structure was looming ahead of them, alight and unfinished. It was the new building where she and Jonathan had taken refuge from the darklings. The construction was going late tonight, it seemed. The grid of steel was brightly lit, big lamps hanging from every girder, swinging in the autumn wind. It looked almost like it had in the secret hour, when the moon was setting and the whole building had suddenly ignited with white light, driving the slithers and darklings away.

"Hey, any new buildings at work?" she murmured softly.

"What?" Constanza asked.

"Nothing. Just something I forgot to ask my mom about."

Jonathan and Jessica had talked a couple of times about what had happened that night and about what might have saved them from their pursuers. Jonathan figured the building must be built of some new kind of metal. Jessica had told Rex and Dess the whole story, but they were busy planning the snake pit expedition and hadn't come up with any answers. Apparently Rex didn't know everything about the rules of midnight.

"I've been meaning to talk to Mom about her new job," Jessica continued. "But she's so busy there, I haven't been able to."

"Yeah, my dad's the same way," Constanza said. "Not that I'd want to talk to him about his job. Oil futures or whatever." She pointed ahead, her smile brightening. "Congratulations, Jessica, you are now leaving Bixby."

The town limit flashed by, and Jessica's stomach tingled. They weren't just leaving Bixby—they were headed out to the badlands.

"Next stop, the snake pit," she said to herself.

She checked her watch. Fifty-seven minutes to midnight.

COORDINATES

Rex and Melissa were late.

Dess looked at her watch. Only three minutes past, but the timing for getting out to the snake pit was getting tight. Melissa's rusty old heap could only get them so far. They'd have to walk the last half mile across the Bottom.

The three of them had gone out to the snake pit after school to set up her hardware. Dess wished now that they'd stayed there; coming home and waiting for all the parentals to go to sleep had been a dumb idea. Getting in trouble with Mom and Dad was nothing compared to getting caught by hungry darklings halfway across the Bottom.

But Rex had to make sure his crazy dad was in bed before he left. As if taking care of Melissa weren't enough.

Dess counted to thirteen, forcing herself to relax. She reached into the guts of Ada Lovelace's music box and pulled out a few gears, rearranging them and visualizing the resulting choreography. She gave the mechanical ballerina a windup and watched her dance, checking her predictions.

Ada jumped into motion, always ready to dance, but the new steps didn't come out as expected. The final, stuttering lift of her left arm went forward instead of back. Dess shook her head. She could see it now: she'd turned one of the gears around the wrong way.

It was Rex and Melissa's fault she was so anxious. If they'd been here on time, Rex would be the one getting all nervous, and she and Melissa could rag on him and be the calm ones. They'd be on their way to the snake pit, where Dess's masterpiece in metal would draw oohs and aahs from all concerned as slithers burned themselves to cinders.

She looked out the window again. Still no crappy Ford cruising to a stop in front of the house two doors down, the usual spot for premidnight rendezvous.

Dess kicked her duffel bag, and it made a reassuring metal clank. All ready to go, filled with state-of-the-art antidarkling weaponry, backups in case the defenses around the snake pit failed. And she'd left a very special new toy on the roof for Jonathan to pick up on his way out. She'd done her bit.

So where were Rex and Melissa?

Dess itched to call, but that would be totally stupid. Melissa's parents let her do whatever she wanted, but Rex's dad was a major psycho. If Rex was creeping out his window this very moment, it would be a bad time for the phone to ring.

Besides, they'd *better* already be on their way.

Eleven-oh-six. In forty seconds it would be exactly forty thousand seconds after noon. More importantly, it would be a mere thirty-two hundred seconds until midnight. Dess could feel the blue time—full of darklings—rushing toward her at a thousand miles per hour.

Okay, she thought. *A bit faster than that, really.* The earth's circumference was 24,860 miles, and a day was twenty-four hours. So midnight would have to move at about 1,036 miles per hour to make it all the way around the earth once per day.

She'd seen it on the Discovery Channel, from cameras on the space shuttle: the terminator line, the edge of darkness that marked dawn or sunset, sweeping across the earth. True midnight must work the same way, an invisible edge cutting across the world, bringing the blue time.

Right now midnight would be about nine hundred miles east of here, in the next time zone. Of course, as far as any of them knew, there weren't darklings or midnighters or blue time anywhere but Bixby. Rex had never figured that one out. Dess wondered if a little less lore and a little more math might solve the puzzle.

She looked out the window. Still no Rex and Melissa.

For a horrible moment she wondered if they had left her behind. Just taken off for the snake pit without her. The old feeling of isolation gripped her.

It was all Melissa the Mindcaster's fault. She'd tracked Rex down when they were both eight years old. Dess was only a year younger, but it had taken Melissa another four years to find her. Melissa's excuse was that Dess lived too close to the badlands and that back then all the darklings and slithers had confused her unformed talent.

That sounded like a load of crap to Dess. Melissa could pick Rex up from a mile away even in daylight; in the blue time another midnighter was like a flare on a dark horizon. She'd found Jonathan and Jessica within days after they'd arrived. But for the four years that Rex and Melissa had been alone together, all Dess had known was slithers, the lonely surety of math, and Ada Lovelace.

She reached into Ada's box and switched the errant gear around, wound her up again. "Dance, my pretty."

Dess was sure that her isolation in those early years had been purposeful. Melissa had played for time while she and Rex explored midnight together, grew up together. The scheme had worked. By the time Melissa finally "found" Dess, Rex and Melissa were so tight that nothing could ever come between them. And Melissa's psychic hold on Rex made it impossible for him to even *think* about what Melissa had done.

Dess swallowed and stared out the window.

They wouldn't dare leave her behind tonight. Even with the snake pit already set up to repel darklings, they needed her in case something went wrong. When it came to steel, only she could improvise. Without her this whole mission would be impossible.

It wouldn't be so bad if Jonathan Martinez hadn't been such a disappointment, flying off to his own little world instead of bringing the group together. Maybe Jessica would bring him around, once the two of them reappeared from the couple zone.

Dess shook her head. She had to stop thinking about this

stuff before they got here. She didn't want to give Melissa the satisfaction of knowing she felt this way.

As she always did to hide her thoughts, Dess let the numbers take over her brain. *"Ane, twa, thri, feower . . ."*

Seconds later something pinged in the back of her head: another mathematical mistake. "Two in one night," she muttered.

Midnight wasn't coming toward Bixby at 1,036 miles per hour. It would only move that fast at the equator, the one line of latitude that went around the earth's true circumference, like a tape measure around the widest part of a fat man's belly.

Dess could see it in her head now. The farther north you were, the slower midnight (or dawn, or whatever) swept across the earth. A mile from the North Pole the daylight would move as slowly as a sick turtle, taking a whole day to crawl in a small circle.

She looked out the window. Still no rusty Ford, and midnight 2,978 seconds away.

Now it was really bugging her: How fast was midnight moving toward Bixby? Why wasn't her brain just telling her, giving her the answers like it always did?

She counted to thirteen, relaxing and letting the calculations move into the conscious part of her mind. Of course: to figure it out, she needed to know how far away from the equator Bixby was.

She turned from the empty window and pulled her social studies textbook off the shelf, opening it to the back. Flipping through it, she found a map of the midwestern

United States. A postage stamp like Bixby wasn't on it, of course, but she knew the town was just southwest of Tulsa.

This was easy: a latitude and a longitude line crossed right where Bixby would have been if anyone had bothered to put it on the map. Thirty-six degrees north and ninety-six west.

"Oh boy," she said softly as the numbers rattled around in her head. All thoughts of midnight's speed disappeared. This was serious.

Thirty-six was a multiple of twelve. Ninety-six was a multiple of twelve. The numerals all added up (three plus six plus nine plus six) to twenty-four, *another* multiple of twelve.

She closed the book and whacked herself on the head with it. Dess had played with the zip code, the population, the angles of the architecture, but it had never occurred to her to look up Bixby's coordinates before.

Maybe it wasn't just the mystical stones and untouched desert that made Bixby different; maybe it was the spot on the globe itself. Just like the thirteen-pointed stars everywhere, the clue had been hidden right out in the open, on every map in the world.

Dess's heart beat faster as the numbers roiled through her. If she was right, this discovery might also answer the other trillion-dollar question: Were there other blue times in the world? Dess closed her eyes, picturing a globe in her mind. The seas and landmasses disappeared until only navigational lines remained, a glowing wire-frame sphere. When you switched around the directions, there would be seven more places with the same numbers as

Bixby: thirty-six south by ninety-six west, thirty-six west by ninety-six north, etc. And probably more combinations with other numbers. Forty-eight by eighty-four followed the same pattern, as did twenty-four by twenty-four. Of course, most of these places would be in the middle of an ocean, but some of them were bound to be on land.

There might be another dozen Bixbys out there.

Or the whole thing might be a coincidence.

Dess bit her lip. There might be a way to check the theory.

She opened the social studies book again and stared at the map of Oklahoma, willing her eyes to become microscopes, to expand the map until she could see Bixby and the surrounding badlands. Where *exactly* did the two lines intersect?

Her dad could find out. As a rig foreman, he had detailed survey maps of the oil fields surrounding town, including the badlands.

Dess looked out the window. Nothing. Sitting here waiting was driving her insane. She had to find out where the center of midnight was. If her theory was right, she had a pretty good idea of where the lines would intersect.

She stood up and crept to her door, opening it a crack. The usual flicker of TV light was absent down the hall, the house silent and still. Dad was working tomorrow, like he did most weekends, so her parents were already in bed. Dess stepped out into the hall, careful not to put any weight on the long-memorized pattern of squeaky boards, moving slowly toward the living room. She left the door open behind her, listening with one ear for the sound of impatient tapping on her window.

This was really stupid, she realized. It could wait until tomorrow. Things were behind schedule enough without a parental confrontation.

But she had to know for sure.

Dad kept his maps in the wide flat file that doubled as a coffee table in the living room. Dess knelt before it and pulled out the top drawer, a yard across. Just folders, pens, and crap in this one. The next one down opened onto maps on thin paper that tried to curl up as she pulled out the drawer, bearing black fingerprints and giving off the familiar smell of Oklahoma crude.

She heard a sound outside and froze, holding her breath.

The car passed by, rattling on the unpaved road and off into the distance.

Dess rifled through the maps, peering at the coordinates in the streetlight glow angling through the front window. The maps were incredibly detailed, showing individual houses and oil rigs. She realized that all of Bixby was contained within a single degree of latitude and longitude, which was subdivided into smaller units called "minutes," about a mile across. Her fingers raced to find the exact point of intersection.

The maps weren't in any particular order. "Thanks, Dad," she whispered to herself.

A sound came from her parents' bedroom, and Dess closed her eyes, heart pounding. Dad hated anyone touching his stuff. But no light went on, and silence slowly settled across the house again.

Finally she found it.

Dess pulled the map out slowly, letting it curl up into a scroll, and carried it with quick, silent steps back to her room.

After a glance out the window at the still empty street, she unrolled the map on her floor, pinning its corners down with four pieces of steel. Her shaking fingers followed the dotted lines to their intersection.

"I knew it," she said.

Thirty-six north by ninety-six west was right in the middle of Rustle's Bottom.

It couldn't be a coincidence. The snake pit really was darkling central. And if a certain longitude and latitude was all it took, there were probably other places in the world where the blue time came at midnight.

A horn sounded outside her window.

"Don't honk at *me!*" she hissed, grabbing her duffel bag.

Morons. Dess was keeping this to herself for the moment. She could check it out on her own. If nothing else, she'd make Rex wish he listened to her more.

Before Dess pulled herself out the window, she glanced at the clock: 11:24.

They weren't going to make it in time.

24

RUSTLE'S BOTTOM

The party was just getting started.

Rustle's Bottom was a broad, flat plain, stretching as far as Jessica could see. It seemed blank and featureless all the way to the mountains, a range of low peaks dimly silhouetted against the dark horizon. It was completely barren, except for the cars parked on the hard-packed dirt. According to Dess, it was the bed of a lake that had dried up hundreds of years ago. Jessica kicked at the dry ground. There was no hint that it had ever been anything but cold, windy desert.

She gathered herself up in the jacket, which wasn't nearly as warm as her own back at Constanza's house. Out here there was nothing to block the wind. The reason why Oklahoma was so windy was its flatness: the air just kept building up speed as it moved across the plain, like a lead-footed driver alone on a long, straight highway. It blew without any change in speed or direction, cutting through the unlined jacket. At least her feet were warm. Constanza had tried to lend her shoes with heels, but she had stuck with a pair of old, reliable boots, which she hoped were snakeproof.

Pulling the coat around her, Jessica looked up, and her eyes widened with awe. The sky in Chicago had never been filled with so many stars. This far from the lights of town, there seemed to be millions of them. For the first time Jessica could see how the Milky Way had gotten its name. It was a winding river of white that ran from east to west (she'd checked her compass as they'd gotten out of the car), full of bright stars and mushy swirls of light.

"*Brrr.* It's practically winter already," Constanza said. "Come on. Let's go get warm."

A couple of miles back they had driven off the road and right across the lake bed, which was like driving across a huge parking lot. Constanza had navigated toward a flickering light, finally pulling up to where a dozen or so cars and pickups were already parked in a ragged line. A hundred feet away was a group of people clustered around a bonfire. The shallow pit was ringed with stones that showed the marks of many previous fires. Someone had dumped in a pile of kindling, a few tree stumps, and what looked like some broken furniture. The fire was still sputtering to life, popping and hissing as new wood dried out.

Jessica followed Constanza over toward the fire.

A big spark popped and flew into the air and was carried away by the wind. The crowd laughed as the flaming projectile bounced crazily across the desert before burning itself out a few seconds later. Music played from a small CD player sitting on the dirt.

"Isn't this excellent?" Constanza said.

"Yeah." The night was beautiful, Jessica had to admit, and dramatic. She wished that a bonfire and a desert sky were the only dramas she would be facing tonight.

"Hey, Constanza." A boy detached himself from the crowd.

"Hey, Rick. How's it going? This is my friend Jess."

"Hey, Jill."

"Hi, Rick. It's Jessica, actually."

"Sure. Come on and grab some fire."

They huddled up around the fire pit. Jessica pulled her hands from her pockets to warm them. Rick offered them a plastic cup of beer each, and Jessica said no thanks. More cars arrived, and their passengers dragged over more wood for the fire. Broken chairs, dried-out tree limbs, a bale of old newspapers that ignited a few pages at a time and lifted up into the sky, carried by the hot air. Someone brought over a stop sign with a clump of concrete clinging to its base, and everyone laughed and applauded when it went on the fire and blackened. Jessica hoped that nobody was going to have a car accident because of this party. Constanza was having fun, and it was a beautiful night, but Jessica felt too young to be here, as if someone was going to ask for ID and throw her out any second.

She looked at her watch: 11:45. In five minutes it would be time to take her walk. Dess had said the snake pit was only a few minutes away, but the idea of being late was too scary to contemplate. She wanted to be safely inside the snake pit before midnight fell.

Jessica rubbed her hands nervously, not looking forward to leaving the warmth of the fire, to being alone out on the desert. She shivered and realized that although the front half of her was roasting, her back was freezing. Jessica turned around and faced out toward the desert. The fire at her back felt like a fur coat slipping on, and she sighed.

"You're pretty quiet."

Jess blinked. As her eyes adjusted to the darkness, she made out the shape of a boy in front of her.

"I guess I am. I don't really know that many people here."

"You're a friend of Liz and Constanza's?"

"Yeah. Jessica."

"Hey, Jessica. My name's Steve."

Jessica could see the boy's face now, lit by the flickering fire. He looked younger than a lot of the guys here.

She smiled. "So, Steve, you're from Broken Arrow?"

"Yeah. Born here. You're standing in downtown Broken Arrow, actually. As you can see, it's a city that never sleeps. Kind of like Bixby but without the skyscrapers."

Jessica laughed. "A burgeoning metropolis."

"Yeah, except I don't know what 'burgeoning' means."

"Oh. It means, um . . ." She shrugged. "Really flat and windy?"

Steve nodded. "Broken Arrow definitely burgeons, then."

Now Jessica's face was getting cold. "I think I'm done on this side," she said, making a space for him next to her as she turned around. She checked her watch again. Two minutes. She held out her hands, trying to store up the fire's warmth for her walk.

"So, you don't sound like you're from Bixby."

"I just moved here from Chicago."

"Chicago? Wow. Real skyscrapers. Oklahoma must seem completely weird to you."

"It's different, yeah. Except for the wind, which is pretty much *just* like Chicago."

"You're really cold, aren't you? You want my coat?"

Steve was wearing a down jacket. It looked incredibly warm.

Jessica shook her head. "No, I couldn't."

"Are you sure?"

"Yeah." She checked her watch. "Actually, I've got to go."

Disappointment flashed in Steve's eyes. "You're leaving the party already? Something I said?"

"No, not at all. I was just going to take a walk. Over to the snake pit."

Steve nodded. "For midnight, huh? You know where it is?"

"Sort of. I mean, I have a map."

"I'll take you."

Jessica bit her lip. She'd never thought of bringing a non-midnighter along. But what would the problem be? Steve would be safe no matter what happened at the snake pit. He'd be frozen for the whole thing. And in the featureless darkness, the idea of walking away from the fire alone wasn't a pleasant one. At least with Steve along she wouldn't get lost.

He was half smiling, waiting anxiously for an answer.

"Sure," she said. "Let's go."

The cold clutched her body from the moment they left the fire, creeping into the borrowed jacket like chilly fingers. Jessica's legs, protected only by tights, were freezing, and her hands grew colder and colder no matter how deep she thrust them into her pockets.

"So who told you about the snake pit?" Steve asked.

"Um, everyone. Constanza was talking about it one day, and it sounded, you know, interesting."

"And you were going alone? Wow, you're one brave girl."

"I have my moments of stupidity," Jessica agreed. She could hear her teeth chattering.

"You *are* cold, Jessica." Steve put his arm around her. The down jacket around her shoulders actually helped, even though it didn't really feel right to be this close to a guy who wasn't Jonathan.

"Thanks."

"No problem."

As they walked across the desert, Jessica wondered how Steve knew where he was going. There were no landmarks that she could see except the Milky Way, which ran in the direction they were walking. That meant that they were headed either east or west. She'd have to check the compass to be sure.

"You sure you know where we're going?"

"Oh, yeah. Born and bred in Broken Arrow, I'm not very proud to say."

"Okay."

She looked at her watch. Five minutes.

"Don't worry, we'll get there by midnight," Steve said. "Right on time for the evil spirit show."

She smiled ruefully. "Wouldn't want to miss that."

There was a flicker of light at the corner of her eye. It was the bonfire, off to their right. She wondered why it wasn't behind them anymore.

Jessica looked up into the sky. Now the Milky Way was spread out sideways across their path. They had turned either north or south.

"Steve? How far is the snake pit?"

"Oh, maybe another ten minutes."

"Ten minutes? But it's almost midnight." A shiver traveled through Jessica, more chilling than the cold. "My friend said it was really close to the fire pit."

"Are you cold? We can stop off in my car if you want."

"Your car?"

"It's right up here," Steve said, pulling her closer to him. "We could warm up."

She pulled away. "But I have to get there by midnight!"

The row of parked cars was visible now in front of them. He'd led her in a circle.

"Listen, Jessica," he said. "The snake pit's no big deal, all right? It's just this old sinkhole full of rainwater and snakes. That's Broken Arrow's idea of magic, I'm afraid." He moved closer. "I can show you something much more interesting."

Jessica whirled around and walked quickly back toward

the fire, thrusting a hand into her pocket for the map and flashlight. Her fingers fumbled, made numb and clumsy by the cold.

"Jessica . . ." She heard his footsteps following her.

She ignored him, unfolding the map. It showed the snake pit almost due east of the fire pit. Jessica pointed the flashlight at Dess's compass and turned away from the fire, heading east.

She heard Steve's footsteps behind her but ignored them, hoping he would lose interest and go away.

Jessica shoved everything back into her pockets, quickening her stride. Dess had said she couldn't miss the snake pit. Supposedly the sinkhole stood out on the desert as a long dark patch.

Steve's hand grabbed her shoulder. "Hey, wait up, Jessica. I'm sorry. I didn't know it was that big a deal."

She yanked herself away. "Go mess with someone else."

"I wasn't . . ." He stopped walking, and his voice faded. "You'll get lost out there, Jessica. The snakes'll get you."

"Better them than you," she said to herself.

"And the evil spirits too, Jessica," Steve called. "It's almost midnight. Do you want to be out here all a—"

His voice was silenced as suddenly as a radio being switched off. The light changed, the familiar blue sweeping across the desert like dawn. The air became still and silent. It was instantly warmer, but Jessica shivered.

Midnight had come.

She started to run.

25

THE SNAKE PIT

As Jessica began to run, she glanced once quickly over her shoulder, grimacing at the sight of Steve. He'd been looking straight at her when midnight had frozen him. Somehow she had to get back here at the end of the secret hour. If she wasn't standing in exactly the same position, it would seem to him as if she'd suddenly shifted place.

But Jessica smiled as she turned away and broke into a headlong run. If she didn't come back at all, he would think she had disappeared into thin air.

She could live with that.

The desert was a blue expanse, broad and flat, as if she were running across an endless ocean. In the midnight light, though, a few features became visible. Wisps of cloud were scattered overhead, and a few scraggly scrub plants clung to the hard earth. The stars were still visible, and Jessica could tell from the Milky Way that she was headed in the right direction.

There was no sign of darklings or slithers, at least. Not yet.

Nor was there any sign of the snake pit.

Jessica felt like an idiot for having trusted Steve. If she had stuck to the plan, leaving the party alone and following Dess's map, she'd have been safely at the snake pit by now.

"I'm such a wimp," Jessica spat through clenched teeth. How was she supposed to survive darklings and slithers if she was afraid of a short walk in the dark alone?

As she ran, Jessica searched the horizon for the snake pit, for anything bigger than a scrubby weed. How far had Steve taken her out of her way? Her watch said she'd been running for six minutes.

Her feet pounded to a halt. That seemed too far, for what was supposed to have been a five-minute walk.

She pulled out the compass. Would it work in the secret hour?

"Come on, come on," Jess whispered. The needle swung lazily in a full circle, then finally pointed the way she had come.

But she'd been running east. North could *not* be behind her.

A sound came across the desert, a chirping call.

Jessica scanned the sky. Directly in front of her, batlike wings were silhouetted against the rising moon. A flying slither, close enough to have spotted her. She had to keep moving. But which way?

She faced the direction that the compass said was east. There was nothing but featureless, blue desert before her. Her eyes fell to the compass angrily.

The needle was pointing in a new direction. It said north was still behind her, but now she was facing a different way.

"What the—"

Jessica turned in a slow circle. No matter which way she faced, the needle pointed straight at her.

"Great, I'm the North Pole now," she muttered. Another one for Rex to ponder.

If she survived long enough to see him again.

She thrust the useless compass into her pocket and looked up at the stars. The Milky Way ran east to west, or at least it had before midnight had freaked out the compass. At one end of the river of light was the rising moon.

"Jessica, you idiot!" The sun rose in the east; why wouldn't the dark moon?

She had been going the right way all along.

Jessica started running again, as hard as she could. If the slither had spotted her, there was no time left to waste. Either she was headed in the right direction or she was dead meat.

The moon was higher now, its baleful face broad enough to fill the eastern horizon. Winged things were gathering in front of her, dark shapes against the cold light of the moon.

Suddenly she saw what looked like a flicker of blue lightning before her. But it seemed to strike in reverse, jumping from the ground up into the sky, spreading out from a thick trunk to many thin fingers of fire, like a huge and leafless tree suddenly revealed by a flash of blue. More streaks of lightning shot up from the ground, and Jessica heard the screams of flying slithers. She watched as one dropped from the sky, touched by one of the branches of blue electricity.

"Dess," she said. The bolts of lightning were the snake pit's defenses, coming to life. Jessica was headed the right way. Safety was close.

She ran harder.

The flying beasts seemed to be testing the defenses, trying to get past the lightning and down into the snake pit. As the cloud of slithers thickened, the lightning grew more furious, forming a stuttering arc of blue flame over the pit. The scrubby weeds around Jessica cast long, flickering shadows.

Another thirty seconds and she would be safe.

A huge, dark shape rose up over the blue arc, too big to be a slither. It came straight toward Jessica and began to descend, its wings almost large enough to blot out the fireworks behind it.

She skidded to a stop, panting. As the darkling landed and its wings folded, she could see its form boil and change, resolving into a crouched black shape of muscles, claws, and flashing eyes. A panther.

The blue arc protecting the snake pit was only a few yards behind it. She was so close.

Jessica pulled off Jonathan's necklace, holding it tightly in one hand. She whispered its name, "Obstructively."

The beast roared, shaking the hard desert earth under her feet. It reared up, saber teeth growing from its maw.

For a moment Jessica was overwhelmed by the same paralyzing fear that had trapped her the first time she'd seen a darkling. But then she remembered how joyfully Dess had dispatched that panther, in a wild burst of sparks from the flying hubcap.

This time Jessica wasn't defenseless.

"You're in big trouble, psychokitty," she said, holding the necklace high.

The beast just growled, unimpressed.

She readied herself to attack, the necklace wadded into a ball in her hand. No point in waiting for another darkling to show up.

The panther arched its back, eyes flashing, as if sensing what she was about to do.

Jessica took a deep breath and ran straight toward it.

The cat reared back, off balance. It was a predator, not used to prey turning on it. But then its hunting reflexes took over. Its claws extended, and it lunged at her with a single bound like the strike of a huge snake, suddenly a bolt of solid muscle.

She hurled the necklace.

The metal ignited the moment it left her hand, the links aflame in a string of blue sparklers. Burning steel and the panther arced toward each other, beast and metal colliding in midair with a thunderous sound. The cat was thrown back, howling. It rolled over once and scrabbled to its feet at the edge of the snake pit, shaking its head.

Its cold eyes locked on Jessica.

A second later the world seemed to explode.

A bolt of lightning shot out from the snake pit, leaping

across the few feet of desert and striking the body of the
panther. The whole snake pit seemed to burst into cold,
blue flame for a moment, with a rushing noise like a building rain, and then a deafening explosion threw Jessica to
the ground. She rolled across the dirt, the boom shaking
the hard desert sand beneath her.

For a moment she couldn't move. Her head rang, and she
could see nothing but the bolt of lightning striking the big cat,
burned into her eyes like the afterimage of a camera flash.

Jessica forced her eyes open and rose shakily, coughing,
not knowing which way was which. Tears streamed down
her face, and as she blinked them away, Jessica saw a blurry
form hurtling toward her through the air.

She took a few half-blind steps backward. The shape
landed in front of her.

Jessica put a hand up to her neck instinctively, but the
necklace was gone. She was defenseless.

A hand grabbed her arm.

"This way, Jess."

Gravity slid away. Suddenly she was made of feathers.

"Jonathan."

With a single, soaring step he pulled her across the crack-
ling boundary. She had been only yards from the edge of the
snake pit. Lights flashed around them, the hairs on her head
standing up as if she'd stepped into a bath of electricity.

Jessica stumbled when they landed inside the sinkhole,
and the moment Jonathan let go of her arm, her feet
slipped down the slope of softer sand. She sat down hard.

"Jess?"

"I'm okay." She blinked away the dirt in her eyes and managed to get Jonathan's face into focus. He was breathing hard, kneeling next to where she sat, loose dirt slipping around them down into the center of the pit.

"I tried to stop the darkling, but it went for you so fast," he said breathlessly. "I thought I was too late."

"No, you were just in time." Jessica shook her head, trying to clear the ringing in her ears. Her fingers and toes buzzed, as if some huge force had moved through her, electrifying her body in its wake. Every breath seemed to fill her with energy. She almost felt like laughing.

"I lost Obstructively. I mean, I threw it at the psychokitty," she babbled.

"I saw the whole thing. That was incredible."

"Is it gone? Your necklace?"

"Blown to bits, but I'll give you another one."

"Oh, good."

Jessica giggled, then forced herself to take a slow, deep breath. The buzzing in her body was fading. Finally her vision cleared completely. Jonathan's face was twisted with concern.

"Are you sure you're okay?" he asked. "You look like you just stuck a fork into a light socket."

"Gee, thanks." Jessica stood shakily, and he reached out a hand to help her up. "I'm okay, really."

In fact, she felt great. She smoothed her hair, which was sticking out in all directions.

"Uh, Jessica . . ."

"Yeah?"

"Are you wearing makeup?"

She dusted the dirt off herself. "Can't a girl get dressed up for a party?"

Jonathan raised one eyebrow and looked around. The bowl of the snake pit was ringed with pieces of metal, junkyard shapes that glowed and sputtered. Sheets of lightning flashed up from them into the sky, where screaming slithers wheeled in tight circles around the pit. Burned and twisted shapes lay on the ground, the bodies of fried, smoking slithers that had ventured too close. Through the blue dome of lightning Jessica spotted a few darklings hovering in the distance, their eyes radiant indigo in the glare of the incessant flashes.

Jonathan laughed. "Some party."

Jessica smiled but then knitted her brows. "Not all the guests are here, though."

"I spotted Melissa's car on my way, at the other end of the Bottom. I guess they're going to be a little late." He looked at the fireworks show around them. "If they get here at all."

Jessica looked out through the arcing blue lightning, past the wheeling cloud of slithers. "How did you get through, Jonathan?"

He pointed to an object on the ground next to him. It looked like an old trash can lid, dented and marked all over with strange signs and patterns. "Meet Purposelessly Hyperinflated Individuality. Something Dess made to help me get here."

"Purposelessly Hyperinflated . . . ?" She laughed.

"What?"

"Nothing. It's just a good name."

"Her new thing is thirty-nine-letter phrases. Packs more of a punch."

"Looks like you needed it," Jessica said. The lid was blackened on one side, as if it had been used to ward off a flamethrower.

"I had flying slithers bouncing off me like bugs off a windshield." Jonathan picked it up. With his fingers through the handle, the trash can lid looked like a battered shield. He looked up at the moon, half risen.

"They should've been here by now."

Jessica could still see part of the Milky Way past the huge moon. "They'd be coming from that way, right?" she asked.

Jonathan nodded and pulled out a candy bar, taking a hurried bite.

They skirted the pit to the other side, the flashes of lightning sending long shadows from them in all directions. The sinkhole was a rounded, irregular crater in the desert, as if a giant shovel had scooped up a load of dirt. Plants clung to its sides, and the earth at its depressed center looked dark and damp. Jessica started at what she thought was a crawling slither underfoot, but it turned out to be a normal snake, frozen by midnight.

"Nice place for a party," she muttered.

They reached the opposite edge and looked out across the smooth plain of the Bottom.

"There they are," Jonathan said.

26

GAUNTLET

"Looks pretty impressive, Dess."

"Thanks, except I was hoping we'd see it from the *inside*."

"Come on," Rex said for the tenth time. "The cops were all over the place tonight. We're lucky we made it to your house at all."

"So how are we supposed to get over there?" she asked.

The blue arc over the snake pit shone brightly across the desert. With his midnight vision Rex could see every slender finger of the cold lightning that leapt from the ring of steel Dess had created. He could see the slithers swirling overhead, drawn to the snake pit and its ancient stones, barely smart enough to avoid the deadly forces they attracted from the clean metal. He could also see darklings overhead, hovering wary and patient, waiting for something to happen.

Everything was in readiness.

Unfortunately, it was all happening hundreds of yards away, across open, defenseless desert.

"I have no idea," he admitted.

"They know we're here," Melissa said. "But they don't care about us. Just her."

Rex nodded. He could see two forms inside the barrier of lightning, looking back at him across the plain. Jessica had made it here, had risked her life to meet them.

"So maybe we can just walk across."

Dess looked at him as if he were nuts.

"After you," Melissa suggested.

Dess had created a small protective perimeter around them, clean steel stakes borrowed from her dad's camping tent, carefully arranged and linked with wire to make a thirteen-pointed star. The wires glistened in the moonlight like a spiderweb around them. It was easy to keep away darklings if you could set up defenses, but moving across open terrain was another matter.

"We can't just sit here." He looked up at the moon. "We've only got another forty minutes or so."

"Less than that," Dess said. "The arc is weakening."

Rex stared at her. "What?" he cried. "You said it would last all midnight."

She shook her head. "I know, but you saw those fireworks a minute ago. Something big must have hit it. Like maybe a darkling threw itself against the barrier. I didn't think even a psychokitty would be that stupid."

Rex blinked. He wouldn't have imagined it either. Darklings were very old, and those left alive were, by simple process of elimination, only the very cautious ones. Self-sacrifice was not in their nature. "Then we can't stand around. We've got to help them."

Melissa raised her head and sniffed the wind. "I don't think they're going away anytime soon."

"No," Rex agreed. "But we have to try. We could run that distance in a couple of minutes."

"And get ourselves killed in thirty seconds," Dess said.

He turned to Melissa. "You said they don't care about us."

"They'll care about us pretty quick if we get any closer to *her*."

Rex clenched his fists. "That's why we have to try. Don't you guys get it? They want to get Jessica because she's important, because she's the key to something. We have to find out what."

"Yeah, I get it," Melissa said. "They hate her. I can taste it like a mouthful of gasoline. But we've never really been enemies with the darklings, Rex. You always said they're like wild animals: stay out of their way and they'll stay out of ours. She's the one driving them crazy."

"So what do you suggest we do?"

"We walk away."

"What?"

"We turn around and go home."

"Melissa," Dess said, "my ring around the snake pit may not last for the whole hour."

Melissa shrugged. "Then all our problems will be solved, one way or another. Maybe Jessica will figure out what her talent is once she really needs it. Or maybe the darklings get what they want, and everything goes back to normal."

Rex looked at his old friend, not believing the words that had just come out of her mouth. "Melissa—," he started, but found that he didn't know what to say.

A sharp laugh came from Dess. "And everything goes back to normal? I thought you didn't like normal."

"Normal might suck, but it's better than dying for her."

"For both of them," Dess said. She turned to Rex. "I'm not going to get stuck with just you two again. Let's go."

Rex watched as Dess knelt by her duffel bag. She unzipped it and pulled out a yard-long metal pole. She twisted something at one end and gave it a flick. Another shaft of steel slid out like a folding telescope until the whole thing was almost a foot longer than Dess was tall. It was decorated with her usual mathematical signs and symbols, but *a lot* of them.

"Resplendently Scintillating Illustrations," she said happily.

Dess turned and walked toward the snake pit, stepping over the shining boundary of taut guitar string and onto the open desert.

"Coming?" she asked over her shoulder.

Rex blinked, then followed. He paused to lift up the duffel bag, which clanked reassuringly at his side. After a few steps he heard Melissa sigh and knew that she would be close behind.

They had gone just over halfway when the darklings noticed them.

A few slithers had flown or crawled near, but Dess's weapon had sparked to life at their approach. None of them had dared to test its power. Rex had almost begun to think they'd make it without any trouble.

Then the darkling came. It swept over them from behind, blocking out the moon for a moment, and landed directly in their path.

It didn't look like a cat or like any darkling he'd seen before. Rex wasn't exactly sure what it was. Its globular body was hairy, with uneven patches of fur sticking out all over it. The wings were broad, with skeletal fingers visible through the translucent skin. Four long, hairy legs dangled from the rounded body, waving and softly scraping the desert as it landed. The creature's bloated belly sagged, resting on the sand.

"Old," Melissa said quietly. "Very old."

Rex dropped the duffel bag and reached into it. His hand closed on a paper bag full of small metal objects—washers, safety pins, silverware, and nails, all clinking against each other. He pulled it out and hefted it in his hand, wondering if Dess had really named each and every one of the pieces inside. It felt as if there were hundreds.

"It doesn't want to fight us," Melissa said. "It wants us to go away."

"Not a chance," Rex said.

The wings were shrinking, being sucked into the creature. A fifth leg sprouted from the body, thrusting out and waving in the air mindlessly. Then another, and then two more, until it could finally lift its bulk up from the earth on eight spindly legs.

Rex shuddered as he recognized the shape. It was a tarantula, a huge version of the desert spider.

The monstrous creature illustrated what he'd tried to explain to Jessica back at the museum. The darklings were the original nightmares, the template for every human fear. Black cats, snakes, spiders, lizards, worms—the darklings mimicked them all in their pursuit of terror.

Spiders, it so happened, were Rex's personal nightmare.

Especially hairy spiders.

The thing's legs twitched and trembled, the hair on them threadbare and matted. It shifted its balance almost nervously, one leg lingering in the air as if testing the wind. Eyes seemed scattered across its body at random, flashing purple in the dark moonlight.

"Doesn't look so tough," Dess proclaimed without much conviction.

"There are others," Melissa said.

Two more darklings hovered in the air above, well away, but clearly ready to join in.

"This one first," Rex said, swallowing his disgust and taking a few steps forward. He reached into the paper bag, took a sharp handful of the metal bits, and threw them as hard as he could at the beast.

They sputtered to life in the air, burning a deep blue, like the base of a flame. The metal pieces struck the darkling and burned themselves out against it. Wisps of smoke rose from it, and a foul smell like singed hair and wet dog reached Rex's nostrils. The beast hardly reacted at all, just shivered and twitched, emitting a slow, liquid sigh, the exhalation of huge and infected lungs.

"Leave this to me," Dess said, "and the heavy artillery."

She ran toward it, the metal shaft over her shoulder like a javelin. The beast reared back on six of its legs, the other two waving in front of it to ward her off.

From a few yards away she threw the weapon, which burst into light even as it left her hand, wailing through the air with the shriek of a Roman candle. The metal buried itself in the spider, tearing a gash in the mottled flesh. Blue fire spewed from the wound.

The thing screamed hideously, its bloated body crashing to the ground as its arms waved uselessly in the air.

"Oh, bleah!" cried Dess. She stumbled back from the spider, putting one hand over her mouth.

Seconds later a horrible smell washed across Rex and Melissa, dead rat and burned plastic mixed together with rotten eggs. Melissa coughed and gagged, falling to one knee.

"Run for the pit!" Rex managed to cry. They were no more than a hundred yards away.

He ran toward one side of the shuddering spider, still clutching the bag of metal bits. Melissa stumbled after him. Dess dashed past the tarantula, whose legs still flailed wildly, heading for the blue arc of the snake pit.

As Rex ran, the desert before him seemed to be moving,

dark sand flowing across his path. The huge spider was sagging, deflating like a punctured balloon.

"Stop, Rex!" Melissa cried, pulling him to a halt. "It's not dead. Just—"

She didn't finish, choking on the stench.

Now Rex could see them. Things were pouring from the darkling's wound, gushing out in a torrent. More spiders, thousands of them. They swarmed in a black river between the two of them and the snake pit.

Dess was on the other side, still running, only a few seconds from the safety of the still flickering lightning. Rex saw her cross the boundary, falling into Jessica's and Jonathan's arms.

The black river of spiders changed course, flowing toward him and Melissa. It made a harsh roaring sound as it moved, like a truckload of gravel being poured onto a sheet of glass.

Rex emptied the rest of the bag of metal pieces, scattering its contents in a rough circle around their feet, a couple of yards across. The crawling host swept up to the patch of glittering steel and broke against it, flowing around them like water.

In seconds they were surrounded, an island in a writhing sea of spiders.

The bits of metal sparked and sputtered, the outermost pieces glowing bright purple. A few spiders dared to move into the steel. They burst into flame, but more came, crawling across the bridge of burned bodies.

"How long do you think the steel will last?" he asked Melissa.

"Doesn't matter," she said. She was looking upward. Rex followed her dumbstruck gaze.

The other two darklings were coming down.

They were shaped like panthers. One was right above them, its saber teeth protruding from its jaw as it dove, wings billowing like a parachute behind it.

"I'm sorry, Cowgirl."

"At least these things got me," she said, "before all those damn, noisy humans drove me insane."

"Yeah." Rex hoped the panthers arrived before spiders were crawling all over him. He put his right fist up to his lips and finally named the steel skull rings on his fingers. "Understanding. Incorruptible. Anticlimactic."

Then he grasped Melissa's arm, knowing this was all his fault, wondering what he had done wrong.

A second later something barreled into the darkling, and sparks flew.

27

PURPOSELESSLY HYPER-INFLATED INDIVIDUALITY

Jonathan caught most of the impact on his shield, but the collision still knocked the wind out of him. The darkling's skin bulged with muscle, as hard as a sack of doorknobs. He heard the thin aluminum alloy of Purposelessly Hyperinflated Individuality crumple with the impact, then the shield burned his fingers as it instantly turned white-hot. Sparks flew from the darkling's flesh, and its scream rang deafeningly in his ears.

For a moment Jonathan grew heavy; contact with the darkling had robbed him of his midnight gravity. He fell toward the ground, but as the icy touch of the creature's flesh faded, Jonathan's body lightened again.

By the time he hit the ground, he was almost back to weightless.

He rolled to his feet, coming up face-to-face with a very surprised Rex.

"Did you see that?" he said. "Direct hit."

On his way out to the Bottom, Jonathan had discovered

that the trash can lid was a great flying aid. It was a surfboard, a wing, a sail—a surface to catch the air and control his direction after he'd jumped. In the moments he had soared toward the darkling, Jonathan had used it to adjust his path like a smart missile homing in on its target.

Something sizzled at his feet, and Jonathan glanced down. The spiders were closing in from every direction, forcing their burning way through the metal. He had landed in the middle of a lake of relentless, poisonous bugs.

Smart was relative, he supposed.

"Smells bad out here," he said to Rex and Melissa. "Let's jump."

"One problem, genius," Melissa said. She pointed.

The other darkling was swooping toward the three of them, skimming across the desert.

Jonathan pulled the still smoldering Purposelessly Hyperinflated Individuality from his hand, hoping its triple-decker name had one more jolt left in it. He crooked the trash can lid in his arm like a giant Frisbee and hurled it at the beast.

He didn't pause to see the result, grabbing Rex. He held out his other hand.

Melissa shrank from him. "I'd rather die."

"That's crap," Rex said, shoving her forward. Her hands came up instinctively and Jonathan grabbed one.

A wave of nausea hit him, and he almost blacked out. He could feel Melissa's mind rushing into his, belligerent and angry but at the same time feverishly hungry, consuming his thoughts and memories, pushing into every corner of his mind. Her emotions swept through him: terror of the spiders, surprise at being suddenly weightless, and, overwhelming everything, horror at the intimacy of being *touched*.

For a moment he was paralyzed, but then an irresistible command surged into his mind.

Jump, idiot, Melissa thought at him.

"*One, two . . . ,*" he started.

Rex hadn't flown with him for more than a year, but the reflexes were still there. They knelt and jumped together, soaring over the spiders. Together they were strong enough to drag Melissa along.

Jonathan heard the second darkling collide with the projectile, and another feline screech echoed across the desert. But there were other winged shapes coming at them—slithers, at least.

Melissa's fingers dug into his, but she managed to fight, snapping off necklace after necklace with her free hand, casting them into the air around the trio as they flew, knocking screaming slithers to the ground. Rex flailed about with his free hand, the metal rings he wore sparking to life.

The first jump carried them to within yards of the snake pit. Jonathan had to hold Rex back or their next leap would have carried them all the way through and out the other side.

They skidded to a stop inside the arc's safety seconds later, and Jonathan let go, letting them drop into the soft sand. Melissa landed badly, an ankle twisting and eyes flashing in the lightning. The venom and agony from her mind drained out of Jonathan, leaving a taste like rotten meat on his tongue.

Melissa doubled over, convulsing once with a pitiful moan, the fingers of the hand he'd touched clawing the hard sand. Still coughing, she managed to stand and face him, and Jonathan braced himself.

Her face held an expression he'd never seen before or perhaps had never been able to see. She was so sad, so hopeless. Then the familiar mask of annoyance descended over her features.

"Thanks," she said.

Jonathan realized that they'd actually made it back to the snake pit. "You're welcome."

Melissa turned to Dess. "And you."

Dess lowered her gaze, shrugged.

Melissa turned away from them all. "Thanks, I mean, Dess."

Jonathan looked at Jessica, who frowned. Rex put his hand on Melissa's shoulder, but she pulled away.

Rex sighed and tenderly pulled off his rings. The fingers looked burned underneath. He glanced up at the moon, almost at its peak.

"We'd better get started," Rex said. "Ready, Jessica?"

Jessica shivered in her jacket. "I guess."

Jonathan took her hand. He felt the muscles relax as midnight gravity flowed through her.

"Jonathan, you help Dess," Rex said.

He bristled for a moment, remembering how Rex always assumed he was in command. But he took a deep breath. "Okay," he said. "Help Dess what?"

Dess cleared her throat. "Help me fix the defenses to keep the snake pit from being overrun by darklings and about a million slithers."

"I thought you said—"

"The defenses are weakening," she explained. "Something big must have been caught in the lightning arc."

"Like a darkling?" Jessica asked.

"Yeah."

Jonathan and Jess looked at each other.

"I did that," Jessica said.

A few yards away Melissa snorted, completely back to her old self.

Dess frowned. "Wow. That's a trick you'll have to show me."

"Just an accident. Like everything I do."

"Later," Rex said. "Buy us some time, Dess." He turned to Jessica. "Jess, are you . . . ?"

"Yes?"

Rex paused. "Are you wearing makeup?"

She rolled her eyes. "Come on. It's Friday night!"

"No, you look great. Really. Let's go do this."

Jessica squeezed Jonathan's hand, then turned away. Rex and Melissa led her down toward the dark center of the pit.

Jonathan took another deep breath, pulling his eyes away from Jessica.

"Okay, Dess, what do we do?"

"First, we need the clean metal I brought, which is . . ." Dess groaned, slapping a hand to her forehead. "In my *duffel bag.*"

Jonathan looked around. "Where?"

Dess pointed out of the snake pit and across the sand, to where spiders still poured from the darkling she had speared, spreading over the desert to form a black, seething sea of legs and teeth.

"Not a chance," Jonathan said.

Dess sighed. "Then I guess we'll have to improvise."

28

CEREMONY

Jessica followed Rex down into the center of the snake pit.

The ground was damp down here. This morning in the library Dess had explained to her how sinkholes formed. Somewhere below them was an underground pocket of water trapped between layers of stone, which had collected back when the Bottom had been a lake. The crust of sand beneath her feet was thinner here than across the rest of the Bottom and had partly collapsed into the pocket of water a few decades ago.

Jessica walked carefully, wondering if the snake pit was planning on collapsing the rest of the way anytime soon. With her luck, it would probably pick tonight.

At the center, the lowest and dampest part of the pit, a shaft of stone thrust up from the ground. Dess had said it had been buried for a long time, maybe thousands of years, before the formation of the sinkhole had exposed it to the sun again. The stone had been important to the people who'd fought the darklings in the old days, before the creatures had retreated to the secret hour.

It was about as tall as Rex, with a flat shelf jutting out from it about halfway up. A little pile of rocks sat on the shelf. Rex swept them away.

"Kids," he said.

"Lucky there's no stiffs tonight," Melissa said. She turned to Jessica. "Some nights you have to crawl over them to get anything done."

"Yeah, I heard about people coming here at midnight."

"They do," Melissa said. "We like to give them a scare, just to keep them out of the way next time, you know?"

"I'm sure you do."

Melissa smiled. "It's for their own good."

Rex was tracing his fingers across the stone, staring intently at it.

"This is one of the places where the lore changes," he said to Jessica. "I try to come here pretty often."

"Changes? You mean, the lore's different on different nights?"

Jessica took a step closer, trying to see the signs that Rex was reading. All she saw was rock, divided into separate layers of different hues. In the blue light they were all shades of gray.

He nodded. "Yeah. Every time I read the signs here, there are new stories." He thumped the rock with one knuckle. "There are a lot of tales stored in here, and only so many show up at once."

"So it's like the screen of a computer," she said.

Melissa snorted, but Rex nodded again. "Sure. Except

you can't make it tell you what you need to know. It tells you what it wants."

"Unless you ask it really nicely," Melissa said.

She pulled a black velvet bag from her jacket and drew a knife from it.

Jessica swallowed. "How does this work, anyway?"

"The rock just needs a little taste of you," Melissa said.

"A taste," Jessica asked. "As in it's going to lick my hand?"

Melissa smiled again. "More of a bite than a lick."

Rex turned to Melissa and took the knife from her hand. "Stop it, Melissa. It's not that big a deal."

He turned toward Jessica.

"A few drops of blood will do."

She drew a step away. "Nobody said anything about blood!"

"Just from your fingertip. It won't hurt that much."

Jessica clenched her fist.

"Come on, Jess," Melissa said. "Haven't you ever become a blood sister with someone? Or made a blood oath?"

"Uh, not really. More of a cross-my-heart kind of girl."

Rex nodded. "Actually, the crossing of the heart was originally a blood oath. They used a knife in the old days."

"The hope-to-die part was a lot more literal back then," Melissa said.

"These are not the old days," Jessica said. "And I don't particularly hope to die."

"What, are you too wimpy to cut your finger?" Melissa asked.

Jessica scowled. After everything she'd been through that night, no one was calling her a wimp. Certainly not Melissa, anyway.

"Okay. Give me the knife," she said with a sigh.

"Let the blood collect right here," Rex said. He pointed at a small depression in the shelf of rock, no bigger than a quarter.

Jessica inspected the knife. "Is this thing clean?"

"Absolutely. Nothing inhuman has ever—"

"Not that kind of clean," Jessica interrupted, trying not to roll her eyes. "Disinfected clean."

Rex smiled. "Smell it."

Jessica sniffed the knife and caught a whiff of rubbing alcohol.

"Just go easy, okay?" Rex said. "We only need a few drops."

"No problem." She looked at her hand and curled it into a fist except for the ring finger. The knife glistened in the dark moonlight, and she could read the tiny words *stainless steel* on its shaft.

"Okay," she said, preparing herself.

"Do you want me to do it for—"

"No!" Jessica interrupted him.

She swallowed, gritted her teeth, and pulled the edge across her fingertip. Pain shot up her arm.

As she watched, blood welled up along the cut. Even in the blue light of midnight it was a fresh, bright red.

"Don't waste it," Melissa said.

"Plenty to go around," Jessica muttered. She held her hand over the shelf of rock and watched as a drop gradually formed on the fingertip, wobbled tenuously for a moment, then fell into the little bowl of stone.

A hissing sound came from deep inside the rock. Jessica jerked her hand away.

"More," Rex said.

She reached out carefully, letting another drop fall into the bowl. The hissing grew louder as the blood ran. She felt a tremor build under her feet.

"Okay," Rex said. "Maybe that's enough."

The shaft of stone in front of Jessica was trembling. Sand was slipping down into the center of the pit from all sides, and she had to pull one foot free, then the other.

"Is this what's supposed to happen?"

"Um, I don't know," Rex said.

"We never actually did this before," Melissa admitted.

"Great."

"I mean, it's usually pretty obvious who has what talent," Rex said, backing away from the stone. It was shaking harder now. Dust rose up from the ground around them, and Jessica heard a huge gulping sound from beneath her feet.

She imagined the water below, cold and dark and waiting for centuries.

"So when should we start running?" she called over the rumble.

With a sharp boom the shaft of stone cracked before them, a fissure splitting it from top to bottom.

"I guess about right now!" Rex yelled.

Jessica turned, scrambling upward. The sand slid under her, carrying her back down the slope.

Suddenly the rumbling stopped.

The three of them came to a halt, looked at each other, then turned toward the stone.

"Nice going," Melissa said. "You broke it, Jessica."

The stone had actually cracked in two, a thin fracture running its entire length, but the trembling had stopped completely. Dust swirled around them, and lightning still flashed from the perimeter of the pit, but it seemed almost silent after the earthquake.

Jonathan landed softly next to Jessica, and she heard Dess running down the slope behind her.

"What happened?" he asked.

Jessica held up her finger. "I cut myself. Then things got earthquakey."

Rex ran back down to the stone. He peered closely at the shelf.

"It worked," he said softly.

Jessica came up beside him, staring into the little bowl. Her blood had twisted into long threads, turning dark and staining the rock. The threads of blood formed a symbol, what looked to Jessica like a crescent-shaped claw holding up a spark.

"What does it mean, Rex?"

He paused, blinking.

"Two words, linked together . . . flame-bringer."

Jessica shrugged. "Which is what?"

He took a step back from the stone, shaking his head. Jessica turned around, looking at the other midnighters. They all looked as puzzled as she was.

"I don't know," Rex said. "Flame-bringer? There's no such talent."

"There is now," Jonathan said.

"Well, it better be something good," Dess announced. "Because in about five minutes we've got company."

29

FLAME-BRINGER

"What do you mean, Dess?" Rex asked.

"When the defenses ate Jessica's darkling, my clean metal got very dirty. It's starting to sputter out."

Jessica looked up at the edge of the pit. The ring of lightning surrounding them looked weaker. The flashes no longer blinded when they shot up into the sky, the bolts of blue pale and tentative.

"I know," Rex said. "But I thought you could fix it."

"We did what we could. I don't have enough clean steel. *Someone* left my duffel bag out on the desert."

"You walked away from your duffel bag," Rex replied, "when you were getting all Amazon with your spear."

"Somebody had to kill that tarantula," Dess shouted.

"You didn't kill it, you turned it into an army," Rex yelled, "which some of us almost drowned in."

"You don't *drown* in an *army*!"

"Stop it!"

Melissa's cry silenced Rex and Dess. Jessica saw that

their argument had drained the color from her face. She was doubled over in agony.

"Sorry, Melissa," Rex said. He took a deep breath.

"There's nothing I can do, Rex," Dess said softly.

Jessica looked up into the sky. Through the sputtering ceiling of lightning she could see slithers swirling around the snake pit. At the lip of the crater a host of tiny eyes gazed down at her. The spiders had surrounded the pit and peered down at them expectantly.

"It's up to you, Jessica."

She looked at Rex helplessly. "What am I supposed to do? You all keep acting like I know something. Like I'm someone special."

Jonathan grasped her hand, and she felt his reassuring weightlessness flow into her. "It's okay, Jess. We'll figure it out."

"What does 'flame-bringer' mean, Rex?" Dess asked.

"I can't be sure. I'd have to do more—"

"There isn't time to go look it up in the lore, Rex," Jonathan interrupted. "What do you *think* it means?"

Rex looked over at the shaft of stone, biting his lip. Melissa pulled her head from her hands and looked up at him.

"You're not serious," she said.

Dess laughed. "You think it's literal, don't you? You think she can use fire. *Real* fire."

"In the secret hour?" Jonathan asked.

"That would kick butt," Dess said. "Red fire in the blue time."

Rex looked at Melissa.

"It makes sense, I guess," she said. "At least it's something that would scare them enough to explain all this."

"But you said fire didn't work here," Jessica said.

Rex nodded. "That's right. That's why they created the secret hour in the first place. The whole point of the Split was to escape technology. Fire, electronics, all the new ideas." He turned to Jessica. "But you've come to make them face fire again. You could change everything."

"Well, don't just stand there making speeches about it," Dess said. "Anyone got any matches?"

"No."

"No."

"No."

Melissa shook her head. "Some flame-bringer. Too bad we didn't get the match-bringer."

"Hey, I asked about matches," Jessica said. "And Rex said they'd be—"

A cracking sound pealed through the snake pit, along with a blinding flash, and a dead slither fell to the ground next to Dess.

"Oh, yuck!" she cried, holding her nose at the smell.

Melissa raised her head to the sky. "They know it's fading. They're coming closer."

"Okay," Rex said. "Maybe we don't need matches. We can start a fire the old-fashioned way."

"With what? Flint or something?" Jonathan said.

"Or two sticks. You rub them together," Dess said.

"Sticks?" Jessica looked around. "I'm not the stick-bringer either, and this *is* a desert."

"Here." Rex pulled off a steel ring from his boot. He picked up a rock from the ground. "Bang these together, Jess."

She took them from him and struck them against each other.

"Harder."

Jessica held the rock firmly and brought the metal down against it as hard as she could.

A spark flew, bright red in the blue light.

"Oh, yeah," Dess said. "Did you see that color?"

Jessica glanced at Rex. It hadn't looked like much to her.

His mouth had fallen open. "Fire," he murmured.

"Yeah, but sparks won't stop an army," Jonathan said. "We need to start a blaze."

Dess nodded. "Too bad there's no kindling out here. Does anyone have any paper?"

Jessica pulled Dess's map to the snake pit out of her pocket. "I'll get this going. You guys try to find something else flammable." She knelt and put it on the ground, holding the rock next to it. She struck at it with the steel.

A few sparks came, but they bounced harmlessly off the paper.

A scream came from overhead. Jessica paused to look up. A darkling hovered right above them, daring the lightning. The blue fingers leapt up at the creature, hurling it back. But it descended once more, testing the defenses again and again. The sparks seemed to be driving it into a murderous rage.

"Keep whacking," Dess said.

Jessica turned back to the rock, trying to connect at a shallow angle. She missed with the metal ring, and her knuckles drove the rock into the sand. Pain shot through her hand.

Jessica pulled the rock from the sand and struck at it again. The sparks wouldn't come. Blood welled up on her knuckles, and the cut on her ring finger began to throb with her heartbeat.

This wasn't working.

"How long before midnight ends?" she heard Jonathan ask.

"Not soon enough," Dess said.

Jessica kept pounding away at the rock. A few more sparks flew, but the paper wouldn't ignite.

"It's not happening," she said. "Maybe two stones?"

"Here." Jonathan knelt next to her, handing her another rock. She struck them together.

Nothing.

She looked at her watch. Twenty minutes before the end of the hour. The flashes of lightning were fading visibly around them.

"Jessica."

"I'm *trying*, Jonathan."

"Your watch."

"What?"

He pointed at the watch. "It's working."

Jessica looked at it uncomprehendingly. She realized that she hadn't worn it in the midnight hour before. She always took it off before going to bed.

"It's working," Jonathan repeated, "and it's electronic—it's not a windup."

"Here they come," Dess whispered.

Jessica looked up. The circle of blue lightning around the snake pit had died, exposing the dark moon over their heads. The darkling overhead was descending warily. The wind from its wing beats stirred the dust around her.

"Jessica," Rex said softly. "We need a fire *now*."

She picked up the rocks again but paused.

She remembered the new building at Aerospace Oklahoma, where she and Jonathan had taken refuge the weekend before. When Jessica had seen it tonight, it had been ablaze with lights. They must be lighting it every night. All night.

"Jessica . . ."

A sound came from all around them, a rushing noise. The tarantulas were pouring into the snake pit from every direction.

"No," Rex said softly.

Jessica pushed the little button on the side of her watch, and the tiny night-light glowed white in the blue light. It said 12:42.

Jonathan met her eyes, his jaw wide open.

"Forget these," Jessica said, dropping the two rocks to

the ground. She pulled the flashlight from her pocket and held it to her lips.

"Serendipitous," she said.

She turned it toward the surging sea of tarantulas and switched it on.

A cone of white light leapt from the flashlight, and the spiders began to scream.

30

TALENT

The white light swept across the crater floor, reducing the spiders to ash in its wake. Shrill, horrible cries rose up from the swarming army, like a thousand whistles blowing at once. The tide of hairy bodies turned away swiftly, pouring back up the snake pit's sloped walls. Jessica pointed the flashlight into the air, and the slithers that crossed its path burst into flame, suddenly red against the dark sky. She shone the light straight up to search for the darkling over their heads, but the creature had disappeared into the distance, howling.

A last few spiders crawled witlessly around the smoking bodies of their fellows, and she burned them one by one with the flashlight.

The white light seemed unreal and uncanny in the blue time, revealing everything in its true colors. The beam drove the blue from the landscape, returned the reds and browns of the desert, and turned the charred bodies of slithers and spiders a dull gray.

Even the moon above them seemed gray now, pale and

unthreatening, washed out and emptied of its menace.

As the attackers retreated from the snake pit, the night grew silent. The clicking calls of slithers and the shrieks of the spider army faded, until only the howls of a few dark-lings could be heard, screams of pain and defeat in the distance.

"Turn that thing off!" Dess complained.

Jessica started when she saw her friends' eyes flashing angry purple in the light. Dess cowered behind her hands. Jonathan, Melissa, and Rex had all covered their eyes, their faces twisted in pain.

Only Jessica could stand the light.

She pointed the flashlight to the ground, then switched it off.

"Sorry."

One by one, blinking painfully, they dropped their hands.

"That's okay," said Rex.

"Yeah. Don't worry about it," Jonathan said.

"Call it even." Dess laughed, rubbing her eyes. "Not being spider food kind of makes up for the temporary blinding."

"Speak for yourself," Melissa said, rubbing her temples. "I had to taste *your* stupid pain along with mine."

"You really can do it," Rex said softly. "You brought technology into the secret hour."

Jessica's head spun. Her vision still danced with the colors revealed in the white light, the afterimages of burning spiders and slithers. The flashlight seemed to be tingling in her hand.

"Fire on tap," Dess said. "You're a darkling's worst nightmare!"

Melissa nodded slowly, looking into the sky. "That's true. They are not happy about this. Not happy at all."

Jessica looked at her, then down at the flashlight in her hand. "Yeah, but what are they going to do about it?"

Dess laughed. "You said it."

Jonathan put his hand on her shoulder. "It's true. You're the flame-bringer. This means you're safe now, Jessica."

She nodded. The flashlight in her hand seemed ordinary now, but when it had shone, something had surged through her, larger and more powerful than anything she had experienced before. She had felt like the conduit of something huge, as if the daylight world were flowing through her into midnight, changing everything.

"Safe," she murmured. Not just safe, though. What she had become felt bigger than that, and scarier, too.

"You know, Jessica, it's probably not just flashlights," Dess said. "I wonder what your limits are. I mean, maybe you can use a camera in the blue time."

Jessica shrugged, looking at Rex.

"There's no way of knowing," he said, "except to try. I mean, film is a chemical process, kind of like fire, I guess."

"Hey, just a flash attachment would kick butt."

"Or walkie-talkies!"

"What about a car engine?"

"No way."

The group fell into silence. Rex shook his head, dazed and happy, then looked up at the setting moon.

"It's late," he said. "We can figure this out tomorrow night."

Jonathan nodded. "I better get going. St. Claire's boys are on the lookout for me these days. Do you want me to take you home?"

Jessica sighed. She wanted to fly, to leave the horrible things she'd seen tonight behind on the ground. But she shook her head.

"I have to get back to the party. Constanza will flip if I just disappear into thin air."

"Okay. See you tomorrow?"

"Definitely."

Jonathan bent forward to kiss her, and gravity left her body at the touch of his lips. As he pulled away, her feet settled back onto the ground, but her stomach still danced inside her.

"Tomorrow," she said as Jonathan turned and jumped, soaring out of the snake pit. Another bound took him high into the air, then he disappeared into distance and darkness.

"We'd better get moving too," Rex said.

"Sure," Jessica answered. "I'll be okay."

"You look better than okay." Dess laughed. "Wipe that smile off your face, Jessica Day."

Jessica felt herself blushing and pulled her jacket tighter.

"Do you know the way back to the party?" Melissa asked quietly.

"Yeah." She pointed. "Moon sets in the west, so back that way."

"Not bad, Jessica," Dess said. "You're starting to get the hang of midnight."

"Thanks."

"Let's clean up some of this stuff, guys," Rex said. "We left a bigger mess than usual." Dess and Melissa grudgingly agreed.

"I should get back to the party," Jessica said. She hefted the flashlight in her hand. "I guess I'll be safe."

Rex nodded. "Thanks for coming here, Jessica. For trusting us."

"Thanks for telling me what I am," she answered, then frowned. "Whatever it turns out to mean in the long run, at least I'm not a totally useless midnighter, you know?"

"I never thought you were."

It wasn't long before she reached the bonfire. Walking directly took only five minutes, just like Dess had promised.

Jessica had never seen a frozen fire before. It didn't look like much. The bluish flames cast no light, were barely visible except as a warping of the air, like ripples of heat in the desert.

She didn't want to look at the frozen people, especially their faces, which seemed ugly and dead, like a bad photograph. So she peered closely at the fire, reaching out a tentative finger to touch one of the flames.

The heat was still there, but muted and soft, like a sound from the next room. Her touch left a glowing mark suspended in the air, as if the red flame were trying to poke its way through into the blue time. She pulled her finger back. Where she had touched it, the frozen flame was red now. That one spark of light stood out against the blue veil that lay across the desert night.

As the moon set, Jessica slipped back into the shadows. Midnight ended.

The cold wrapped around her suddenly, and she shivered in the light jacket.

The fire pit jumped into motion—conversation, laughter, and music blurting to life as if Jess had opened a door onto a party. She felt smaller; the world had suddenly grown crowded, pushing her back into the shadows.

"Jessica?"

Constanza was peering out at her from the fireside.

"Hey."

"I thought you were 'taking a walk' with Steve," Constanza said, smiling. "Didn't think I'd see you for a while."

"Yeah, well, he turned out to be kind of a creep, actually."

Constanza took a few steps nearer, hands disappearing into pockets as she left the fire behind her.

"He what?" Constanza looked closer, her eyes widening as she saw Jessica's electrified hair, her bloody knuckles, the dirt on the jacket and dress. "Are you okay? What happened?"

"Oh, I'm sorry about your clothes. I didn't—"

"That creep!" Constanza cried. "I'm so sorry. I had no idea."

"Well, it wasn't exactly his—"

"Come on, Jess, I'm taking you home."

Jessica paused, then sighed with relief. The last thing

she wanted was any more partying tonight. "Yeah, sure. I'd really appreciate that."

Constanza thrust her arm through Jessica's and walked her toward the cars.

"These Broken Arrow boys are really too much sometimes." Constanza sighed. "I don't know what anyone sees in them. They think they're so cool, but they're so out of control."

"Nice fire, though."

"You like bonfires?"

"Yeah."

"Well, good. Maybe sometime we'll—"

A voice came from the darkness in front of them. "Hey, there you are."

Jessica's feet froze in midstride. It was Steve, making his way back from the cars where he'd led Jessica. She felt Constanza's hand tighten on her arm.

"You totally disappeared there, Jess. Kind of freaked me out." He took a few steps closer. "Hey, what happened to your—"

He never saw it coming; Jessica hardly saw it herself. In one fluid motion Constanza released her, took a step forward, and punched Steve in the face.

He stumbled backward, tripped on his own feet, and landed on his butt on the hard ground.

"Hey!" Constanza took Jessica's arm and resumed their march toward the cars, continuing where she had left off.

"We'll get together with some decent Bixby boys and have a party out on the salt flats."

Jessica blinked and felt a laugh gurgling up inside her. "Uh, yeah, that'd be fun."

Steve's protests faded behind them.

"Nothing like a desert bonfire to keep warm," Constanza proclaimed.

Jessica smiled and pulled her friend a bit closer for warmth.

"Great idea," she said. "I'll bring the matches."

31 | 12:00 A.M.
NIGHT WATCH

"They're still out there, in the distance."

"Cowering, you mean." Rex leaned back on the hood of Melissa's car, propping his head on his hands.

She tasted the air. "No, something else."

It was two midnights after the flame-bringer had come to Rustle's Bottom, and the blue-lit desert looked as if nothing had ever walked on its hard earth. The vast emptiness of the place covered Melissa's tongue with a dry, lonely taste like powdered chalk and sand. But she could still sense the darklings and their allies hidden among the low mountains on the other side of the Bottom.

"Waiting," she said.

"For what?"

Melissa shrugged. It was a taste, nothing more specific.

"For the next thing to happen, I guess."

"They must still be in shock," Rex said. "I know I am."

She shook her head again. "No, they were expecting her."

"Are you kidding?"

Melissa opened her eyes and turned to her old friend.

"You've never tasted the darklings, Rex. Maybe you have to be a mindcaster to understand them, but they aren't like us."

She lay back next to him, looking up at the moon.

"They're so old, so frightened."

"Until last week they never struck me as the frightened type," Rex said. "More in the frighten*ing* category, actually."

Melissa smiled. She had felt Rex's fear of the spiders two nights before, a terror as deep and mindless as any kid's nightmare.

"They've been chased to the edge of the world, Rex, squeezed into one hour of the day. Pursued by the daylight, by fire and math, by an age of new technologies. Scared into hiding by a species they used to eat for breakfast. Literally."

"I guess so."

"I know so. I can feel it from them. *We're* their nightmare, Rex. Clever humans with our tools and numbers and fire. Little monkeys that started hunting them one day and have never given up. Ever since they ran away into the secret hour, they always feared, even *knew* somewhere deep inside, that one day we'd come after them here in the blue time. Just like *you* always know that somewhere under your house there's a spider crawling, coming for you."

She felt the shiver crawl up Rex's spine and giggled.

"Hey, cut that out," he complained. "I don't eavesdrop on your nightmares, Cowgirl."

"Lucky you," she said with a snort, then continued. "So they always knew in the pits of their darkling souls that

Jessica would come. A flame-bringer, invading their last refuge."

"That's why they were so anxious to kill her."

"Were?" she said softly, and smiled.

Melissa could feel it from across the desert, the hatred out there, cold and unyielding. It was as focused and bitter as the tip of a lead pencil resting on the end of her tongue. Not helpless at all, or stupid, the intelligence that waited in those hills was patient and well prepared. Its animal side had attacked blindly at first, as darklings always did, but it wasn't beaten yet. They had made plans for this situation, backup plans for every contingency. Every dark and ancient mind out there waited in constant, paranoid readiness.

They had been planning for this day for ten thousand years.

They would come again for Jessica Day.

They stayed at the edge of the Bottom for the whole secret hour, waiting to see if the darklings would dare to venture back.

Melissa yawned. This guard duty was Rex's useless caution at work, but after the last week she was happy for any midnight that turned out boring.

She could taste Dess out at the snake pit, measuring the cracks in the stone that Jessica had made, trying to work out the mathematics of its new asymmetry. Dess was also on some new navigation trip, doing star sightings with a homemade sextant, excited about some new numerological secret she was keeping from the rest of them, her mind wrapped up in the pure world of angles and ratios.

She could feel Jonathan and Jessica back in Bixby, flying together for a while, then perching on some high spot to look down on the world. Happy, as simple as that, and Jessica thrilled with her new power. So different from the fearful, alien minds who hated her.

She could feel Rex next to her, his mind spinning with questions, with the need to read more and know more. And underneath it all, the quiet, joyful realization that Rex Greene would be the seer who wrote the lore for these strange and exciting days.

Everybody happy, blissfully ignorant that this battle had hardly begun.

Midnight ended.

Dess returned right on time, just as the car rumbled to life beneath Rex and Melissa. She had kept the old Ford running—an engine frozen at midnight didn't use up any gas.

They jumped off the hood and got in, Dess opening a rear door with a dazed expression on her face. When her head was really in the numbers, she didn't talk much, so Rex and Melissa maintained a respectful silence.

Melissa drove them home through back roads, avoiding police cars by feel. At midnight on Sunday there were very few humans awake in Bixby, so the cops were easy to taste. But every once in a while Melissa did catch a snatch of thought here or there, a sleepless worry, a late night argument, an eruption of a dream or nightmare.

There's no way I can pay this bill. . . .

How was I supposed to know she was allergic to peanuts?

I can't believe it's Monday again tomorrow. . . .

We must have Jessica Day.

Melissa started, her hands gripping the wheel tightly at the last intense burst of thought. She searched for the source, tried to distill it from the noise of worries and night terrors and dream stuff, but it had disappeared back into the chaos of Bixby's mental terrain as quickly as it had surfaced, a stone dropping into a churning ocean.

She took a deep breath, realizing that it was 12:17 A.M., not midnight. That thought had been human.

"What was that?" Rex asked.

"What was what?"

"You tasted something. Back there. You practically pulled the steering wheel off."

Melissa glanced at Rex, bit her lip, and shrugged, turning her eyes back to the road.

"It was nothing, Rex. Probably just some kid's nightmare."

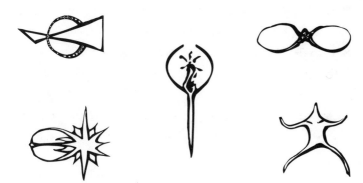